This book is dedicated to:

Phillis, Leslee, Diana and Jackie

How I wish we could enjoy one more book discussion.

CHAPTER 1

The squealing brakes of the arriving school bus formed an odd harmony with a distant siren. I bent over to pick up the newspaper on my driveway as the bus came to a stop, its warning lights blinking from yellow to red. Seven children lined up at the door, the older ones hunched under the weight of their backpacks. Off to one side, mothers formed a tight circle, no doubt discussing the latest in school gossip—who wasn't speaking to whom, which teacher was giving unreasonable homework, why so-and-so wasn't invited to a birthday party.

At least I no longer had to deal with those issues. Emma, my ten-year-old neighbor, shouted to her mother and waved good-bye, but Lauren failed to respond, apparently too engrossed in conversation to notice.

"Have a good day, Emma!" I called. The girl turned my way, smiled and waved back.

I slapped the newspaper against my palm, contemplating the possibilities of what I might do if someone attempted to snatch one of the children. The potential harm inflicted by a fifty-eight-year-old woman beating someone with a rolled-up newspaper was laughable, but it might buy some time, create enough of a distraction for the child to escape. Roy always warned me about the personal danger of injecting myself into such a situation, but saving a child would be worth the cost. I'd become certain of that truth over the past twelve years.

The last student climbed the bus steps. The driver closed the door, then waved in my direction before the bus roared on to the next stop, leaving behind a pungent cloud of diesel exhaust. Across the street, Amanda Fisher tossed her purse and backpack into the car then climbed into the driver's seat. At twenty, she was looking more and more like her mother, Nicole. Had it already been five years since that beautiful woman died of breast cancer? Amanda tapped the horn and waved to me as she left for class at the community college.

I brushed grains of sand and dirt from the newspaper's wrapper before pulling my sweater tight against the morning chill and retracing my steps to the front door. Weeds had sprouted overnight in the flowerbed, and I stooped to tear at them. May was starting out warmer than usual this year despite the winds that give Chicago its nickname. My flowerbeds needed immediate attention if they were to be ready for the summer growing season. I could plant the vegetable garden this week—tomatoes, cukes, and muskmelons—and still have time to play with my ideas for the flower gardens. That "Yard of the Month" sign always looked so nice surrounded by colorful beauties.

Lauren called my name as I reached my front door. Now that the mommy committee had dispersed, she hurried along the sidewalk waving an envelope in the air.

"I meant to run this over to you yesterday, but I didn't get a chance. The mail carrier left it in our box by mistake. Might be just junk, but I thought it looked like a real letter." She handed me the envelope. I didn't recognize the return address, but I thanked her and pushed the door open.

"Oh, before you go—" Lauren held out her hand, then drew her finger to her mouth and nipped at her fingernail. "Didn't you say you used to teach math?"

"Yes." I transferred the letter to the same hand as the newspaper, and tried to think how I might dodge the request that was sure to come.

"I wondered, would you be willing to tutor Emma? She really struggles with math, and I'm not very patient when it comes to helping her. She has a little friend who needs help, too, if you'd be willing to work with both of them one or two nights a week after school. Of course, we'd pay you the going rate for tutors." She rushed to get it all in before I could respond.

"I'm sorry, but I haven't done any teaching in over a decade." *Twelve years, one month and some odd days, to be exact.* "I doubt I'd be competent."

"I thought Roy said you won Teacher of the Year once."

"That was a long time ago, my dear. Teaching has changed a lot since then, especially methods for teaching math, from what I hear. Check with your school. I'm sure they can recommend a more capable tutor than me. But thank you for bringing this over." I held up the envelope and stepped inside.

"Okay, well..." Clearly disappointed, Lauren gave a small wave and turned toward her house. "Have a nice day, Elaine."

I closed and locked the door, then examined the envelope as I made my way to the kitchen. The neat cursive style of the handwritten address suggested a personal note. The Chicago return address in the upper left corner was also handwritten.

In the kitchen, I found Roy pouring himself a cup of coffee. He lifted the pot in my direction and raised one graying eyebrow. "Want some?"

"Yes, please." I dropped the newspaper on the table before using a paring knife to open the envelope.

"Kind of early for the mail, isn't it?" Roy set my cup on the table.

"Lauren brought it over, said it was left in her box yesterday." I slid the card out and checked the signature at the end of the handwritten message. "It's from a former student. I didn't recognize her married name." I read the note silently.

Dear Mrs. Sutterfeld,

I've heard that one can't fully understand what parenting is like until you become a parent yourself. I believe the same is true of teaching. I wanted you to know how often I've thought of you over the years that I've been teaching special ed. I'll be forever grateful to you for getting me help with my dyslexia. So many years, I thought I was too stupid to learn to read and do math. But your encouragement and patience made all the difference, and I know other kids felt the same way. Each day, I try my best to do for my students as you did for me. Thank you. A thousand thank yous! Forester Junior High School lost its best teacher when they let you go.

"What does she say?" Roy sat down at the table and sipped his coffee.

"Not much. It's just an update on what she's doing." I slipped the notecard back into the envelope and tossed it into the bottom drawer of my desk, along with other notes from students and my Teacher of the Year award—all ancient history.

"Did I hear Lauren ask you about tutoring Emma?" Roy slid the newspaper from its protective sleeve, keeping the first section and the sports for himself. I nodded in answer to his question. "Why not try it? You enjoy little Emma so much, it might be good for you."

"I'm neither a tutor nor a teacher."

"Lainey—"

"Roy, we've been over this before. I'm not a teacher. Teachers don't lose their students."

Roy sighed the way he always did when we had this conversation. I didn't appreciate him bringing it up again, but the way he blinked and turned his eyes in a slow arc from me to the floor and back to his newspaper softened my anger. He was my protector, my encourager. I offered a truce, planting a kiss beneath his white mustache. Since he'd turned sixty, the hair was thicker above his lip than atop his head. It made for a slightly scratchy kiss.

Roy reached into his shirt pocket and withdrew two tickets, holding them out to me. Squinting through my glasses, I read the tiny print on the strips of heavy stock paper.

"The symphony?" I threw my arms around his neck and kissed both of his cheeks. His mustache twitched the way it did when he was trying not to smile.

"Happy birthday, Lainey. I thought you'd like that." He snapped the newspaper to attention, then took another sip of his coffee. "It still feels odd not giving you a real present though, the kind you unwrap. Isn't there anything else you'd like?"

I grabbed up the plastic wrapper from the paper and stashed it in the recycling before washing my hands at the sink. "I've been thinking I could use a new purse." Then, realizing what I'd said, I quickly added, "But I need to do that myself. A symphony concert is perfect. It's all I need or want."

Unlike most men, Roy never forgot a birthday or anniversary. His knack for remembering details like a suspect's brand of cigarettes had made him a successful police detective, and more recently, a private investigator. But his talent didn't extend to choosing tasteful gifts. I still cringed at the ugly gifts he'd presented me over the years, especially that yellow and black sweater that made me look like a "Caution" sign in a road construction zone. Last year, I started to request outings instead of physical gifts. Best idea ever. And oh, how I love the symphony. A tingle of excitement ran through me as I dried my hands. Funny how the same music that stirs and inspires me has Roy snoring well before the intermission.

I took my usual seat across from him, and he slid the rest of the paper over to me. I'd get to the crossword puzzle after I paged through the state and local news, though sometimes I wondered why I bothered. Today's reporting included the usual depressing fare—a fire in an apartment building that left several families homeless, a young teen shot outside his home, another politician indicted on charges of some illegal nonsense.

Halfway down the third page, a picture caught my eye. A young girl held a certificate of accomplishment from the city's anti-gang initiative, a program started by one of Roy's boyhood friends. Judge Ted Owens had done well for himself, rising from the public defender's office to become a powerful force in the city's political scene. After he won a seat on the county bench, the number of teens coming through his courtroom on gang-related charges prompted him to establish a citywide program aimed at keeping kids out of gangs.

I studied the picture of the dark-skinned teenage girl. She looked about thirteen, the same age as Jenny when she disappeared. But something in this girl's expression struck a dissonant note as surely as a violin out of tune. I raised the coffee cup to my lips, my gaze drifting down to the girl's necklace. A pendant hung on a cord, an asymmetrical heart with a teardrop appearance. I could barely make out the design in the center, but it looked like someone's initials.

Inhaling a sharp breath, I sucked hot coffee into my windpipe. It burned down my throat and into my chest, sending me into a fit of coughing. The cup in my hand hit the table, bobbling and splashing dark brown spots onto the newsprint. I clamped one steadying hand over it while a coughing spasm threatened to expel my insides. Roy eyed me as I covered my mouth with both hands, my cough deep and wrenching.

"Are you all right?"

Unable to speak, I shook my head and pointed to the picture, swiveling the page toward Roy. His gaze dropped to the image, then rose back to me.

"Tiana Brown? Am I supposed to know her?"

I jabbed my finger at the girl's chest, croaking between coughs. "The...pendant."

Roy picked up the paper and examined the picture up close. "I don't get it. What about the pendant?" His eyebrows crowded together. "Are you sure you're okay?"

Each breath I inhaled prompted another round of coughing, but I managed to choke out two words. "Jenny. Ortiz."

Roy shook out the paper, stood, and moved into the morning light streaming through the window over the sink. "You're sure it's not one of those mass-produced junky things they sell at the mall?"

I whipped my head from side to side and whispered, "Custom." Inhaling long and slow, I waited for another cough, then tried speaking in my normal voice. It sounded raspy and uncertain even to me. "It was a gift from her father for her thirteenth birthday. His hobby was woodcarving, and he carved it for Jenny. Those initials are hers."

Roy looked skeptical, but studied the photo again. "And you remember that after how many years?"

I cleared my throat several times and inhaled deeply. "I know that pendant is Jenny's. She was so proud of it. And, Roy," I waited until his gaze locked with mine, "she was wearing it the day she disappeared."

Roy chewed the tips of his mustache along his upper lip and gazed back at the picture. "So someone out there knows what happened to her, maybe even knows where she is."

I pulled in a breath, then slowly released it. "Is it possible?

After twelve years, will we finally know what happened to that poor child?"

"Don't set your hopes too high. It might not be anything." Roy folded the page of newsprint, swallowed the last of his coffee, and hurried from the kitchen to his office. "Anthony'll be coming over when he finishes his shift," he called over his shoulder. "We were supposed to go out for breakfast. You'll have to let him know I've been called out."

I followed him, stopping in the doorway of his office. "What are you going to do?"

"First, I want to meet with Jenny's dad to verify the pendant is hers." Roy pulled open a drawer, then banged it shut. He shuffled through a stack of papers in a file folder.

"It's been years since you've had contact with Gary Ortiz." My legs wobbled like gelatin and I leaned against the doorframe. "What if he's moved?"

"If he's still alive, I can find him. And last time I saw him, he was very much alive." Roy pulled a manila envelope from his file cabinet, opened the flap, and shook it upside down. A small, gray memory card dropped onto his desk. He fitted it into his laptop, waited for the screen to change then scrolled through the pages that popped up. A dozen clicks later he grabbed a pen and scribbled on a notepad.

"Got it." He dropped the pen onto the desk. "Same address as ten years ago." He ejected the card, dropped it back into the envelope, returned that to the file cabinet, then shoved the drawer closed. I moved to stand at the corner of his desk.

"I"m coming with you."

"No, Elaine." He pulled on his jacket, slid a notepad into his pocket, and snatched the newsprint page from his desk.

"But she was my student." I blocked the door to keep him from going out.

"I understand that, but it's very likely I'll be going into

dangerous parts of town. I wouldn't dare take you anywhere near them." He adjusted the back of his jacket collar and angled his way between me and the doorframe. "I want you here where I know you're safe."

"How long will you be gone?"

"Depends on who's willing to talk. I'll try to check in if it gets late."

"What am I supposed to do while you're out? I can't just sit here twiddling my thumbs."

Roy clamped his papers under his arm and put his hands on my shoulders. "You can pray. I have a hunch we're going to need all the help we can get." He bent to kiss me, then hurried out the door. I listened until the sound of his car faded as he backed out of the garage and the overhead door closed.

Pray? I'd given that up years ago, almost as long ago as teaching. What's the use when there's never an answer? When you beg and plead and cry and nothing changes?

Still, we finally had a solid clue, the first one since Roy was on the police force. An icy chill blanketed my shoulders and without even thinking, my hands clasped together beneath my chin. Prayer might not help, but it couldn't hurt. I only hoped God still recognized my voice after all this time.

After cleaning the coffee pot and cups in the kitchen, I moved to the bedroom and made the bed, wiped down the bathroom and straightened my shoes in the closet. Minutes later, I found myself staring out the window as if expecting to see Roy's car coming up the street. Chiding myself for thinking I could piddle the day away until he came home, I turned away from the window and changed into a pair of grubby jeans and a faded long-sleeved shirt. After slipping my cell phone into my jacket pocket, I grabbed my sun hat and some tools from the garage and planted myself beside the front beds.

Last fall's mulch had melded together in the winter's cold and snow, forming a tough layer that required jabbing and pulling and raking to break it up. I stabbed the garden rake into the hardened mulch, the perfect remedy for releasing the tension in my back and shoulders. Trading the rake for a trowel, I dug down beneath the mulch to the soil, turning it over and mixing it all together to form a nice loose bed in which to plant some impatiens. Once they were in, I'd cover the ground with another layer of mulch.

A large shadow fell across the bed, and I jumped at the sight of Amanda's father standing almost at my elbow.

"Anthony!" I put a hand to my chest and sat back on my ankles, catching my breath. "What are you doing sneaking up on me like that? You'll give me a heart attack."

A laugh rumbled up from deep in Anthony's chest. "Sorry, Ms. Elaine. Wasn't trying to sneak up on you." Born and raised in Texas, Anthony Fisher still held to that endearing habit of putting a title in front of a lady's first name. "I called you twice, but you're working so hard you didn't even hear me. You must be concentrating on winning Yard of the Month again."

I reached behind me, feeling for my garden stool, and Anthony helped me onto it. My knees thanked me.

"I needed to dig in the dirt today," I said, brushing the soil from my gloves and drawing them off my hands.

"Therapy, huh?"

"Dirt therapy—the best kind." I pushed back my floppy straw hat to better see him. Nearly six feet with a solid build, Anthony presented a formidable sight, especially in his police uniform. The blue looked striking against his dark skin. He gave me a hand and helped me to my feet.

"Is Roy inside?"

"No, he said to tell you he's sorry, but he got called out on a case." I swished my gloves against my knees to dislodge the dirt clinging to my pant legs.

Anthony inclined his head toward the patch of dirt I'd been working. "Does that case have anything to do with this dirt therapy session?"

My joints were starting to make me feel like the Tin Man without his oil can. Mentally railing against the aging process, I moved over to the sunny garden bench and sank onto it. I slapped my gloves together, debating how much to tell him. Anthony was like a son to both Roy and me. No reason to hide anything from him.

"In my younger days when I taught junior high school, I lost a student on a field trip." The memory never failed to choke me up. I clenched my teeth, hoping Anthony didn't notice my quivering chin. He sat beside me, laying his hand on my shoulder.

"You don't need to say any more. Roy told me all about it, how one of your students disappeared and was never found."

I pulled a crumpled tissue from my pants pocket. "How long have you known?"

Anthony tipped his head back, gazing into the oak tree that shaded half the front yard. "Around the time we found out about Nicole's cancer. We were talking—Roy and me—trying to think about anything besides the cancer. I asked how he got into private investigations, and he told me about getting fired from the department. Said he always suspected someone didn't want the girl's disappearance solved." He rubbed the sole of his shoe back and forth on the spring green grass. "He'd been over the files so many times, he pretty much had them memorized by the time they fired him. Said every now and then, he'd look over his notes in hopes of finding that one missing piece of the puzzle." He shifted and turned to face me. "Has he found it?"

"We think so." I blew my nose and stuffed the tissue back in my pocket. "This morning's Tribune carried a picture of a girl about the same age as my student. She was wearing the exact pendant Jenny was wearing the day she disappeared."

"A necklace? You still remember that?"

"It was unique. Her dad was a hobbyist woodcarver. He entered shows and had won a few awards. He carved it especially for her, and she treasured it."

Anthony leaned forward, elbows on his knees. "So Roy's out investigating?"

"He was going to Jenny's dad first to make sure it's the same pendant."

Anthony's jaw worked side to side, then jutted forward. "If he can track down the girl in the picture, find out how she got hold of it, and trace it back to your student"—Anthony whistled—"he could be stirring up a snake pit if there really was a cover-up." He straightened, ran his arm along the back of the bench and touched my shoulder. "What about you? How are you doing?"

I slid my hands into my gloves and pushed off the bench. "Like I said, dirt therapy. It's cheaper than a psychiatrist." Easing down onto my hands and knees again, I picked up the trowel and jabbed it into the ground.

CHAPTER 2

My hand explored the empty space on Roy's side of the bed. Last night, he'd come home and eaten supper, but he had remained tight-lipped all evening. His creased brow, his habit of chewing the tips of his mustache told me he was deep into the case. Sometime during the night, he left our bedroom. A faint glow from his office lit the hallway.

The clock radio on our bureau read 3:57 a.m. as I turned onto my back and stared at the ceiling. Jenny's dad had positively identified the pendant. Roy told me that much after meeting Mr. Ortiz on Monday, but he refused to say anything more. He always grew intense in the midst of an investigation, but now, four days since I'd recognized the pendant, the wrinkles on his forehead seemed deeper than usual, the set of his jaw firmer. His expression alternated between sadness and anger. At supper, when I asked if he wanted more potatoes, he looked at me in surprise, as if he hadn't realized I was there.

I threw back the covers, slid my feet into slippers, and grabbed a robe from the closet, tying the sash around my waist on the way to Roy's office. He sat with his elbows propped on his desk, forehead resting on his hands. A halo of light from the lamp on his desk encircled him. I took a tentative step into the office, thinking maybe he'd fallen asleep there.

"Roy?" I whispered. His head jerked up, then sank back onto his palms. "Is there anything I can do?"

"No, Lainey. Go back to bed. I didn't mean to wake you." He sounded as fatigued as he looked.

"You didn't wake me." I moved behind him to massage his neck and shoulders. "Something's bothering you more than usual. What is it?"

He peeked at me over his shoulder. "I've never discussed cases with you. Not about to start now." His shoulders rolled, and he rotated his head under my ministrations.

"This is different. I've never been personally involved in your cases before." My fingers pressed, kneaded, and released the muscles around his neck. "Have you found out what happened to Jenny?"

His delayed answer came out hushed. "Yes."

"And?"

Roy sat forward in his chair, ending my massage. He rubbed his eyes, then dragged his fingers down the sides of his face. "I doubt she lived more than twenty-four hours after she disappeared, but I still haven't located her remains." He slammed his palms on the desk.

Bile climbed into my throat, burning its way up inside my chest. Squeezing my eyes shut, I wrapped my arms around my waist and stumbled toward the nearest chair. Roy jumped up and guided me to the seat. I rocked forward and back, using the sleeve of my robe to blot the tears on my cheeks.

Roy rubbed my back. "Later today, I'm meeting someone, hoping he can tell me where she was...disposed of. I believe he's responsible for Jenny's disappearance. And her death."

"Why not just turn him in?"

"I want to look in his eyes before I turn over the evidence. Besides, I still don't know who can be trusted in the police department. Most everyone I worked with has moved on, but that doesn't mean the corruption has died out." Roy moved back to the desk and sank into his chair. "Maybe I can persuade him to turn himself in. Every man deserves a chance to preserve a shred of dignity."

I gasped. "You can't be serious! You just told me he murdered an innocent young girl." I stood, planted my hands on his desk, and leaned down to make eye contact. "What if he kills you, too?"

Moments passed in silence before he finally said, "I don't think he'll do that, but it's a chance I have to take." He covered my hands with his own. "I'm sorry, Lainey. Go on back to bed. I'll be there in a minute."

I pulled my hands away from his and left the office. Any attempt to dissuade him from meeting with the suspect would be futile. He was a law officer to the core of his being, one of those who ran toward danger while everyone else ran away. His forced exit from the police department had been unjust and difficult to swallow. But though I'd never admit it to Roy, a part of me had rejoiced that I'd no longer dread the sight of a squad car stopping at my house, an officer arriving to deliver the news that my husband was never coming home.

The memory of those uncertain days and nights rushed back in an overwhelming, choking flood as I shuffled down the hallway. Going back to bed was useless. Despite the time, I'd never be able to sleep. Might as well start some coffee. On second thought, a little tea might settle the queasiness in my stomach.

In the kitchen, I filled the teakettle and lit the burner. Twelve years, I'd prayed for this day, always wondering what happened to Jenny. Had she run away? Was she kidnapped? Was she still alive somewhere? Now that I knew the answer, I somehow wanted to go back to my life before I saw that photo, before I recognized the pendant. Before I knew the potential danger to my husband.

I tore a teabag from its wrapper and dropped it into a cup. Was justice for Jenny worth the risk to Roy? Of course, it was. How selfish of me. Justice wasn't only for Jenny, but for her parents and siblings as well. They deserved to see the culprit apprehended and punished. Roy's insistence on solving the case had cost him his job. He, too, deserved the satisfaction of finally bringing it to a close.

Jenny's image came to mind, long black hair framing a round face with serious eyes the color of rich milk chocolate. She'd been an average student and never a behavior problem, though the divorce of her parents brought a noticeable drop in her grades. How could I secretly want this precious child's fate to continue undiscovered and unpunished?

Thunder crashed overhead, its shock waves rattling the windows and sending tremors through the floor. Rain formed an opaque curtain between Anthony's house and ours. A chorus of muffled hammers drummed the roof, and dark, heavy clouds brought the look of early evening to the middle of the afternoon. Weather like this always snarled traffic on the roadways leading into and out of the city. Surely that explained why Roy was late. Nearly two hours had passed since he called to say he was heading home. I'd heard nothing since. I tried calling his cell phone, but it went to voice mail.

I checked the time again. Barely three minutes had passed since the last time I looked. Needing something to occupy my mind, I picked up the remote and punched the button for the television. Even the noise of sitcom reruns was better than listening to the grandfather clock tick off the seconds.

The ringing of the house phone startled me. I snatched up the receiver, realizing too late the number on Caller ID wasn't one I recognized. I listened for the customary pause before answering the sales pitch.

"Hello?"

"Yes, this is Sergeant Bruckner with the Chicago Police. I need to speak with," he paused, "Elaine Sutterfeld."

The room swayed, and I grabbed hold of the table. "This is Elaine. Is something wrong?"

"Are you the wife of Mr. Roy Sutterfeld?"

"Yes. Where is he?"

"I'm afraid there's been an accident. The ambulance has taken him to the hospital. Do you have something to write down the address and phone number?"

"How bad is he?" My heart pounded while I scrambled for a pen and a scrap of paper.

"It's best if I let the hospital give you that information. Are you ready to write this down?"

"Just a minute." I found a pen in the junk drawer and grabbed the empty return envelope for the electricity bill. "All right, go ahead." My hand shook, making the numbers and letters look all squiggly. I hung up, forgetting to thank the officer for calling, then dialed the hospital's number from the envelope. An operator answered.

"Yes, can you tell me the condition of a patient named Roy Sutterfeld, please?"

"Do you know his room number?"

"No, I don't. He was just recently brought in."

"Hmm, I don't see his name anywhere. You say he was brought in recently? Let me transfer you to Emergency and see if he's still there." Some music came on that was supposed to be soothing. I found it annoying. At last, someone came back on the line, and I repeated my request.

"I'm sorry. I'm not able to give out that information over the phone."

"But I'm his wife! The police just called me—" I tried to argue with her, but those silly privacy rules prevented her from telling me anything useful.

I slammed the receiver down, then picked it up again to call for a taxi. After gathering my purse and a jacket, I kept watch for the cab near the picture window in the living room. I could barely see Anthony's house through the heavy rain. He'd be sleeping after his night shift, and Amanda's car was gone. Minutes ticked by on the grandfather clock. At last, the cab pulled up in front of the house, and the driver sounded his horn. I grabbed an umbrella from the coat closet and hurried out, stopping to lock the door and set the alarm before sloshing through sidewalk puddles to the cab. The driver jumped out to open my door, and I fairly dove for the back seat, leaving him to collapse my umbrella and drop it on the floor.

Back in his seat, the driver slammed his door, shook the rain from his hair and shoulders, and peered at me through the rearview mirror.

"Where're we going?"

Before I could answer, someone pounded on the window. We both jumped, but I recognized Anthony making a cranking motion with his finger. The driver jerked a thumb at him.

"You know this guy?"

"He's my neighbor. See what he wants." I scooched forward on the seat, but the driver hesitated.

"You sure he's all right?"

"He's a police officer. Open the window."

The driver mumbled something and cracked his window open. "You want a ride, too? There's room—"

"Roy had an accident." I cut off the sales pitch. "He's in the Loyola Emergency Room in Maywood."

"How bad?" Anthony peered at me through the barely open window. Rivulets of rainwater poured from his hair down his face and dripped from his chin.

"They won't tell me. I need to get over there now."

Anthony yanked my door open. "Come on, I'll take you."

The cabbie jerked around in his seat. "Hey! What about my fare?"

Anthony pulled a twenty-dollar bill out of his pocket and slapped it over the driver's shoulder. "That should cover any tip. Tell dispatch it was a fake call." He held my umbrella open, covering me while I climbed out. We hustled across the street and tumbled into his car.

Anthony scraped his hands over his hair and face to remove the worst of the moisture and pulled his wet shirt away from his shoulders.

"Do you want to grab some dry clothes? You're soaked through."

"I'll be fine. We need to go find Roy." He gunned the engine out of the driveway, and the tires spun on the pavement until they finally found traction. I clutched the armrest and pressed my feet to the floor as Anthony wove in and out of traffic like he was in one of those high-speed chases I'd seen on television. My knuckles returned to their normal coloring when he stopped at the emergency room entrance.

I inquired about Roy at the desk while Anthony parked the car. A sterile antiseptic smell mixed with something unidentifiable twinged my nostrils.

"Are you a relative?" the receptionist asked.

"Yes, I'm his wife."

"He's been taken up to surgery."

"Where is the surgery unit?"

"I need you to sign some papers first." She grabbed a clipboard and shoved a stack of papers under the clamp at the top.

"Can you at least tell me his condition? What's the surgery for?"

"I'll ask the doctor to come out and talk with you." She handed me a pen and the clipboard. "Fill out the first two pages, initial, and sign wherever I've placed an X. I'll see if the doctor can come out."

I huffed to let her know I didn't appreciate the delay before I retreated to a chair along one wall. Across the room, a Hispanic woman rocked a fussy infant. Another couple stared at the television on the wall, the woman keeping a hand on a whimpering child curled up in a chair next to her. A man who looked to be in his twenties or thirties paced back and forth, cell phone to his ear, making no apparent effort to keep his voice low.

I concentrated on the forms in my lap and managed to fill out the first few spaces. Name, address, birthdates, relationship to patient. After that, my mind went blank. I looked up as Anthony sat down beside me.

"They've taken Roy to surgery, but I have to fill out these forms—" I choked on the words. My throat burned from holding back the tears.

Anthony took the clipboard, looked it over, and made a few notations on it. "Sign here and here. I'll tell her you'll come back later and fill out the rest."

The simple act of scrawling my name took more concentration than it should have, but as soon as I finished, Anthony whisked the clipboard away and strode over to the receptionist's desk. He spoke to her in low, clipped tones. Her lips pressed together in a frown as she labored to get up from her chair then disappeared into the back.

Moments later, she returned to her seat, glaring at Anthony while a man in green scrubs emerged from behind the locked door that led to the examining rooms. A jerk of her head in my direction sent the man over to me.

"I'm Doctor Lee. You're Mrs. Sutterfeld?" He took the seat next to me, glancing at Anthony who came to stand beside me.

"This is my neighbor, Anthony Fisher." My fingers ached from their grip on my purse. "How is my husband? Why are they operating?"

Dr. Lee expelled a breath. "You haven't heard what happened?" The warmth of Anthony's hand on my back brought only a tiny measure of comfort. "Your husband was in a very serious accident. We've had a few with this rain. Roy was critical when they brought him in. We stabilized him, but he needs the surgery to stop some internal bleeding." His gaze shifted from me to Anthony and back again. "I'll let OR know you're waiting for him, but I should warn you there's a chance he won't survive."

"Won't survive?" I parroted his last words, and the doctor glanced up at Anthony with pursed lips. Anthony's arm encircled my shoulders. He took my hand in his. "Come on, Ms. Elaine. Let's go wait for Roy."

His gentle pressure brought me up from the chair, and I clung to his strength as we made our way through a maze of hallways to the surgery waiting room. Several other people occupied the various groups of couches and chairs around the room. Anthony led me past them to a corner seat and lowered me onto it.

"Let me get you something to drink," he said, heading for the coffee nook.

I sat unmoving with my purse in my lap, knuckles white. *An accident.* Both the police and the doctor had called it that. Entirely possible in this kind of rain. But Roy was a careful driver. I needed more information. Where did it happen? Was his the only car involved? Were there any witnesses?

Questions swarmed through my head like pesky mosquitoes. When Anthony returned, I set my coffee on the end table and fired my first question at him.

"Where did Roy's accident happen?"

Anthony briefly halted his descent to the chair. "You're asking me?" He completed his downward motion and stretched out his legs.

"You're a police officer. Can't you find out?"

He switched his cup to the other hand and tugged at his wet shirt. "I suppose I could."

I waited, but he showed no sign of doing what I asked.

"Well?"

"You mean now?"

"Yes, now. Unless you have something better to do while we wait."

Sighing, he set his coffee on the table next to mine and took the phone from his belt holster. Punching in a number, he rose and wandered out to the hall to carry on his conversation. I followed him, adding my own questions to his.

"Ask if anyone else was involved. Were there any witnesses?"

Anthony held his forefinger to his lips, and I bit my tongue, listening to his side of the conversation. At last, he clicked off the phone and snapped it back into the holster.

"They'll have the officers call me when they file their reports."

"How soon will that be?" I trailed after him back to our corner of the waiting room.

"A couple weeks."

"Weeks?" My outburst turned several heads in my direction. I took my seat and hissed, "I need to know now!"

Roy had given me no indication when he called whether or not the suspect agreed to turn himself in. Had my husband been targeted because of what he'd uncovered? Or was my imagination creating something sinister out of a normal accident caused by rain-slick roads and decreased visibility?

With nothing else to do while we waited, I mulled over the

possibilities. Anthony took several calls, but none of them answered my questions. Every so often, the doors opened and a doctor came out to speak with someone in the waiting room. My pulse rose in anticipation—or dread—until the proper waiting party was identified. The news station on the television ran through a full cycle of programming and started the next cycle before the doors parted and I heard my name.

"Mrs. Sutterfeld?"

A man in scrubs shuffled farther into the room, surgical mask dangling from one ear. The coverings on his shoes whispered against the terrazzo floor. His somber gaze scanned the room until his eyes met mine.

Pulse pounding in my ears, I rose to meet him. "Yes. How's Roy?"

The doctor ushered us into a consultation room and stood with his back against the closed door. "I'm very sorry..."

CHAPTER 3

My world tilted, spun. Strong hands slowed my descent, guiding me into a chair. Anthony murmured something that sounded like gibberish, thanks to the thrumming in my ears. He kept one hand on my shoulder as the surgeon pulled a chair up close to mine.

"Your husband's injuries were severe. We took the risk of operating because we thought he had a chance of surviving." His hands moved around his body as he described Roy's injuries, the internal organs affected by the accident. "We did the best we could, but there was too much damage." The surgeon paused before asking if I had any further questions.

Formulating a question is impossible when your brain has turned to slop. I didn't respond, so Anthony thanked the doctor, who stood and reached for the door.

"A social worker will be here shortly to help you make final arrangements. You can pick up your husband's personal effects in the ER before you leave," he said. "Again, Mrs. Sutterfeld, I'm very sorry for your loss."

He opened the door and left, back to his surgery, back to his life—leaving mine shattered. Anthony took his place on the chair before me, sandwiching my cold fingers between his dark palms. "I'm so sorry, Ms. Elaine." His voice wavered and he rubbed his cheek against his shoulder. "I loved Mr. Roy like my own daddy."

The simple act of breathing strained my chest, brought searing pain. How could I go on?

Be strong, Lainey.

That's what Roy always told me, but I didn't want to be strong. I wanted my husband back, alive.

A mental fog closed around me. I don't even remember answering the social worker's questions. At last, Anthony stood, wiping his eyes with his now dry shirt. Weaving his arm under mine, he helped me stand, lending his support for my lack of balance. "Come on, Ms. Elaine. Let me take you home."

He deposited me in the front seat, pulled the seat belt across, and buckled me in as if I were a child, then set the bag from the ER in my lap. I opened it and pulled out Roy's wallet, his wedding ring, and some small change. I held his ring on my finger as we exited the parking lot, and it occurred to me that I was leaving him with strangers who cared little for who he was or what he had accomplished. Roy was gone. His spirit, his personality, everything that made him Roy Sutterfeld no longer existed.

Anthony tried to make conversation on the drive home through gray drizzle, but I remained silent. Eventually, he gave up. What words could possibly fill the void? He pulled the car into the driveway, stopping at the flagstone path to the front door that Roy had carefully planned and laid. Anthony helped me out of the car, unlocked the door with my key, and followed me into the living room. I stood there like a mindless idiot while he took my jacket and purse and laid them on the coffee table.

What do I do now?

"Can I fix you anything to eat or drink?" He looked so hopeful, I hated to turn him down, but my stomach rebelled at the thought of food.

"No, thank you. If you'll excuse me, I think I'll go lie down."

"You do that, Ms. Elaine. I'm going home to change, but I'll be right back."

I started down the hall then stopped. "What for?"

"It's not good to be alone when the one you love dies." He held my gaze. "Trust me. I know."

"Aren't you working tonight?"

"I'll nap here on the couch while you're resting." He opened the door. "You go ahead and lie down. I'll be right back."

In the bedroom, I collapsed onto the bed where Roy and I had slept together for thirty-two years. But I'd abandoned him back there at the hospital. I should've stayed with him, if only to say good-bye.

Sleep seemed to hover just beyond my grasp, and at some point, I sat up to remove my shoes. Shivering, I crawled under the covers only to see Roy's empty side of the bed. I scooted over, burying my face in his pillow, inhaling the lingering scent of his hair crème. I might never again wash this pillowcase, these sheets.

I gazed about the room, noting Roy's open closet door. He'd been meticulous about everything. Clothes hung neat and orderly in his closet—a few pairs of pants and a couple of extra shirts. Two suits still hung along one side, barely used these days except for the rare funeral. His shoes, all three pairs of them, were lined up against the back wall in a neat row. And back in the corner, a spot of color. Bright, sunny yellow. I'd noticed it in his office early this morning, but was too distracted to pay attention.

What in the world...?

Squinting, I threw back the covers and padded over to the closet. All his shirts and pants displayed quiet blues and browns with an occasional dull red or forest green thrown in. Bright yellow didn't exist in Roy's color palette. What could it be? Parting the pants that hung beside the suits, I discovered a gift bag about the size of a paper grocery sack. Polka dot tissue paper ballooned out the top and curly white ribbons secured the handles at the top.

A birthday present in addition to the symphony tickets?

I clutched my throat at the sentiment, hardly able to breathe as I tugged the bag out of its hiding place and set it in the middle of the closet floor. My birthday wasn't until next week, but with Roy gone, why should I wait? I pulled at the ribbon. The knot held fast. A pair of scissors lay in a drawer in the bathroom, but retrieving them required more energy than I could muster at the moment. I tore out the tissue paper and split the bag from top to bottom. A purse fell out. A cloth bag, the perfect accessory for jungle combat fatigues. The ugliest green I'd ever seen in a handbag, it left no doubt Roy had chosen it himself. The last ugly gift I'd ever receive from him.

I clasped it to my heart and crumpled to the floor, tears flowing like a river through a breached dam.

CHAPTER 4

In the living room of a dingy apartment, the girl stood alone, pinching the denim of her jeans between her fingers and biting the inside of her cheek.

"Tiana, do you remember what I told you when I gave you that necklace?" He regretted getting rid of one so beautiful and satisfying. Entirely necessary, though, given the nature of his visitor this morning.

She whispered her answer. "Yes."

"What did I tell you?"

"That it was special for me and no one else."

"That's right, a secret just between us. And what else?"

Tiana pressed her lips together, rolling them in. If not for her dark complexion, he felt certain he'd see a hot flush on her cheeks.

"I...I don't remember." The way her gaze darted to one corner of the floor gave away her lie. Her fingers rubbed the pendant hanging from a cord around her neck.

"I think you do remember, but you don't want to admit it. Hmmm?"

"I wasn't supposed to wear it anywhere except here. Only when we—"

"Were you supposed to take it out of this apartment?"

"No." Tears filled her eyes, and she fell to her knees. "I'm sorry. It won't happen again. I promise. I'm really sorry."

For a moment, he enjoyed hearing her beg. "All right, enough. Get up." He turned on the television to one of those idiotic afternoon sitcom reruns, then grabbed two bottles of root beer from the refrigerator and brought them to the couch. Making sure she saw him pop the lids, he noted which one opened easier and held it out to her, gesturing to the spot beside him. "Come sit with me. Let's just relax a bit."

Tiana rose to her feet. She accepted the bottle from him and sat on the edge of the couch, half facing him, seemingly wary of his arm stretched along the back of the couch. He tipped his bottle toward her.

"Drink up." He winked, took a long draft himself, and watched her follow his lead. "Taste good?"

"Mm-hmm." She nodded and lifted her bottle for another swallow. Gradually, she turned her attention to the television, sat back, and pulled her feet up under her. Before the show's final credits, she was leaning against his shoulder, out cold.

When he'd finished with her, he removed the pendant and cord, and left the apartment, giving a single nod to the young men loitering at the building's entrance. They grinned and raced up the stairs while he climbed into a car waiting to take him home.

How different his life might be if that drug had been available when he was Tiana's age. His twin brothers' mocking laughter still echoed in his mind. A full ten years older, Jack and Lester excelled at everything—sports, academics, popularity. By comparison, he consistently looked inept and incompetent. Eventually, he understood the age difference was to blame, but by then, it was too late to salve the embarrassment and humiliation embedded deep within. The twins' college years brought relief from their constant abuse, except for summer vacations when they returned home.

The year he turned thirteen, they noticed his interest in girls. One girl in particular, a seventeen-year-old neighbor. The fact she was older didn't stop him from developing a crush on her. Her age only added to her allure. He should've suspected his brothers' sudden interest in 'developing his manhood.' Instead, he drank in their attention, savoring it like a glass of fine wine. Pretending to take him into their confidence, they kept him supplied with provocative girly magazines and provided detailed instructions on seducing girls, promising to make a man out of him. He eagerly accepted their challenge to prove himself with the current object of his affection.

She'd strung him along at first, pretending a reciprocal interest. But when he moved in for the reward, she deftly frustrated every one of his bumbling efforts, then laughed at him. Jack and Lester had clued her in, once again setting him up for failure so they could ridicule and tease him.

The embarrassment of that one encounter kept him from dating until near the end of high school. A smile tugged at his mouth now, remembering the young girl, naïve and easily impressed with the attentions of a high school senior. The success proved addictive. No matter how many times he'd tried to give it up, he always came back.

He pulled the pendant from his pocket and examined it. A heart carved from some kind of exotic red wood, the shape distorted as if two unequal apostrophes conjoined to share one tail. A lighter-colored wood inlaid on the face formed initials. He'd altered it just enough to make the trinket his personal charm, like a class ring, marking a girl as his.

CHAPTER 5

The shock of Roy's death brought a blessed numbness to the next several days. Amanda, Lauren, and others brought food I knew I'd never eat. What would I have done without Anthony to help me make the hundreds of decisions required?

"Ms. Elaine? You 'bout ready?" Anthony's voice boomed from the living room all the way down the hall.

Has any woman ever been ready to attend her husband's funeral?

"Almost. I'll be right out." I attached earrings to my ears, slid my feet into black pumps, and reached for my sweater lying on the bed along with my new purse. I brushed my hand across the coarse grain of the fabric the way I imagined Roy had done when he selected it. Olive green didn't exactly complement my black dress. A small clutch might better fit the occasion, but this last gift was a comfort I sorely needed.

My heels tapped the hardwood floor along the hall until I met Anthony in the living room. He looked every bit as impressive in his dark suit as he did in his police uniform. Was it the same suit he'd worn for Nicole's funeral five years ago? Roy and I did our best to help him through his wife's cancer and death, never imagining a circumstance where he'd repay the favor.

"Is Amanda coming with us?"

"No, she's cutting out of class just for the service then heading on back to school."

I took his strong, solid arm. My hand trembled on his sleeve and he covered it with his other hand. I avoided looking at him as we walked out to his car.

"How did you survive Nicole's funeral?"

Emotion intensified his deep baritone voice. "It ain't easy, that's for sure. Never figured I'd be attending another memorial service so soon for someone I care so much about." He helped me into the passenger seat, then walked around and slid into the driver's side.

I dug through my purse for a tissue. "This must bring back a lot of painful memories for you."

"Can't say it doesn't." His habit of backing into a driveway allowed him a clear view before pulling into the street. "But today's about Roy. And you. I just wish I could've been around to help you more. Boss wouldn't let me have any extra time off with my vacation coming up end of the week. I know Mama would understand if I cancelled. I hate to leave you alone at a time like this." He turned the corner and headed for the funeral home.

"Don't you dare cancel your vacation. You've already done more than I could've asked. I appreciate your kindness, but you need to go on and visit your mother. And tell Ruby I said hello. Someday, I want to meet that lady."

"Who's going to look after you while I'm gone? Remember, Amanda's at school all day."

I twisted to face him. "You think I'm some helpless old woman?"

His hesitation spoke for him. "It would make me feel better to know you're not having to do everything alone. Isn't there anyone who can stay with you?"

"I'll be fine. I don't need anyone staying with me, making sure I eat and worrying over my odd sleeping hours and making me feel awkward when I cry."

If only I felt as confident as I sounded. The house seemed so empty without Roy. I couldn't remember it feeling this lifeless in the past when his investigations occasionally took him out of town. A fresh pang of grief stabbed my heart with the realization he'd never again come through the door and call out, "Lainey, I'm home." I knew I didn't need to hide my grief from Anthony, but I couldn't let myself go. Not today. Not now.

The car bumped over the curb as he made a sharp turn into the funeral home's parking lot. He found a spot with an easy exit, and we walked up to the double doors. Holding one door open, he motioned me inside, but I froze. Everything within me wanted to run from this place, this time, this scene. His arm came about my shoulders.

"Be strong, Ms. Elaine. You know that's what Roy would say if he could."

Drawing a breath deep into my lungs, I stepped through the door. Anthony tucked my arm under his, and a funeral director soon led us up the center aisle to the front row. Whispers and soft murmurs behind us blended together in an incoherent mix. Or maybe I was the incoherent one. I settled the purse on my lap, flexing my cold hands and wiggling my toes inside my shoes like I'd taught my students to do when they were nervous during a test. It probably hadn't worked for them either.

The simple memorial service was a good idea. I couldn't have endured seeing Roy in a casket. Even now, I clung to my composure with white knuckles amid the depressing canned organ music and the eulogy for a man who should not be dead.

Anthony said the officers investigating the crash found

several witnesses. They reported a car going way too fast for conditions had forced Roy off the road as he approached an overpass. They'd found the other car abandoned several miles from the accident site. It had been stolen, raising suspicions the driver had committed a crime somewhere else and used it as a getaway vehicle. Certainly, it was a tragic accident, but nothing to indicate an intentional hit.

At length, Anthony rose and stood before the podium. He glanced at me, then looked out over the room and cleared his throat.

"Five years ago, I sat next to Ms. Elaine here while Roy spoke about my wife, Nicole." He paused, and inhaled deeply. "Roy Sutterfeld was a man of high integrity. The police department lost a respected and honest cop when he left the force. A gifted and compassionate investigator, he refused to give up until he'd found the answers. He was a faithful husband, a loyal friend, and I looked up to him as much as my own father. I hope he meant it when he said I was the son he never had. He was a mentor who will be severely missed by all who knew him."

Anthony's lips pressed together in a straight line. He swallowed hard, shifted from one foot to the other and back again, then cleared his throat. He hesitated, as if he had more to say, but shook his head, stepped down, and sat beside me. I slipped my arm under his and whispered in his ear.

"Thank you."

Anthony pulled a handkerchief from his suit pocket and wiped his eyes. He blew his nose then stuffed the cloth back in his pocket as the funeral director finished up and waited for us to exit. I thrust my wrist through the purse handles and trusted Anthony's arm to keep me from collapsing on the way out. In the lobby, Amanda rushed up to hug me, tears streaming down her cheeks.

"I'm so sorry. I miss him so much." She cried on my shoulder then stepped back and wiped her cheeks, smearing the tears. "I hate to leave, but I'm missing class."

"You go ahead and don't worry," I said. "I know how much you loved him. Thank you for coming."

She fled out the door, and I was directed to a spot to greet the guests. *Be strong, Lainey.*

Why? Why did I have to be strong when I'd rather go home and cry my heart out again?

But that's not what Roy would expect of me. I stiffened my back, raised my head, and determined to get through this without dissolving into a puddle on the carpet.

I must admit, it was nice to see several fellow officers Roy had served with on the police force. Lauren and other neighbors offered to help if I'd let them know what I needed. Clearly, they had no understanding of the muddled state of mind the death of a loved one creates. One long-time friend from my teaching days understood, having lost her husband two years ago. She promised to pick me up for dinner one night next week, but another teaching friend acted like widowhood might be contagious. I hoped she never found herself in my shoes—married, but no longer in a relationship. A Mrs. with no Mr.

At the end of the line, a familiar figure approached, tall and distinguished-looking with his prematurely silver hair and confident posture. He'd been out on the golf course more than once, judging by his tanned face, and the lines of age accentuated his handsome features. Ted Owens opened his arms and drew me in. "Elaine. I'm so sorry."

I moved into the warm embrace of an old friend. His breath tickled the hair on top of my head. I stepped back but held tight to Ted's hands.

He looked deep into my eyes and frowned. "I was stunned to hear of Roy's death. How are you holding up?"

I searched for an appropriate answer, but words could never

adequately describe the devastation of my loss. And I didn't want to burden anyone else with my grief. "As well as can be expected, I guess. It was quite a shock."

"Yes, I can imagine. Is there anything I can do to help? Anything at all?" The smooth compassion in his voice no doubt contributed to the reputation he had in the courtroom for delivering harsh sentences with the softest of tones.

"I can't think of anything right now." I glanced at Anthony standing nearby. "My neighbor, Anthony Fisher, is taking good care of me. He's been a good friend to both Roy and me. I don't know what I'd have done without him these last few days."

The two men exchanged greetings and handshakes. Ted retrieved a business card from inside his tailored suit coat and handed it to me. "Take this, and please don't hesitate to call me if there's anything I can do for you."

I took the card. "It's good to see you again, Ted. Thank you for coming. I know it would mean the world to Roy."

Eyes downcast, he pressed his lips together in a frown and gave a slight nod.

After returning to the refuge of Anthony's car, I clicked my seatbelt into place and leaned my head against the backrest. Exhaling the tension of the past hour, I took a moment to study Ted's card before tucking it into my purse. No doubt his office in the downtown Chicago area allowed him to keep his pulse on the city's movers and shakers.

Anthony pulled onto the street. "Are you and the judge good friends? I had no idea you knew him."

I fluttered my hand. "Roy's known Ted since they were kids. They were best friends growing up."

"Is that right?"

I nestled into the comfort of the seat. "They parted ways after high school. Not that they had a falling out, but Roy enlisted in the army, then entered the police academy when he got out. Ted went to college and law school. They were never as close as they had been, although they've always maintained a certain loyalty. We used to see him and his wife occasionally at social events."

"He's married?"

"Divorced. That came as a shock to us." I peered out the window at the passing storefronts. "He and Dorothy separated shortly after he defended me in a negligence lawsuit after Jenny disappeared. He'd opened his own practice as a defense attorney after several years as a public defender. By then, he was running in different circles than we did, and the friendship sort of naturally fell by the wayside. But when Ted heard I'd been slapped with that lawsuit, he called Roy and offered to represent me at no charge."

Anthony glanced my way, one eyebrow raised. "Pays to have friends in high places."

I fiddled with the handles on my purse. "It probably wasn't as altruistic as it sounds. I think he already had higher aspirations and figured my case might provide the name recognition he needed. He won the case and a year or two later, he won the election as a county judge."

"He's definitely built his own empire since then. Not many people with as much political power as Judge Owens. I'm a little surprised I never heard Roy talk about him." Anthony turned the corner onto our street.

"Like I said, we travel in different social circles, but I'll always be grateful for what he did for us, for me."

"I'm surprised he never remarried."

"I guess he enjoys playing the eligible bachelor. He always seems to have some high society lady on his arm for public events, but I never hear his name connected with anyone special. He's a very charming personality. I'm surprised some woman hasn't been able to snag him." Anthony grunted, and I gathered my purse and jacket as we pulled into the driveway. Remembering something, I dug into my purse and came up with the two symphony tickets. "Think you could find someone to use these?"

Anthony inspected the tickets. "This Friday night? That's when I leave to visit Mama."

"How is she doing? Has she adjusted to the assisted living home?"

"It hasn't been easy, but my sister thinks she's learning to accept it. The doctors are pleased with the way her hip is healing." He flipped the tickets over and back. "I'm not really a symphony kind of guy. You sure you don't want these?"

"They were a birthday present from Roy." I almost choked on the words.

"Aw, Ms. Elaine. When was your birthday?"

"It's Friday."

Anthony blew air between his lips and tucked the tickets into his inside suit pocket. "How about if I check around at work and find someone who wants them?"

"Perfect. I hate to see them go to waste."

Anthony escorted me to the front door and waited while I opened it. I waved him off, locked the door, and set my purse on the occasional table. I stood there, staring stupidly at my empty house, trying to think what to do next. Disconnected, unrelated thoughts wandered through my brain like children lost in a maze. The few that made sense played tag, racing away before I could catch hold of them. Too often in the past few days, I'd found myself standing in the middle of a room like I was now, trying to remember why I was there, what I'd been doing just moments before.

I noticed my jacket still in hand, so I opened the door to the coat closet and hung it next to Roy's woolen trench coat. My fingers slipped down his sleeve. If only I could feel the strength of his arm within.

Silence weighed heavily as I closed the closet door. The

steady rhythm of the grandfather clock that always comforted me before now seemed a mocking reminder of the way life continued on after my own world came to a screeching halt. Tick. Tick. Tick.

I moved to the hallway and stood outside the door to Roy's office. Anthony had closed it at my request after we returned from the hospital. I didn't want the reminder every time I walked the hall. Now, I wrapped my palm over the cool, round doorknob, desperate for the memories held in this room while fearing the crush of accompanying emotions. Swallowing hard, I turned the knob and pushed. The door swung open, an inch at a time in sync with the clock's ticking.

I gasped. There'd be no sentimental reminiscing here today.

CHAPTER 6

File drawers gaped open, their contents strewn about the room as if a whirlwind had passed through. Papers and folders littered Roy's desk, the floor, and every surface in between. Bits of shattered glass from the computer monitor caught reflected light from the ceiling fixture. Overturned desk drawers lay in every corner.

Anthony came as soon as I called. He surveyed the scene from the doorway, his arm blocking my entrance.

"I hope you didn't touch anything."

"No, I turned around and called you as soon as I saw it."

"Good." He punched numbers on his cell phone and spoke to someone, giving them my address. "Burglary's coming out," he said, pocketing his phone. "Do you know how they got in?"

I tried to remember if I'd set the alarm when we left for the funeral, but I couldn't even remember whether I'd reset it when I came home ten minutes ago. I must have looked as befuddled as I felt.

"Don't worry about it. The investigation will figure it out, but they'll want to know if anything's missing."

I looked around the room. How I could tell? I'd have to collect all the files, reorganize them—

No, wait. I knew which file was missing. I also knew they wouldn't find what they wanted in it, nor on the hard drive they'd taken. Roy never kept sensitive information in such obvious places. All the evidence, all the information about who abducted Jenny and what happened to her would be on that memory card he'd kept in an envelope. But even if the burglar found the envelope, the card wouldn't have been there.

Ordinarily, Roy would've carried it with him that morning. But then, why wasn't it returned to me with his personal effects? I alone knew of this particular habit of Roy's. But even if whoever ran him off the road happened to find it before the emergency vehicles arrived, why do this? Were they making sure nothing incriminating was left behind? Or was this a warning to me?

The burglary squad performed a thorough investigation, dusting for fingerprints and checking for points of entry. While they worked, Anthony urged me to check for anything else that might be missing—jewelry, medications, cash, Roy's guns. Everything appeared to be in place, and the investigators suggested it looked like a professional job done by someone who knew how to bypass the security alarm.

After they left, Anthony made sure I engaged the alarm before I sent him home, though I questioned what difference it would make when someone knew how to disable it. He urged me to call someone to come stay with me. Even offered Amanda, but I wasn't in the mood for company of any kind. I closed the door after him, and returned again to my empty house with plenty of vacant hours to fill.

That was the problem with being a widow. My days lacked the rhythm they had when working around Roy's schedule. It mattered little what time I went to bed or what time I awoke, when I ate supper or whether I ate at all. There was no one here to care. Each day stretched endlessly before me with no purpose, no one to take care of and no schedule to plan around. Maybe I needed a job, but what could I do besides teaching?

Earlier today before the funeral, I'd cleaned the bathroom, straightening the medicine cabinet that held Roy's shaving kit and other toiletries, and throwing out his medicines. I even left the toilet seat up to make things look normal. But it wasn't normal, and it never would be again.

The clock chimed five o'clock. Time for supper. In the few days since Roy's accident, friends and neighbors had filled my refrigerator with casseroles and sandwiches, but I rarely felt hungry. Grief caused so many changes. Besides the lack of appetite, there were the emotional swings. Sometimes I cried for hours, other times I couldn't force a tear. I'd wake at odd hours, unable to sleep. Other times, like now, I wanted nothing more than to sleep forever.

As the clock finished chiming, I walked back to the bedroom and crawled onto the bed still wearing my black dress. My shoes fell from my feet, hitting the floor as I pulled the covers up to my chin and closed my eyes. With any luck, I'd never wake up.

The digital clock on the dresser read 3:30, but was it a.m. or p.m.? Darkness at the windows indicated morning, early morning, but I struggled to recall what day it was.

Wednesday?

No. That was yesterday, so today must be Thursday. Six days since Roy's death. The day of the week might give me trouble, but I knew exactly how many days since the accident.

Lights blazed overhead and in the hall, though I'd gone to bed while the sun still shone. Without Roy, I'd taken to leaving a few lights on all the time, mainly for comfort. Back when I was teaching and a school program or event kept me out late in the evening, I hated coming home to a dark house. I'd trained Roy to leave one light on for me somewhere in the house, one light to welcome me home and let me know I was expected and not forgotten.

After changing out of my dress clothes, I threw on my fleecy bathrobe against mid-May's chill. I stopped at Roy's office on my way to the kitchen, debating whether to enter or not, but decided to make some coffee first. When I came back, I reached in to flick the light switch, holding my breath against finding another intruder.

Light flooded the empty room. I exhaled in relief and surveyed the damage, formulating a plan of attack. A couple of commendations from Roy's days on the police force hung at odd angles on the otherwise bare walls. Manila folders and papers littered the floor, the desk and the chairs. Shuffling through the mess, I set my cup on a corner of the desk and retrieved a broom and dustpan to sweep up the broken glass from the picture frames lying on the floor. Righting the overturned wastebasket beside the desk, I dumped the glass in there, then collected the files and papers into one pile on the desk.

I lowered myself into Roy's chair, expecting a sense of his presence—a whiff of his aftershave maybe, something that made this room his. But whatever I'd hoped for never materialized. Destroyed by the prowler maybe? I pulled my mind back to the task at hand, sorting folders from papers and matching them as best I could—until I uncovered the page of newsprint that set everything in motion. I skimmed over it, my gaze locking onto Jenny's pendant right there in plain view. If she were alive, she'd be a grown woman by now, but in my mind, she remained a thirteen-year-old girl, a child.

With Roy gone, would I ever know what happened to her? Could I find the memory card that held the evidence? If I did, who would I trust to handle it? The supervisor who fired Roy might be gone by now, but the politics would remain. This was Chicago after all, and I was beginning to think someone out there still didn't want this case solved.

Maybe Roy had already given the card to someone. But who? Anthony? Surely Anthony would've told me about it, especially after all this. He wasn't a detective like Roy had been, but a patrol officer would know what to do with evidence. He'd also know whom to trust in the department. Solving the case might even earn him a promotion. Or a dismissal, like Roy's.

I'd worry about that later. First, I needed to find that card. A manila envelope sticking out of one file drawer caught my attention, and I pulled it out, checking for the name Ortiz on the outside. It was empty, holding none of its former contents—no newspaper clippings or photocopied articles about the girl's disappearance, and no memory card.

Where did you put it, Roy?

I vowed to find it. I had to, not just for Jenny, but for Roy, too.

The doorbell rang, followed by a firm, familiar rap on the door. Without my noticing, the sun had risen, and the clock now read a little after eight.

I opened the front door, and Anthony, still in uniform, held up a bag from a local bakery. "I brought breakfast. Thought we could eat together." He set the bag on the kitchen table while I started some fresh coffee.

I set out a couple small plates. "I've been up since 3:30 putting Roy's office back together."

"Not sleeping well, huh? I remember after Nicole died, I waited forever to fall asleep, then woke at odd hours." He crumpled the bag and stuffed it in the wastebasket beneath the sink.

"You think whoever broke in yesterday found what they were looking for?"

"I doubt it. Roy never kept sensitive information in obvious places. He stored Jenny's information on a memory card, one of those little chips like they use in cameras and phones. He must have hidden it somewhere. There was nothing like that in his personal effects from the hospital. Did he happen to mention anything to you about the case?"

Anthony shook his head as he chewed a bite of cheese Danish. "Nope. He didn't tell you anything?"

I poured two cups and set them on the table, sitting down in my usual spot. "Roy always kept his investigations to himself. Confidentiality and all that. The only thing he told me, other than that Jenny was...gone...was that he had all the evidence, but he wanted to give the suspect a chance to turn himself in."

Anthony frowned, his thumb mashing crumbs on his plate. "No name?"

"No, and he never made it home from that meeting."

The crumb smashing halted. "That's why you wanted to know the details about his accident? You think the perp had him killed?"

"It crossed my mind." I rubbed my finger around the rim of my cup. "Years ago, when he was pushed out of the department, he suspected someone didn't want the case solved. That's still possible, isn't it?"

Anthony pushed his plate away and eyed me with one raised brow. "You need to find that card with the evidence. Did he have a safe deposit box or anything like that?"

"Not that I know of." I gathered up the plates and set them in the sink. "I've searched his office but found nothing so far. I'm not even sure what to do with all those files now that he's gone."

"Shred 'em." He stood and took his cup to the sink, tossing

the last of his coffee down the drain. "If you can afford it, hire one of those companies that shreds private documents."

"Good idea. I'll check into that."

"By the way," Anthony stopped at the door, "I haven't found anyone yet for the tickets."

"Well, keep trying. I certainly can't use them."

Friday morning, I choked down a piece of toast as the sun brightened the kitchen window. A vine's tendrils clung to the screen, reminding me of my outside chores. Bushes needed trimming, and more weeds had sprouted in the flowerbeds after the rain earlier in the week. Some dirt therapy might be what I needed to help sort out the pieces of my puzzle. Who had Roy met with? And where was that memory card?

I cleaned up the crumbs from my meager breakfast and changed into gardening clothes. The house phone rang before I made it out the door. I answered on the extension in Roy's office.

"Elaine, this is Ted. I've been thinking of you since Roy's memorial service. How are you holding up?"

I shifted the receiver to my other hand and fiddled with some papers I'd left on the desk. "Just trying to get through each day, Ted. I appreciate your thoughtfulness in calling."

"Don't mention it. This was such a shock when I heard the news, and I didn't have much time to chat with you the other day. I'm sorry now that I didn't make more effort to stay in touch with Roy. He was a good man. I just can't believe he's gone."

I couldn't talk past the tightening in my throat, and I sank into Roy's desk chair.

Ted sighed. "We sure had fun together as boys."

"He used to tell me about the trouble the two of you got into."

Ted chuckled. "The good old days. I remember one year at

homecoming, I dared him to climb the water tower and spray paint our class year on the side."

"Did he do it?"

"He not only did it, he left my initials under it. So, guess who took the punishment." Ted laughed, and I smiled in spite of myself. That sounded like something Roy would do.

"Well, listen," Ted continued, "is there anything I can help you with? Maybe I could bring over some supper or something."

"That's not necessary. My neighbors have crammed my refrigerator with more food than I'll ever be able to eat. And to be honest, I really don't feel up to socializing just yet."

"I understand. Do you have someone to look after you in case you do need something?"

"Anthony is just across the street. You met him at the memorial service." Might Roy have talked Jenny's case over with Ted? His experience defending and presiding over criminal cases might have been valuable for shedding light on anything Roy uncovered. No, Roy would've mentioned seeing his old friend.

Lost in my musings, I'd missed what Ted was saying and asked him to repeat it.

"I said I'd like to see you, if only to satisfy myself you're all right. I wouldn't need to stay long. Is tomorrow a good time to come out and visit?"

I hesitated. "Could you make it in the afternoon?"

"Saturday afternoon it is. I'll see you then, but please call if there's anything at all I can do for you before then."

The papers I'd been fingering gave me an idea. "Actually, there is something I'd like to ask you. In your legal career, you must have disposed of private files before. Is there someone you can recommend for that?"

"Are we talking about disposing of Roy's files?"

"Yes. I'm sure there are privacy issues with things like this."

"Absolutely. Why don't we take a look at them when I come over tomorrow? I'll be glad to help you with that."

After I hung up, I collected my tools from the garage and headed outside. The warm sunshine lifted my spirits as I trimmed away the unruly vine and eradicated the weeds in one bed. Anthony arrived home after his night shift and backed into his driveway. I waved my clippers at him and stood back to survey the shrubs before I started pruning.

"When you're finished there, you're welcome to come over and work on my yard." Anthony crossed the street and came to stand beside me. "Looks great. Wish I had your green thumb." He glanced behind him where neglected flowerbeds hugged the front of his house, looking sad and forlorn.

"I might be up for that challenge after I finish my work here. You need something to liven things up over there."

"Nah, I was just teasing. You don't have to do that, Ms Elaine."

Mizzy Lane. That's how it sounded when he said my name, and I loved hearing it.

"I'd do it because I want to. It would give me something to occupy my time now that Roy's gone. Gardening isn't a chore for me. It's relaxing. I enjoy it." I bent down and yanked out a weed hiding in back of a shrub. "Aren't you leaving to visit your mother today?"

"I am, but I thought you'd like to know I found someone to use those tickets."

I stepped up to a shrub and cut off a branch that stuck out. "That's good. I'm sure they'll enjoy it. I wish I could've gone but —" I brushed a hair from my face with my forearm.

"Yes ma'am, I know you'd like to go, so I expect you to be dressed and ready when I pick you up at five o'clock."

I dropped the clippers to my side and twisted to look at him. "Where are we going at five?"

"I thought we'd go downtown and have a nice dinner out before the concert."

"What concert?"

"The symphony."

"I thought you said you found someone—"

"I did. You!"

"But—"

"I figure Roy wanted you to go, or he wouldn't have bought the tickets. You just said you'd like to go, so I'm taking you as my date. I've never been to a symphony concert before. I figure it's about time."

I stared at him. "I thought you were leaving for Texas tonight."

Anthony shrugged his massive shoulders. "I'll leave after the concert. Mama's not expecting me until Sunday anyway."

I laid the clippers on the ground and collapsed onto the garden bench. "Oh, Anthony. I don't know. It doesn't feel right going out so soon after Roy.... I'd hate to waste a nice dinner. I don't feel much like eating these days." I pulled off the gardening gloves and pressed my fingers to my eyes.

Anthony knelt on one knee in front of me. "Ms. Elaine, I know I'm a poor substitute for Roy, but I'd consider it an honor if you'd let me escort you to this concert. I like to think Roy would want me to do this for you. Please?"

I blinked the tears from my eyes, sniffed, and nodded my assent while my chin quivered in protest. Anthony wrapped me in a gentle bear hug, then stood and headed back across the street to his house.

"See you at five sharp!"

CHAPTER 7

"Anthony, you've kept me out way past my bedtime, but that was wonderful. The food, the music..." My ears still rang with the silken tones of the violins and the thrumming of tympani. My neighbor's deep chuckle filled the car as he maneuvered onto the Eisenhower Expressway taking us out of downtown Chicago.

"I'm sorry Roy isn't here instead of me, but I'm glad you enjoyed it."

"Did you like it?"

He took his time answering while accelerating past several cars. "It's not exactly my type of music."

"Well, at least you stayed awake the whole time. I always had to wake Roy up for intermission." Anthony laughed, and I smiled with him, even though the memory brought a stab of pain.

"Any more ideas where he might have hidden that memory card?"

I threw my hands up. "I've looked everywhere. The day I recognized the pendant, I saw him take a manila envelope out of his file cabinet. The card was in it then, but I found the envelope when I was putting the files away and it was empty."

"Do you think the burglar took it?"

"No, I don't. Roy wouldn't have left it in there. Not after he'd solved the case."

"And he didn't tell you anything about what he discovered?"

Streetlights flashed past as we sped along the expressway toward home. I looked down at the purse in my lap, my fingers tightening around the edges. "Roy kept his investigations to himself until they became public knowledge. Even this one. He told me Jenny probably hadn't lived long after she disappeared, but that's all."

Anthony pulled a toothpick from one of his pockets and stuck it in his mouth. "You don't think he might've already turned it over to someone." He made it sound like a question.

"Possibly. I thought maybe he'd given it to you. But if he did turn it in, wouldn't it be all over the news by now?"

"Not necessarily. Whoever he gave it to would investigate it thoroughly before making any moves. That could take a few days."

I relaxed against the car seat and stretched my tense fingers. "Maybe I'm getting all worried over nothing."

"If you'd like, I can go through Roy's office when I get back from Texas. Sometimes a fresh pair of eyes helps."

"That won't be necessary. Ted Owens is coming over tomorrow afternoon to check on me. I asked him to look over the files and decide what to do with them. Hopefully, they'll be gone by the time you get back."

I yawned, covering my mouth with my hand. The enjoyable evening, the late hour, and the motion of the car all combined to make me drowsy. Maybe I'd be able to sleep through the night.

Anthony exited the freeway and took the surface roads to our neighborhood. A siren blared somewhere nearby. A second one wailed behind us, and Anthony pulled aside to allow the fire engine to roar past with lights flashing.

"Does that start your adrenaline flowing, like Pavlov's slobbering dogs?"

Anthony grinned. "Sometimes, but not when I'm officially on vacation."

I peered through the windshield. Lights from street lamps, businesses, and signs reflected off a haze hovering above the rooftops. Or was that smoke? An acrid odor filtered through Anthony's window that he'd lowered an inch.

"Must be quite a fire," I said.

"Seems close, too." Anthony turned into our neighborhood, and I leaned forward as a swirl of blinking red, white, and blue lights invaded our car. A police cruiser barricaded the entrance to our street. A house on our block, burning? I tried to guess which neighbor. *Please don't let it be Lauren's.* I hoped she and Emma and her husband were safe.

Anthony slowed the car to a crawl as we passed the end of the street, straining to see which house was burning. Halfway down the block, two fire trucks lined the curb. One firefighter perched on the truck's ladder, aiming water at the roof of the house. Others on the ground fought flames that seemed to grow from the windows of—

"My house!" I gasped and scrambled for the door handle.

Anthony cursed under his breath and stepped on the gas. The car shot forward, throwing me against the seat.

"Stop! Stop the car!" I grabbed his arm with my left hand, my right one still searching for the door handle. "I have to get out."

"Ms. Elaine, you don't need to be seeing this." Three blocks past our street, he finally pulled over to the curb. He took hold of my hand on his arm and drew me away from the door.

I resisted, clinging to the handle I'd finally found. "I have to see it. That's my house burning." I looked through his rear window. An orange glow filled the sky above the neighborhood's ranch style homes. A whimper escaped my lips. "How could this happen? Oh, Roy. Not our home, too."

I let go of the door handle and fumbled to release my seatbelt. Anthony grabbed my arm before I could open the door and escape. "Please, Ms. Elaine. Don't go back there."

"I have to know what happened." I twisted my arm, turning it every which way to break his hold.

"Let *me* go. I have my badge. They'll talk to me. But you need to stay here."

"It's *my* house!"

"I know that, but do you really want to see it going up in flames?" His deep voice filled the car, and he expelled a breath that sounded a lot like exasperation. Lowering his voice, he pleaded with me, "Ms. Elaine, don't make this the last thing you remember about your house, about you and Mr. Roy's house."

The fight left me. I sank back into the seat and covered my mouth with my hands. Tears cascaded down my cheeks. "Let me make that choice. Please take me back there."

Anthony pounded his fist on the steering wheel, blowing air through his nostrils. Finally, he offered me a deal. "I'll drive back and park where you can look down the street. But only if you promise to stay in this car." He emphasized the last four words. "If you don't think you can do that, I'm taking you away from here, and we'll go find a hotel room for you."

As much as I wanted to see my house, Anthony was right. This wasn't how I wanted to remember it. I agreed to his offer, and he pulled the car around in a U-turn. Cars now lined both sides of the street as people gathered to watch, leaving no room for him to park. He drove slowly past the end of our street until the officer in charge of crowd control motioned us to move on.

"There's no parking spots close enough where you can watch."

"Park wherever you can. I'll wait here."

I'd seen enough already as we passed by. The roof was gone, but flames still soared from the living room windows that faced the street. Had the fire affected Lauren's house or any of the others? It was so late, children would be sleeping. I turned in my seat to watch Anthony pick his way through the parked cars. He showed his badge to the officer managing a crowd of gawkers, then turned down the street and disappeared from view.

Slumped against the seat, I took off my glasses and rubbed the moisture from my eyes. How could this be happening? Losing Roy was bad enough. Losing the house we'd shared for thirty-two years sharpened the pain, drove the knife deeper. I'd have nothing left—no photos, no mementos. Only memories. My grip tightened around the handles of my purse. It didn't look quite so ugly with the glow of the streetlight softening the drab green. At least I had this, Roy's last gift.

I waited, torn between seeing what was happening and holding onto a more pleasant memory of our home. If the flowers I'd planted weren't scorched by now, I was certain they'd been trampled by firefighters. The temptation to slip out for a closer look grew. If I saw Anthony returning, I could hurry back here before he caught me. But as I opened the door, one glance down the block brought the sight of him striding toward the car. I closed my door and refastened my seat belt.

A moment later, Anthony yanked his door open and slid into his seat, bringing with him a smoky odor that filled the car. He blew a long, heavy breath between his lips and looked at me before starting the car, fixing his gaze on the street outside the windshield.

"It's bad, Ms. Elaine. Fire commander says they're trying to keep it contained, keep it from spreading to other houses. Your house was already engulfed by the time they got here." His chest rose and fell with each breath.

I pressed my fingers to my temples. Had I left the coffeemaker on? "I can't imagine how it started. I always leave a few lights on, but except for the microwave and the coffeemaker, I haven't used any appliances for a week or more. I did use the washer and dryer, but that was last week."

Anthony looked at me again, the whites of his eyes clearly visible, but looking yellow in the light of the street lamp. "Ms. Elaine, it's suspicious."

"Suspicious? You mean arson?"

"The captain won't know for sure until they have a chance to investigate. That'll be tomorrow. But with Roy's death, the burglary and now this"—he ticked them off on his fingers—"I'm thinking you need a safe place to stay for a while."

I stared at him, trying to comprehend his meaning. "You think someone's trying to kill me?"

He held his palm out, fingers wide. "I hope they're only after the evidence Roy uncovered in your student's case. But if they think you know anything, they'll come after you as well."

My fingernails dug into the stiff fabric of my purse, and I dragged a breath into my lungs, a smoky breath from the air filtering through the vents. An icy chill raced up my spine, bringing on a shiver. Even my voice shook.

"Get me out of here."

Anthony dropped the gearshift into drive and pulled away from the curb. "Where to?"

I blinked at him. "I have no idea."

"Any friends you could stay with?"

Friends? My world had shrunk to a few acquaintances since Jenny's disappearance. Friends and co-workers dropped off quickly in the weeks and months after my termination. I'd hidden from neighbors and others and avoided social situations so I wouldn't have to explain losing one of my students. Roy became my lifeline. Of the few people I considered friends anymore, I couldn't name one I'd call in an emergency.

"Ms. Elaine, you've got to tell me where you want me to take you."

"Just drop me off at the nearest hotel."

From Ogden Avenue, Anthony made a left turn into the Jewel-Osco parking lot. Cars still dotted the lot even this late on a Friday, but he pulled into a slot well away from them and turned to face me.

"I'm not leaving you at a hotel. You've lost your husband and now your home in the space of a week and a half, not to mention someone breaking in. You need to be with people you know, people who care about you." He pounded the steering wheel again. "If I wasn't going to visit Mama... What about outside the city? Out of state even. Any cousins or other relatives?"

I fiddled with the clasp on my purse—open, shut, open, shut. "Even if I knew of someone, I wouldn't want to put them at risk if someone is trying to kill me." My arms and legs went limp, and I looked to Anthony. "Where can I hide?"

He shook his head from side to side, lips pressed into a hard, straight line, nostrils flaring. He stared out at the night, the glaring lights overhead creating shadowy corners.

"Best to get you out of the city, away from the area. The farther, the better." Gradually his features relaxed. His eyes moved side to side and back again, and he seemed to be considering an idea. With a decisive nod, he wiggled into a comfortable position in his seat, put the car in gear, and steered toward the exit.

"Where are we going?" I asked.

"To the perfect hiding spot. Just until we know you're safe."

"Where are you taking me?"

"Ms. Elaine, you are about to visit the great state of Texas."

"Texas?" I sputtered. "I can't go to Texas!"

"Why not?"

"I'm meeting Ted tomorrow."

"No need. The files are taken care of."

"But what about insurance—Roy's life insurance and the house insurance?"

"I'll take care of those for you when I get back. Why can't you go to Texas?"

"Because..." I groped for an answer. Why not? I no longer had a home or anything of value here. In fact, I had only this crazy purse and the clothes on my back. Speaking of which—I gathered and held up the folds of my long skirt. "For one thing, I have nothing to wear."

Anthony glanced over at my side of the car. "Hmm. That's a problem, but you'd have to get new clothes anyway. I doubt anything survived that fire."

"What about you? Don't you need a change of clothes?"

"I threw my suitcase in the trunk before we left tonight. How much cash do you have on you?"

I dug through my purse for my wallet and counted the bills. "A little under fifty dollars."

"That's not enough." He mumbled, more to himself than to me, but peered out the windshield as if looking for something. "Which bank do you use?"

"Community."

He made a quick U-turn in the middle of the street and soon pulled up next to the Community Bank's ATM machine. "You got your card?" He took it from me and shoved it into the slot. "What's your pin?"

"I'm not telling you."

He rolled his eyes and exhaled. "Ms. Elaine, I'm a cop. I'm only trying to make sure you have enough money for the trip."

"Doesn't matter. I don't give my PIN to anyone." I might have complied if he hadn't talked to me like I was a stubborn five-year-old. Instead, I exited the car, swished my skirt around the front end, and squeezed in between his door and the money machine.

"Do you know how dangerous it is for a woman to be standing outside a cash machine at midnight?"

"You're a cop. I have complete confidence in your ability to protect a helpless female in need of some late-night cash." I moved my body to block his view then punched in my secret numbers. Moments later, I grabbed the cash and my card, and returned to the car. He huffed as he drove toward the street.

We followed Ogden Avenue to the I-355 tollway and turned south toward I-55. The streetlights grew sparse, fading into deep, endless darkness, and I fought to keep from dozing off. My eyelids drooped as the motion of the car lulled me to sleep. More than once, my head rolled onto my chest while my body slid sideways. I jerked awake at the sensation of falling and straightened in my seat. After the third time, Anthony touched my arm.

"You want to lay down in the back seat? I've got a blanket." He pulled to the side of the road and stopped. Only an occasional set of headlights brightened this stretch of highway. "It's more comfortable back there. You might's well get some shut-eye 'cuz we got us a long road ahead."

I yawned. "I accept your offer, but when did you start talking funny?"

He laughed. "Happens ever' time I go home." He came around the car and helped me navigate from the front seat to the back. "Gravel's soft here. Watch your step. I threw a pillow back there too, in case I wanted to stop for a snooze. So you should be all set." He shut both doors and a moment later slipped back into the driver's seat. "Let me know when you need a rest stop. Otherwise, I'm gonna keep driving 'til we need gas."

I removed my shoes and set them on the floor. My toes rejoiced at being able to stretch and wiggle again. Pulling my knees up under my skirt, I lay down and stuffed the pillow under my head. It smelled like Anthony—not unpleasant, but then again, not Roy. I turned the pillow over and found the aroma not quite so strong. After wrapping the blanket snugly around my legs and feet, I pulled the rest up over my shoulders.

And there I lay, wide awake. Now that I was prepared for it, sleep refused to come. A seat belt receptacle jabbed my hip with every bump, and my body swayed with the motion of the car. Worse than that, every time I closed my eyes, an image of hungry flames appeared inside my eyelids—tongues of fire devouring my house, billowing out the windows, and climbing to the roof. Was it really arson or my own careless mistake? More than once in recent days, I'd lost track of what I was doing when something else came to mind, sometimes right in the middle of a task.

I hadn't used the iron all week, and I remembered washing out the coffee pot at lunch, setting it upside down in the dish rack to dry. No stove burner had been left on. With all the food in the refrigerator, there'd been no need to use anything other than the microwave. I'd turned on lights in the living room before leaving for the symphony, and one in the bedroom and another over the sink in the kitchen. Could a socket have shorted out and caused the fire? Or was someone out there trying to destroy me to keep the evidence in Jenny's disappearance a secret? That idea made some sense in light of Roy's accident and the burglary. Was the fire set to destroy any evidence that might've been hidden elsewhere in the house? Or was it meant to destroy me?

CHAPTER 8

"Ms. Elaine?"

Anthony's voice rumbled through my dreams and dragged me back to wakefulness. The seat beneath me no longer vibrated, the car's engine fell silent. I pulled the blanket away from my face.

"Ms. Elaine, we're stopped for gas. Soon as I fill up, we'll try that McDonald's across the street. You can use that restroom there, and we'll get us a little something to eat."

"Where are we?" My voice croaked.

"Other side of St. Louis." He opened his door and got out, then stuck his head back in. "I'm thinkin' we don't look much like mother and son. Folks might remember seeing us if someone comes around asking questions. And there's still a few people who might not like seeing us together. Prob'ly best to stay out of sight as much as possible." He closed his door and proceeded to fill the car's gas tank.

I yawned and pushed myself to a sitting position, keeping my face averted from the only other car filling up at the second bay over to the right. Beyond the bright lights of the station, darkness still hung in the air. I lifted my arm to the light to see the time on my watch, then fumbled around for my glasses that had fallen to the floor. Looked like it was approximately 4:30. Stretching, I arched my back and massaged the spot where the seat belt receptacle had likely left a nasty bruise on my hip. My teeth felt fuzzy, my eyes gritty, and my hair probably resembled Albert Einstein's. Running my fingers through the graying strands, I tried to coax them into some kind of order using the rearview mirror. If Anthony didn't hurry, I might not be able to avoid leaving a puddle on the car's floorboard.

Gas tank filled, windshield and side windows washed, and oil checked, Anthony finally returned to his place behind the steering wheel. "I'll drop you off at McDonald's, then park in back. Inside, let's act like we don't know each other. The less people see us together, the better off we'll be."

I pulled myself up close behind his seat. "Drop me off as close as you can to the ladies' room. And don't waste any time getting there."

Anthony chuckled. "Yes, ma'am."

He let me off at the restaurant's side door, which of course was still locked this early in the morning. I scurried around to the front door, holding my long skirt up to keep the hem from getting dirty. Inside, the overnight workers and two customers at the counter eyed me as I passed. One glimpse in the bathroom mirror explained why. How many middle-aged women went out for fast food at 4:30 in the morning in formal dress and informal hair?

I took care of business, then surveyed the damage. A wet paper towel freshened my face along with some touch-up cosmetics. I combed my hair into some semblance of order, quelling the unruly top and fluffing up the flat sides and back.

Anthony was already enjoying his breakfast by the time I approached the counter. Without his suit coat and tie, he looked like any ordinary businessman. The fragrance of warm coffee and scrambled eggs awakened my appetite, and I carried them to a table near the door. But the eggs turned to sawdust in my mouth as I recalled my reason for being here at this hour. Was someone out there trying to silence me for good?

Anthony stood and stretched, wadding up paper wrappers and stacking foam containers on the orange tray. He slid the waste into the trash bin near my table. Without looking my way, he whispered. "Take your time. I'll be in the car out back. No hurry." With that, he pushed open the door and disappeared around the corner.

By the time I finished, the sky showed the first rosy tinges of light. I swallowed the last of my coffee and made one more trip to the restroom before exiting. The locks on the car clicked open as I approached. Anthony leaned across the front seat to push the door open, finished up a conversation on his phone and slid the phone into his shirt pocket. I cleared my long skirt from the door before closing it.

"Aren't you going to rest?"

"I'm still good for awhile. I slept all yesterday after my shift."

Arranging the skirt around my feet, I brushed at spots of dirt already clinging to the hem. "I need something to wear that's a little more appropriate for daytime. How soon can we stop somewhere?"

Anthony pulled out his phone and tapped away at the screen. "Discount or department?"

"Discount is fine for now." I still had plenty of cash, but no sense wasting it. Who knew how long it might need to last? "When will we reach Texas?"

Anthony checked the time on the dash as he pulled onto the road. He squinted, and his mouth pulled to the side as he calculated. "With stops for shopping, gas, and meals, we should get to Waco sometime after supper."

"Where are we staying?"

He glanced sideways at me. "I hadn't thought that far ahead. I've got a hotel reservation, but..."

"You weren't planning on a roommate. And like you said, we don't exactly look like we're close relations. So where am I staying?"

"It would be perfect if you could stay with Mama and the other ladies. Think you could fake a health problem?"

"Do I look like nursing home material?"

Anthony pulled a toothpick from his pocket and held it between his teeth. He chewed on it, switching the slender sliver of wood from one side of his mouth to the other every minute or so.

"I talked to Mama yesterday morning after I got home from work. She was worried about Gabby, the girl who helps with cooking and keeping an eye on everyone. I shouldn't say girl. She's a young woman, pregnant with twins, but it's not going well. Doctor put her on bed rest, and Mama was all worried about her losing the babies. You might-could fill in for her."

I frowned. "Is that my only option?"

"Unless you want to dress the part of an elderly woman and bluff your way in. Or pay rent on an apartment or hotel room for however long you need to stay here. I'm just trying to figure this out as we go, Ms. Elaine."

Hours later, I carried my purchases into the bathroom of a discount store. The restroom provided a welcome escape from gawkers, and the handicap-accessible stall afforded plenty of room for changing out of the long dress. I'd have welcomed a shower, but the clean underwear alone lifted my spirits. Not knowing when I might shop again, I'd picked out a few extra tops to go with my new slacks and shorts.

Now what to do with the dress? It wouldn't fit in the bag, and I didn't want to raise suspicions by carrying it out of the store. Besides, what possible reason would I have to wear it in Texas? I held it over the trash bin, hesitated then pulled a cheap hanger from one of my bags and hung the dress on it. The hook swiveled to fit over the door of the stall, and I left it hanging there in plain sight of anyone who walked in. Someone would get some use out of it.

More cars had filtered into the parking lot, but I spotted Anthony's silver Buick parked under a shade tree along one side of the lot. We'd passed each other near the electronics section, pretending to be strangers, but he was waiting in the car when I settled into the front seat. Getting in and out proved much easier without the long skirt.

He scrunched a plastic bag and stuffed it beneath his seat then held out a small flip phone. "Your new cell."

"I already have one." I dug through my purse for the phone Roy had insisted I carry, though I rarely used it. Anthony exchanged the old for the new.

"I'll hang onto your old one until later."

"Why do I need this?" I examined the new phone. Without all the bells and whistles, it looked fairly easy to operate.

"I'll need some way to contact you after I get back to Chicago."

"Don't they have a house phone? What's wrong with my old one?"

Anthony fitted the key into the ignition but didn't start the car. He stared out the windshield. "Ms. Elaine, we're going to make you disappear."

That word sent a shiver down my spine, reminding me too much of Jenny.

Could Anthony be responsible...?

Of course not. Way too much of a coincidence. Besides, ten

years ago Anthony would've been in his late teens or early twenties, a few years older than Jenny. Making him about the right age for a young man of questionable morals looking for a pretty young girl to take advantage of.

I edged closer to the door, my fingers wrapping around the handle in case I were forced to make a fast exit.

Anthony didn't seem to notice, though he turned to face me. "If someone really is after you, they may be savvy enough to trace your whereabouts by activity on your phone as well as your credit card, bank accounts, any number of ways. You'll need to stop using all of your accounts."

I gasped and nearly dropped the new phone. "How do you expect me to live, to pay for things?"

"You've got some cash. I'll loan you some more before I leave. Anytime you need more, you call and let me know." He tapped the phone in my hand, then pulled out his own and held it up between us. "We need to change your identity, too. Look this way." He snapped a picture and examined it. "Not the best, but it'll do." He punched several buttons, then tossed his phone into the cup holder, started the car, and headed out of the parking lot.

"What name do you want to use?"

"I'm sort of attached to the one I have. It's worked well for decades."

"This is only temporary until we find out who's after you. You're used to answering to Elaine, so pick something that sounds similar."

"Like Eleanor or Ellen?"

"Or Charmaine. Think of something that rhymes."

I considered my few choices. "Lorraine?"

Anthony bobbed his head. "That works."

"Am I going into some kind of witness protection program?"

"Not enough time. Even there, you could still be traced if

someone knew what they were doing and had the power to pull strings."

Someone like a police officer?

My breath came short and fast. Had I traveled hundreds of miles from home with the man responsible for Jenny's disappearance? Did Anthony set the fire that destroyed my home?

Nonsense. He was with me when it broke out.

But terrorists used timers and cell phones to set off bombs all the time. Couldn't an arsonist set off a fire the same way? What about Roy's death? Anthony normally slept during the day after his night shift, but he'd been awake enough to notice the taxi in front of my house. He'd talked about making this trip to visit his mother, but what if he was planning all along to take me to the same place where he disposed of Jenny's body? If we hadn't been accelerating onto the freeway, I might have opened the door and jumped out.

Once we reached cruising speed, Anthony punched the phone button on the steering wheel and waited. A voice interrupted the third ring.

"Hey, Fish."

Anthony picked up his phone and listened a moment before continuing. "No. No worries. I'm calling in that favor you owe me. You got any contacts in Dallas?" He glanced my way. "I'll be through there later today, probably late afternoon. I need an ID for a Caucasian woman in her fifties. First name Lorraine. Last name's up to you. I've texted you a picture. Let me know where to pick it up, preferably somewhere along I-35."

I loosened my grip on the door handle and let my shoulders relax. Surely a killer wouldn't order an ID if he were only planning to dispose of the body.

My goodness, what's wrong with me to suspect Anthony of such a terrible thing? Roy and I trusted him completely. We've watched him and Nicole raise Amanda. We saw his struggle and grief during Nicole's fatal battle with breast cancer. He'd been more help and comfort than I could've asked for since Roy's accident. Besides, who wouldn't trust a man willing to travel all this way to visit his mother for Mother's Day?

"Tell me about this place where your mother lives."

Anthony stashed his phone in the cup holder. "In Texas, they're called personal care homes, independently owned and operated, usually in a private home and no more than three residents. The woman who owns and operates this one is named Kim Caraway. Nice lady. Very competent. She's a nurse. Took care of her grandmother after a stroke, and Grandma willed the house to her. After Grandma passed away, her doc persuaded Kim to care for a diabetic patient of his, a recent amputee who doesn't watch her sugar." A grin spread across his face and he wagged his head. "Maxine's a character—a tough old broad. She doesn't like following the rules for her diabetes, so she flirts with every man who comes into the house. Trying to snag herself a husband who'll take care of her and get her out of there. But she's mainly got the hots for Kim's dad, a pastor of a small Baptist church in town. They're complete opposites." His deep chuckle made me smile, too.

"Is he married or single?"

"Stan's a widower. He helps Kim with mowing and maintenance kind of things. His wife, Kim's mom, died of heart problems while Kim was caring for the grandmother. And Kim's divorced. Husband took off with some sweet young thing about the time Grandma died."

I shook my head. So many losses in such a short time. I understood that pain. "How long has your mother been there now?"

"Since last fall after she broke her hip. She only needs a little supervision, but the house we grew up in wasn't handicap accessible. She sees the same doc as Maxine so, when he suggested Kim, we contacted her. Kim seemed like a good fit for Mama. It took some adjusting, but she loves Kim. I haven't met the newest resident yet. I think Mama said her name's Jean or Joan, something like that. Some sort of dementia or Alzheimer's, I think."

It sounded depressing, a bunch of women coping with loss—husbands and loved ones, health, and home and independence. Not to mention one lost leg.

Dallas at 4:30 on a Saturday afternoon made me wonder if we'd taken a wrong turn onto the Indy 500. I'd driven Chicago freeways but didn't remember traffic this fast. Anthony seemed unfazed by it all. He accelerated to the speed of light and kept up with the rest of them, apparently unconcerned about the distinct possibility of serious damage should any one of the vehicles around us make a mistake. I gripped the armrest and held tight until he exited the freeway.

"How about some good ol' Texas barbecue for supper?" He aimed for the parking lot with a Rudy's BBQ sign, and I finally let go of the armrest. "Their brisket is the best, but they also have chopped beef, pork loin or turkey sandwiches. It's pretty much self-serve except for the meat, so pick up your slaw or potato salad on the way to the counter. I'll give you a few minutes before I come in."

He let me out on the side of the western-looking building, then drove around to the back. The temperature had risen noticeably since our last stop, but inside the rustic restaurant, a tangy aroma of barbecued meat tantalized even my grief-numbed taste buds. The way my mouth watered, maybe my appetite was coming back. I carried my order to one of the picnic style tables and sat down to eat. Alone. I'd be glad when this little charade was over. Eating alone ranked high on the Worst Parts of Widowhood list. No wonder my appetite played hide-and-seek.

I'd finished half of my turkey sandwich, wrapped up the remains, and sat nursing my Sprite when Anthony finally sauntered in. I watched him walk through the line. Roy used to swagger like that. Was it something they taught at the police academy, that unhurried, confident stroll that says *I'm in command*?

An ache stabbed the middle of my chest. I'd never again see Roy's swagger, never find comfort in our home. What was I doing in Texas of all places? Ever since the morning I recognized Jenny's pendant, my life had not only turned upside down, but inside out as well.

Anthony swallowed his sandwich in about three bites and winked at me on his way out. Minutes later, I tossed my waste in the trashcan and searched the parking lot until I found his car on the opposite side near the back of the lot. As I climbed into the front seat, he handed me a new ID card.

"I wondered what took you so long. You must have met your contact out here."

"Yes, ma'am. You are now Ms. Lorraine Johnson. We were going to give you a Houston address, but we decided to use a fictitious Chicago address because of your accent."

"What accent?"

He ignored my question and started the car. "The more I think about it, the more I like the idea of you taking Gabby's place. You know how to cook, and you know how to manage a classroom full of kids. A few elderly ladies shouldn't be any problem."

"Kind of like Mary Poppins? All I need is an umbrella and a strong wind to deposit me on their doorstep. What about references? Unlike the movie, Kim's not going to hire someone off the street without checking me out." We pulled out of the parking lot and sped onto the freeway again.

"I'll vouch for you. Kim knows me well enough. I think if I

give you a thumbs-up, she'll bite. Especially if we all agree it's only temporary until Gabby comes back." He pointed to a mileage sign for Waco. "You've got about two hours to memorize that address and practice your new name."

I studied the card with "Texas" written in attractive blue lettering in the top left corner. Not a very flattering picture, but then I had slept in the back seat of a car the night before.

"I thought you told your friend how old I was."

Anthony glanced my way. "He's not exactly a friend. I said you're in your fifties, but Mama taught me never to ask a woman's age. Is something wrong?"

"If he was going to make me younger, couldn't he have made me fifty-one instead of fifty-seven?" Answering to a different name was bad enough, but memorizing a whole different birthdate and a fake address? At least the eye color stayed the same.

"Lorraine Johnson." I rolled the name around in my mouth, getting used to the feel of it. "My name is Lorraine Johnson. Hello, my name is Lorraine Johnson."

"You ever do any acting?"

I clutched the armrest again as he stepped on the gas to pass a small box truck. "Ages ago when I was in high school. I was a nurse in the sanitarium for the play *Harvey*. Not exactly a starring role."

"You'll be on stage 24/7 once I leave you at the house. Pull this off and we'll see if we can't get you an Oscar."

My stomach twisted, the barbecue threatening to stir up trouble. "You really think I can do this? What if I make a mistake and they suspect something's up?"

"If worse comes to worst, tell them the truth. Have Kim call me, and I'll corroborate everything. Hopefully, it'll only be for a week or two. Give me time to get back to Chicago and figure out what's going on. I programmed my number into your phone under the name Ann. Don't accept calls from any other number. But don't hesitate to call or text me if you need anything."

"Pajamas."

Anthony shot a glance at me. "Pajamas? What does that have to do with anything?"

"I forgot to buy some. I'll need a nightgown or something for tonight."

"No problem. We've got time to stop. If I remember right, there's a Wal-Mart right off the freeway in Bellmead, this side of Waco."

Is this something Lorraine Johnson would wear?

I held a nightgown at arm's length, debating briefly before grabbing a similar one in a different color and tossing them both into my cart. A few more necessary toiletries and I headed for the checkout stand. Between the clothes, toiletries, food, and chipping in for gas, my cash was already running low. I pulled out my credit card, but hesitated when I recalled Anthony's warning about someone tracking my whereabouts. It seemed ludicrous that someone might be trailing me.

What kind of threat could a fifty-eight-year-old woman pose?

But I couldn't argue with the fact they'd taken Roy's life and burned my house to the ground. Roy always said desperate equals dangerous. I put the card away and pulled out more cash.

Several miles down the road, Anthony pointed out Baylor University's McLane stadium perched on the banks of the Brazos River. Across the river, steeples rose from the university's buildings.

"Welcome to Waco." Anthony exited the freeway. Fast food restaurants and hotels crowded the street near the university, their signs lighting up as the sun dropped low behind the trees.

Anthony drove a scenic path along the river, pointing out the paved walking path and a park with food trucks, bigger-than-life-size sculptures of longhorn cattle, and a historic suspension bridge that once served as a cattle crossing for cowboys taking their herds to the stockyards in Ft. Worth.

Before long, we entered a neighborhood. Minutes later, he stopped the car in front of a white, two-story plantation-style house. Large yards surrounded the homes, and I warmed to the idea of living here. Anthony peered at the houses.

"This was quite the place in its day. Doctors and lawyers lived here when I was growing up. Now the homes are either sold as fixer-uppers or torn down to make room for fancy new ones like this." He looked at the white house then pointed to the one next to it. "That house up there is where Mama lives."

I squinted to see the place that would likely be my home for the next week or two. Narrow burnt-orange bricks on the exterior and a copper roof attested to its age. All on one level, the house stretched out long, one wing jutting off at an angle. It reminded me of...

"A nursing home! You want me to hide out in an old, run-down nursing home?"

CHAPTER 9

"It's not a nursing home, Ms. Elaine. I promise." Anthony raised his right hand in pledge. "My mama would take a switch to my back side if I put her in a nursing home. Miss Kim runs this place like a family home. I know the outside's ugly, but the inside's completely renovated. And what you can't see from here is a beautiful backyard with a little pond and big old oak trees spreading their branches for shade on a hot summer day. You'll eat at a dining table beside floor-to-ceiling windows where you can enjoy the view. On lazy afternoons while the weather's still nice, the ladies sit out on the shaded patio sipping lemonade and sweet tea. Except for Maxine. She drinks Dr Pepper. Did you know a Waco pharmacist invented Dr Pepper?"

"No, I didn't. No wonder it tastes like cough syrup. What's sweet tea?"

"Iced tea with lots of sugar in it. It's a Southern tradition."

My stomach knotted. I twisted my hands together in my lap, studying the house in the shadows of twilight and reviewing my choices. My own home was nothing more than a pile of ash by now. Staying in a hotel for a week or two was too expensive, and I certainly didn't want to bring calamity to anyone kind enough to take me in. But could I play this role as Lorraine Johnson for a week, maybe two?

"I-I don't think I can do this. Isn't there any other way?"

Anthony untangled my hands and held them in his large ones. "You trust me, don't you?"

I drew in a long breath and released it, looking for reassurance in his dark eyes. "Yes, but I don't like this."

"Ms. Elaine, I don't like anything that's happened in the last couple weeks. But someone's after you, and I give you my word I'll look out for you. Roy would want me to, and I'd never forgive myself if anything happened to you. This is the only way I know to make sure you're out of harm's way. We'll solve this puzzle and find out what happened to your student and to Roy. We'll catch the perp who torched your house. But for now, your life may depend on this right here." He tipped his head toward the house.

I pulled my hands from his, took hold of my purse, and willed my stomach to unclench. "All right then. We'd better get going before I change my mind." I gathered my jacket and the plastic shopping bags that held all my worldly belongings.

Anthony stopped me before I opened the car door. "Wait a minute." He pulled out his wallet. "Here's some extra cash. I'll send more whenever you tell me you need it."

I stashed the bills in my purse and reached for the door handle.

"One more thing. Give me your driver's license, your credit cards, bankcards, Social Security card if you carry it. Anything that might identify you as Elaine Sutterfeld."

"Why?" I glared at him, suspicion creeping into the dark corners of my mind.

He draped one beefy arm along the top of the steering wheel. "Whoever wants to silence you will be watching your accounts. What if someone here discovers your ID and hears about you on the news? Or you mistakenly pull out your credit card and use it to pay for something? Boom! They know you're in the vicinity of Waco, Texas, and they'll come looking for you. This isn't Chicago. It's a small town where people know people, and they watch what goes on."

I clutched my purse to my chest, making no move to retrieve the cards he wanted, until an edge of exasperation tinged his voice.

"A minute ago, you said you trusted me. I'll put everything in a safe place and you'll have them back as soon as we figure out who's behind all this. I'm not going to run off with your money. You know where I live. You've got my number. It's the only one programmed into your phone, so you can call or text me any time you want."

If looks could kill, I intended to seriously wound him, but his argument made sense. So why did it feel like I was losing every bit of who I was? I dug out my credit cards, my bankcard and my Illinois driver's license and handed them over. He slipped them into his wallet and shoved that into his hip pocket.

"Remember, Ms. Elaine. We're doing this for Roy as much as for Jenny."

I pushed my door wide open and stepped out onto the curb then leaned down to make eye contact before I shut the door. "It's Lorraine. My name's Lorraine Johnson." I slammed the door.

He laughed out loud. "Yes, ma'am, Ms. Lo-raine. I won't forget." He climbed out of the car and joined me on the sidewalk as a yellow cab drove past. My bags made that crackly plastic sound as they bumped against my legs on my way to the house.

Lorraine. My name is Lorraine Johnson, and I'm here to help. Actually, I'm here to hide from someone who's trying to kill me, but that's probably more information than you need or want.

Some of the house's unsightliness disappeared in the deepening darkness. The wing closest to us angled away from the street toward the backyard, and as I drew closer to the front of the house, a matching wing on the far side became visible. A detached two-car garage sat across the driveway from that wing, and from the sidewalk, the house looked like three-fifths of a pentagon. Wide shallow windows set below the eaves along the length of each wing contributed to the nursing home appearance. I shot Anthony another deadly look as we turned onto the walk leading to the front door.

The cab had parked at the curb in front of the house, and as we walked past, the driver tooted the horn and lowered the passenger-side window.

"Hey, would you mind letting them know their cab is waiting?"

Anthony waved acknowledgement. We approached the front door, dodging June bugs and moths flirting with the outside light. Before he could ring the bell, the door opened, and a woman called, "Good-night, Dad."

"Good-night, honey. I'll see you in the morning." An older gentleman emerged, tugged a green ball cap over his head, and nearly plowed into Anthony. "Excuse me! I didn't see... Why, Anthony, it's good to see you. Are you here for Mother's Day?" He embraced Anthony, then called through the open door. "Kim, look who's here." Turning to me, he offered his hand. "And you are?"

"Lorraine." I croaked, cleared my throat and tried again. "Lorraine Johnson."

The man's mostly gray hair curled out from under his cap, which had a gold BU embroidered on the front. He possessed a friendly, open face, and when we shook hands, he covered mine with his.

"Welcome. Welcome. Did you come down with Anthony?"

Before either of us could answer, a woman appeared on the threshold wearing white capris and a blue sleeveless top. Wavy, reddish hair fell just below her shoulders, and I guessed her to be in her late thirties. A smile lit her face when she saw Anthony, but another toot of the cabbie's horn brought a teasing glint to her eyes.

"Anthony, did you forget to pay the poor man?"

"Not me." Anthony held up his hands in surrender. "Someone here in need of a ride?"

The woman I assumed was Kim squinted at the cab. Her eyebrows pinched together as her gaze swung from Anthony, to the cab, and back to us.

"He's not with you?"

"No." Anthony shook his head.

She stepped outside, closing the door behind her. Her flip-flops slapped the pavement on her way to the street as her father said goodnight and headed toward an old pickup truck parked next to a van in the driveway.

The taxi driver leaned toward the passenger window. "I got a call to take someone here to the airport. Is that you?"

"Nope." Kim bent down to his level. "Are you sure you have the right address?"

The driver checked his computer. "Supposed to be a Ms. Jean Lebow. You know who that is?"

Kim's shoulders drooped, and she rested her forearms on the frame of the open window. "Yes, she's a resident here, but she's not going anywhere. She must have used my office phone when I was busy with Maxine. By now, she probably doesn't even remember doing it. I'm sorry you've wasted your time."

"So no one's going to the airport from this address?"

"No one. And tell your dispatcher to make a note that legitimate calls from this address will only come from me, Kim Caraway. Ignore anyone else asking for cab service at this address." She tapped her fingers on the door. "I apologize for wasting your time."

The driver raised the window, did a U-turn, then roared up the street.

"Sorry," Kim said, returning to where we stood by the door. "I didn't mean to leave you standing out here. I think Ruby's getting ready for bed, but come on inside." She opened the door and waved us in.

Anthony held back. "I'll just wait 'til tomorrow, but she said you were needing some help. Something about Gabby going on bed rest?"

"That's right. Not the best timing with my Mother's Day luncheon tomorrow." She frowned and swatted at a mosquito buzzing her head.

"Well, ma'am, we're here to solve your problem. Let me introduce you to Ms. Lorraine Johnson." Anthony urged me forward, and I nodded at Kim. "She's a personal friend of mine in need of a place to stay and a job. I thought maybe she could help you out."

Kim looked me over and shook my hand. "Nice to meet you, Lorraine, but"—she looked at Anthony—"you know I can't take anyone without references and a background check."

"Not even if I vouch for her? You wouldn't even have to put her on your payroll. Just an informal arrangement for a week or two. She really just needs a place to stay."

"Where would she sleep? I don't have an extra bed."

I couldn't blame her for trying to wiggle out of this unexpected intrusion, but my lack of sleep and the stress was overwhelming, making me feel dead on my feet.

"May I make a suggestion? Allow me to sleep on your couch tonight, and tomorrow, I'll help with the luncheon. Afterward, if you're satisfied with me, we can work out the details then. If not, I'll leave and find something else."

Anthony rocked back on his heels while Kim considered the idea. Her expression, fixed in his direction, made it clear she was not happy to have this sprung on her. At last, she sighed.

"All right, we'll try it, just for a day. Come on in, Lorraine. I'll introduce you to the ladies." Anthony said good-night and returned to his car. Kim closed the door behind us and ushered me into the living room where a woman in a wheelchair leaned toward the television in rapt concentration. A conversational grouping of armchairs joined a sofa on the far wall. An armchair and rocker, both empty, faced the television in a different corner of the room. The TV blared a baseball game as we approached the woman in the wheelchair.

"How's the game going, Maxie?" Kim rested her hand on one of the wheelchair's handles.

The woman in the wheelchair licked her thumb, then pointed it at the floor and gave a Bronx cheer. "They're stinkin' it up. My grandson plays a better game than these guys."

Kim's eyes narrowed, and she frowned as she peered down into the woman's lap. "Where'd you get that bag of chips?"

"Not chips." Maxine kept her gaze glued to the TV but held up an orange snack bag. "Cheese curls." She licked more orange powder from her thumb and fingers, then dipped into the bag again.

"We'll have to check your blood sugar before you go to bed." Kim tapped the woman's shoulder and tried to speak over the television announcer. "Maxine, this is Lorraine Johnson."

The woman held up a hand for silence and leaned even closer to the television as the pitcher went into his windup. Bright red lipstick stood out against her pale complexion, and the lines on her broad face hinted at a hard life. She might've been that color blonde once, but that was decades ago. A stump of one leg ended below the knee and hung over the edge of her seat. Curse words spewed from her mouth as the last batter swung and missed.

"Maxie, watch your language. We have a guest." Kim apologized to me.

Maxine crumpled the snack bag and punched the remote to turn off the TV. Defiance twinkled in her eyes as she looked at Kim. "Girl's gotta let off steam somehow when her boys give the game away. Besides, Stan already left, so there's no one I need to impress." She eyed me up and down. "Nice to meetcha, honey. Kim's place here ain't too bad, if this is where they put ya." I imagined a cigarette hanging from her mouth and wondered if Kim allowed smoking.

Kim patted her arm. "Thanks for the glowing recommendation. I'll be back to check your sugar in a few minutes." She led me toward a hallway that corresponded to the wing I'd seen from the car. The first door was slightly ajar, and Kim raised her hand to knock when a shout burst from a room farther down the hall.

"Get out!"

Kim stepped to the third door and knocked.

"Jean? Is something wrong?"

"Get this strange woman out of here!"

Kim shot a confused look my way. Me? How did she know I was here without even seeing me? And what made her so anxious to get rid of me? Kim shrugged and jiggled the doorknob.

"Jean, open the door for me."

"I told you to get out. Now go! No! You go."

Kim pulled a ring of keys from her pocket and unlocked the bathroom door, pushing it wide open. "Jean? What's the matter? Who's in here with you?"

"She is." A lean woman stood before the sink, tall and dressed in a white cotton bathrobe. With bits of her hair in pin curls, I decided she must be nearing eighty. She pointed at the mirror. "I've told her to get out. She keeps watching me, but she doesn't belong in here when I'm using the bathroom."

"Jean, that's you. It's your reflection." Kim stood next to Jean and waved at the mirror. "See? There's me, and there's you."

Jean wasn't buying it. "Make her get out of here and leave me alone."

Kim cupped her arm around Jean's shoulders and guided her to where I stood in the hallway. "Come on out here for a minute and let me introduce you to Lorraine Johnson. She's our guest tonight. I didn't want you to be upset seeing someone new here."

Apparently, a strange woman in the hall didn't bother her as much as a strange woman in the bathroom.

Jean came nose to nose with me, clutching her bathrobe close to her chest. "Did you see her? She won't let me have any privacy."

I offered my sympathy. "Yes, I heard. Maybe if you keep your back to her, she'll stop looking at you."

"I tried that, but every time I look to see if she's watching, she's peeking right back at me."

The first door on the hallway opened, and a dark-skinned woman emerged. Bearing a strong resemblance to Anthony, she leaned on a walker, her nightgown hanging loose on her thin frame. Jean moved to plead with her for help getting the woman out of the bathroom, then turned to Maxine who was coming down the hall in her wheelchair.

"She sees her reflection and thinks it's some strange woman," Kim explained.

Maxine rolled her eyes. "Throw a towel over the mirror so she can't see it. Now move aside and let me through." She wheeled past us and disappeared into the last room at the end of the hall.

Kim grabbed a large bath towel and made several unsuccessful attempts to hang it over the mirror. When that didn't work, she called for thumbtacks. I volunteered to retrieve them from her office. When the towel hung securely in place, she called Jean into the room.

"How's this? Better?"

Jean tiptoed into the bathroom and peeked at the mirror. Her grip on her bathrobe relaxed. "She's gone. How did you get her out?"

Kim patted her shoulder. "Never mind. You let me know if she bothers you again." Kim closed the bathroom door, leaving Jean inside. Her lips pressed tight together until the corners turned up ever so slightly. Finally, she said, "Vascular dementia. It comes and goes. Some days, she's so lucid you'd never know she's had a stroke." Her eyes brimmed with tears. "Other times, you have to laugh to keep from crying."

CHAPTER 10

Ruby objected to Kim's plan.

"She don't need to sleep in the living room. Put her in here with me." She nodded toward her room, but Kim refused. I couldn't blame her for keeping me away from her clients, even if I did come with a police officer's recommendation.

"She'll be fine on the couch for one night," Kim said. "It's too late now to find someplace else for her."

Ruby eyed my plastic bags. "Is that all you brung with you?"

"Yes, I'm traveling light." Easy to do when one has nothing left.

Ruby continued observing my odd luggage while Kim grabbed some bed linens from the laundry room. "You can use the bathroom for dressing. Breakfast will be at 7:00 tomorrow. The other ladies leave for church at 9:30. Usually, I join them, but with Mother's Day tomorrow, we're having a family brunch. So you and I will stay home to prepare for that." She headed for the living room. "Give me a minute, and I'll have the couch made up for you."

"We all go to Brother Stan's church," Ruby said. "Are you Baptist, by any chance?"

"No. No, I'm not." I'd grown up Methodist, but hadn't entered a church in years except for weddings and funerals.

"Well, that's okay, but I think you'll enjoy it when you can join us." Ruby looked up the hall toward the living room and whispered, "I really wouldn't mind if you want to stay here in my room."

I reached out and squeezed her hand. "That's very kind. Thank you, but I'll be fine. See you in the morning."

Kim finished making up the couch. "I have a night nurse who comes on duty at 11:00. She'll need some of the lights on. I hope that doesn't bother you, but this is the best we can do for now."

I assured her I'd be fine, and she excused herself to check Maxine's blood sugar. By the time I finished changing and getting ready for bed, the rest of the house was quiet, the lights turned low.

I sank onto the couch, thankful I didn't have to wrestle with a seatbelt receptacle. The stress of traveling, of pretending to be someone I'm not, of seeing my house in flames—it was all too much. Nothing sounded better than to close my eyes, shut everything out, and sleep for hours or maybe days. I exhaled and concentrated on relaxing each part of my body. But half an hour passed and still, I lay there staring at the pattern on the ceiling from the dimmed lights in the adjoining room.

Yesterday, I was Elaine Sutterfeld, a recent widow looking for the evidence Roy collected against the person who kidnapped and killed my student a decade ago. Now, a mere twenty-four hours later, I was Lorraine Johnson, hiding among the ladies of a care home in Texas and running from someone who killed my husband, broke into my home, and burned it to the ground. My thoughts zipped one way then another, like a crazy carnival ride, as I tried to process it all.

If only I could fall asleep and wake up to find it was only a bad dream. But whenever I closed my eyes, I saw flames gushing up through the windows of my home, scaling the walls, and devouring the roof. What kind of evil person would set fire to a widow's house? Did they know I wasn't home? Had they intended to kill me too?

A soft *ding* alerted me to a text message. I got out of bed and rummaged through my purse for the cell phone. A message from Anthony asked how things went.

> Sleeping on the living room couch. It's better than your car, but not by much. Met Ruby. She's anxious to see you.

> I'll be there in the morning to take her to church.

Knowing Anthony was nearby provided some comfort, but the noises of an unfamiliar house coupled with the events of the last twenty-four hours kept sleep at bay. Overwhelming loneliness settled around me, but I refused to give in, clamping my jaw tight in resistance to the threatening tears. I missed my home, and I missed Roy something fierce. Without him, I had no one with whom to discuss my suspicions, my fears, my ideas. Anthony might be like a son, but he was no substitute. I trusted Roy's knowledge and judgment completely. Then again, his judgment in confronting the person responsible for Jenny's disappearance hadn't proven all that great. No, I should've known better than to let him go off that morning. If I'd questioned him more, pressed a little harder, Roy might still be alive. It was my fault.

Anthony was right about one thing. Dining was elegant with the view of the backyard through those full-length windows. They'd been covered by drapes last night when I arrived, but this morning I was taken in by the scenery as Ruby and I arrived for breakfast.

The grassy yard sloped away from the house to a pond at the edge of a wooded area. Unlike my old neighborhood where shabby-looking weathered wood fences surrounded small yards and kept neighbors apart, there was nothing here to denote property boundaries, and every angle offered a pleasant view. To our right, gnarled limbs from three ancient oak trees bowed low to the ground like gentlemen proposing on one knee. I pictured a Victorian tea party with ladies in long flowing dresses and handsome young men playing a game of croquet. The only thing missing was a colorful flower garden.

Ruby nudged my arm. "You should have seen it in March when the bluebonnets and Indian paintbrush were blooming. They just cut the grass last week. Y'know, you have to wait 'til they go to seed if you want 'em to come back next year."

The tantalizing scent of bacon wafted in from the kitchen, and I offered to help Kim. She pointed out the plates and utensils and asked me to distribute them around the rectangular table covered by a white tablecloth. I set serving bowls of cut fruit and salsa at opposite ends, adding a nice touch of color.

Maxine rolled up to one end of the table and made no effort to cover her yawning mouth. A scarlet silk robe covered most of her cleavage, but clashed with her red lipstick. Daylight exposed gray roots in her hair, pulled back in a ponytail, and accented the lines on her face. She struck me as someone not to be tangled with, even if she was missing half a leg.

Jean took the chair next to Maxine. At first glance, she appeared more lucid than last night as she smiled at me and unfolded her napkin to lay it across her lap.

"Good morning, Elaine. Did you sleep all right?"

"I can't complain about a place to sleep and a roof over my head." It was honest, if nothing else.

Maxine squinted at me. "I thought your name was Lorraine."

I stiffened, thinking back over Jean's words. "It *is* Lorraine."

"Then why's she calling you Elaine?"

Was this a trick? How could anyone know my real name? Heat crept up my neck to my face as I looked at Jean.

She laid a hand on my wrist. "I'm so sorry. What's your name again?" She looked every bit as embarrassed as I felt.

"Lorraine," I said. "Lorraine Johnson." Jean tapped her fingers on the table.

"Lorraine. Forgive me. My memory is worse than ever since my stroke, and I've always had this bad habit when it comes to people's names. If I can't remember someone's name, I come up with the name I think best fits them. I never get it right, but you look like a perfect Elaine to me." She gave a little laugh. "That was my sister's name. You must remind me of her."

I gave her shoulder a reassuring squeeze. "I never even noticed until Maxine said something. You're welcome to call me anything you like. As long as it's decent, of course."

We both laughed, but I couldn't help comparing her performance last night with the seemingly intelligent woman sitting next to me this morning. I wondered if she was aware of how her mind slipped out of gear, or if she lived in a blessed ignorance?

Maxine hollered toward the kitchen. "What's for breakfast?"

Kim brought out a platter of scrambled eggs and bacon. "You get Chef Kim while Gabby's out, which means you'll have to settle for plain old scrambled eggs and bacon. Lorraine, would you bring in the coffee?"

While I filled each cup on the table, Ruby asked a blessing on the meal. Jean bowed her head, but Maxine huffed and made no effort to keep the serving spoon from tapping the platter as she scooped a generous serving of eggs onto her plate. Almost before Ruby finished the *Amen,* Maxine asked her to pass the salsa.

"So, are you in here for life, or will you get time off for good behavior?" She added a dollop of salsa to her eggs.

Kim rolled her eyes as she set her own plate on the other side of the table. "This is not a prison, Maxie."

"Coulda fooled me. I go in for a bum leg, the doc cuts it off, and sentences me—"

"Would you rather he let you die from infection and gangrene? Pay attention to your diabetes, show me you'll take care of yourself, and you're free to go home."

Maxine looked at me. "Isn't that what I just said? They let you out for good behavior, but if you don't cooperate, you're in for life."

"Well"—Ruby dabbed her mouth with her napkin—"it's a nice place if you have to be here."

"Lorraine may not be staying long," Kim said.

"Oh? Why?" Jean offered me the fruit bowl.

"She's going to help me with the luncheon today, since Gabby's on bed rest. After that, we'll see what happens." Kim helped herself to the eggs. I selected a few chunks of honeydew melon and some grapes.

"I'm looking for a place to stay for a short time, and something to keep me busy. I've recently lost both my home and my husband. We had no children and I have no other close relatives." Was that vague and general enough to satisfy their curiosity? I didn't want them to hear something about me on the news and make the connection.

Ruby's head nodded in time with her chewing. "Gets a mite lonely, doesn't it?"

Maxine plunked her elbow onto the table and flicked her spoon up and down. "Where'd you say you were from?"

"Illinois." I couldn't remember the address on my new card,

and hoped that answer would satisfy Maxine's curiosity. But just in case, I changed the subject. "Looks like you could use a gardener."

A couple neglected flowerbeds dotted the edges of the yard. On the patio, dried plant carcasses hung over the edges of pots in varying sizes.

Kim swallowed some coffee before answering. "You met my dad last night at the door. He takes care of mowing and edging, but he hasn't tackled any gardening yet. I used to do it when I took care of my grandmother, but since evolving into a care home, I haven't had the time."

"I've always had two brown thumbs," Jean said, holding up her fingers.

"Did you garden before you came here?" Ruby asked.

"Yes, a little." Ideas for flowers in the gardens and planters were already percolating in my head. But of course, I wouldn't be here long enough for those ideas to germinate. Still, gardening helped to stimulate my thinking—something I'd need if I were going to figure out who was trying to silence me.

The doorbell rang, and Anthony's familiar knock sounded as Kim cleared the dishes from the table. Without thinking, I opened my mouth to call *Come in*, but caught myself in time. Kim answered the door. Anthony's deep voice carried on a one-sided conversation in the living room, but upon entering the dining room, he clicked off his phone and slipped it into his belt holster.

"Good morning, ladies! How's everyone this fine day?" He walked straight over to Ruby and bent to kiss her cheek. "How's my favorite mama?" Her dark face beamed as he wrapped his strong arms around her thin shoulders.

"If you're passing out kisses, lay one on me." Maxine tapped her finger against her uplifted cheek.

Anthony chuckled. "Sorry, Ms. Maxie. Only for my best girl."

Maxine grunted and put on a pout. "Thought I was your best girl."

"Second best." He winked at Maxine, then turned his attention to Jean. "And who is this young lady?"

"Jean Lebow." She offered her hand, and Anthony shook it.

"Pleased to meet you, Ms. Jean. Is Kim treating you all right?"

"Yes, but I'd really like to go home. Do you think you could take me?"

"I'd love to take you home, but we'll have to make it another time."

Jean looked disappointed, but quickly asked, "Have you met Elaine? She's filling in for Gabby."

Anthony stiffened. His gaze darted to me, but before I could respond, Maxine intervened.

"Jean, we just went over this. Her name's Lorraine, not Elaine."

I touched Jean's hand. "It's okay. Anthony already knows I'm Lorraine. He's the one who brought me here." I greeted Anthony and explained, "Jean thinks I look a little like her sister, Elaine." His shoulders relaxed, and he chuckled.

Jean waved her hand in front of her face and apologized. "But really now, don't you think she looks like an Elaine?"

Anthony raised one eyebrow and gave me an appraising look. "Maybe, but I definitely see more Lor-raine in her than E-laine." He put his hands on Ruby's shoulders.

"Mama, you need to get yourself ready for church?" He pulled her chair out from the table, moved her walker into place, and held her elbow as she pushed herself up.

Kim called from the kitchen. "Anthony, you can ride in the van if you want. I asked Dad to drive today since I'm staying home to fix brunch. I'm sure he'd enjoy some male company."

"Is that okay with you, Mama?" Anthony pushed her chair in under the table.

"Whatever you decide is fine with me. Come on, Jean. We'd best get ourselves ready." Ruby shuffled on down the hall with Jean following. Anthony moved to the patio door and unlocked it.

"Here comes Stan now."

The man who'd bumped into Anthony at the door last night was striding across the backyard from the direction of the pond. Maxine shrugged one shoulder out of her bathrobe. She aimed a red smile at the door and waited for Kim's dad to finish rubbing his shoes on the mat outside the door.

Anthony slid the patio door open. "Mind if I ride with you today, Stan? Kim said you're driving."

Stan stepped into the dining room and clapped his hands. "Of course. The more the merrier."

"Good morning, Stan." Maxine's voice dripped with sweetness. She pushed away from the table, then stopped. "Honey, would you check this wheel for me? It won't move."

A blush touched Stan's cheeks, but he moved to kneel and check the problem wheel. He pushed a lever on the chair's front leg.

"Simple fix," he said. "You forgot to take the brake off."

Maxine giggled like a teenager and leaned forward, exposing more of her cleavage. "How silly of me. I'm as forgetful as Jean." She whirled her chair around and headed down the hallway to her bedroom, waving her fingers over her shoulder. "Don't leave without me."

Stan rose to his feet, his gaze falling on me.

"I don't believe I properly introduced myself last night after running into Anthony. I'm Stan Graham, Kim's father." He held out his hand in greeting.

"Nice to meet you, Stan. I'm Lorraine Johnson." His soft, warm hands clasped mine briefly.

"Are you joining us for worship this morning?"

"Thank you, but I'll stay here and help Kim get things ready for the Mother's Day lunch." My decision wasn't solely because of my trial period with Kim, or my distant relationship with God. Church clothes hadn't been on my shopping list yesterday.

After church, Kim suggested the ladies might want to change clothes since we'd be outdoors. Only Jean headed to her room. One of Anthony's sisters arrived from Houston, and Kim shooed everyone out to the patio to wait for Maxine's daughter and her family before eating. We'd covered three round tables with festive pink tablecloths. A single, long-stemmed rose in a bud vase stood in the center of each table.

Soon, the rumble of a diesel engine sounded in the driveway beside the house. It shut off abruptly, doors opened and slammed shut, and a couple of angry adult voices competed with the excited squealing of children. A younger version of Maxine rounded the corner followed by a young man carrying a child draped over each of his shoulders.

His expression contrasted sharply with the youngsters' laughing protests, and he lengthened his stride to keep up with the woman. "There's just no pleasing you, is there? No matter what I do, it's never good enough. You said we didn't have enough money. So I got a better job, and you're still complaining."

The woman tossed her blonde hair back from her face. "I'm not complaining about the money or the job. It's that woman. Would you like it if one of the salesmen at work was hitting on me?"

"She's not hitting on me. She's just friendly. When did you get so jealous?"

"Gee, I don't know. Maybe it was when I found not one, not two, but three cigarette butts with lipstick on them in your truck. How long did it take you to get to and from lunch that she had time to smoke three cigarettes?" The woman slammed a plate of brownies onto the closest table, then moved over to Maxine, anger still lacing her voice.

"Happy Mother's Day, Mom." She dropped a bouquet of flowers in front of Maxine. The older woman picked up the flowers and shoved them back at her daughter.

"Go back and try that again. This time, say it like you mean it."

The younger woman deflated.

"Sorry, Mom. Happy Mother's Day." She placed the flowers in Maxine's hand, gave her a quick hug and kissed her cheek. "Riley and Micah. Come say hello to Grandma Maxie before you run down to the pond."

The man unloaded the children at the edge of the patio, and Maxine spread her arms wide. "Come give ol' Maxie a hug and kiss." She grabbed the boy and girl in a tight hug and planted loud, sloppy kisses on their cheeks.

"Happy Mother's Day, Maxie."

"Happy Mother's Day."

The children broke away and hurried down to the pond, smearing red lipstick marks into wide swaths across their faces.

"Be careful," their mother called. "You fall in, you'll be wearing wet clothes the rest of the afternoon." Pointedly turning her back to her husband when he approached Maxine, she used a more pleasant tone to greet everyone else.

"Thanks so much for doing this today, Kim. Great idea. Anthony! It's so good to see you. How long are you here? Miss Ruby, don't you look nice? Is that a new dress? That color really suits you. Hey Stan. How was church this morning?" She took a second look when she came to me. "I don't believe we've met. I'm

Brandi Bullard, Maxine's daughter." She held out her hand to shake, and I took it.

"Nice to meet you, Brandi. I'm Lorraine Johnson. Anthony brought me here, thinking I might be able to fill in for Gabby while she's incapacitated."

"I'm sure Kim appreciates that. You saw my kids." She pointed toward the pond. "The girl is Riley, and Micah's the boy. And I guess you figured this is my husband, Travis. Sorry you had to hear our little discussion. You stick around long enough, you'll find out we're just one big family."

Travis smiled and shook my hand. A scraggly growth of whiskers did nothing for his handsome face, but that seemed to be the current fashion among young adult men. He wore his light brown hair long enough to curl over the tops of his ears and touch the back neckline of his t-shirt. Anthony offered him a glass of tea, and Stan greeted him with a handshake.

"Daddy! Come here. You gotta see this." Micah summoned his dad with vigorous hand waving.

Setting his glass on the table, Travis excused himself. "I'll be right back."

I offered Stan a cold glass of tea. He took it, thanked me, and raised it to his lips, his gaze traveling beyond my shoulder. His eyes widened, his back stiffened, and the tea sloshed from his glass onto his white shirt as he spun away.

"Kim!" He jabbed his thumb repeatedly over his shoulder toward the patio door behind us. "It's Jean."

The screen door slid open, and Jean stepped out wearing her bra and panties, a pair of flip-flop sandals and a sunny smile. A towel dangled over one arm.

"Excuse me," she said, "which way is the pool party? I'm supposed to meet some friends there."

CHAPTER 11

Kim nearly dropped the tray of sandwiches we'd carefully arranged. I set the last glass of tea on the nearest table and hurried over to grab the towel from Jean's arm and wrap it around her.

"I'm afraid the pool party has been canceled, dear. Your friends went to get dressed for the luncheon. Let me help you get ready so you won't be late." I hustled Jean inside, but not before I heard Maxine snort.

Ruby voiced a heartfelt prayer. "Lord, have mercy on that poor woman."

I helped Jean dress and returned her to the luncheon. Before following her outside, I checked the kitchen to see if anything else needed to go out. Anthony stood at the refrigerator, holding his glass under the ice dispenser.

"How's everything going?" He poured a refill of his iced tea.

I checked to make sure no one was within earshot. "As well as can be expected, but remind me how this is helping us find the person responsible for killing Roy and Jenny." I grabbed the potato salad from the fridge and hurried outside.

Anthony joined Ruby and his sister at one table, along with Kim and Jean. Brandi settled her kids at another table while Maxine joined Travis and Stan at their table, though it sounded like she had a difficult time distracting them from their conversation about car repairs. I sat with the children and urged Brandi to go fill a plate for herself.

"Hello, Riley, Micah. How old are you children?"

"I'm six." Micah bore a strong resemblance to Dennis the Menace, complete with white-blonde hair, a cowlick, and several strands that stuck up in the back. "I'm in first grade now, but pretty soon, I'll be in second."

"I'm in fourth grade," Riley volunteered. She looked a lot like her daddy, with soft brown hair hanging below her shoulders.

"And do you both enjoy school?"

They exchanged uncertain looks before Riley answered. "Kind of."

"I don't like homework." Micah wrinkled his nose. Riley offered a more detailed explanation.

"It's fun seeing my friends at school, but sometimes it's hard."

"She got an F on her math test." Micah pointed his finger at her, and Riley slapped it down.

"So! You can't read as fast as I can."

"Our brains work differently, don't they?" My diplomatic skills were a bit rusty, but I used to be able to defuse situations like this. "Some of us are good at one thing and some excel in other ways. Many times, our brains simply need to grow and mature a little more before we can understand certain ideas, especially math concepts."

Brandi returned with her food and sat down beside Micah. "Did you kids introduce yourselves to Ms. Lorraine?"

"She already knew our names, but she didn't tell us hers." Micah snuck a glance at me after receiving a warning look from his mom.

"You're absolutely right, Micah," I said. "I should've told you I'm Mrs. Johnson."

Micah picked at his ham sandwich. "Are you a teacher?"

"I used to be, but it's been a long time, before either of you were born."

"How old are you?"

"That's enough, Micah," Brandi interrupted. "It's not polite to ask grownups how old they are. Finish your sandwich and fruit, and then you two can go play again." She brushed a crumb from his cheek.

"Can Daddy play soccer with us?"

"You'll have to ask him."

Riley poked his arm. "I guess not. Looks like he and Pastor Stan are going somewhere." She tipped her head toward the departing men and frowned.

"Maybe when he gets back." Micah bit into his sandwich as Maxine rolled her wheelchair over to our table.

"It's impossible to catch Stan's attention with Travis talking his ear off." She harrumphed.

Brandi's gaze followed the two men to Travis's pickup at the side of the house. "I hope some of Stan's influence will rub off on Travis." Her attention returned to the table, and she asked the kids if they were finished. "You can go play now."

As soon as they left, Maxine asked, "Is he cheating on you?"

Brandi threw her napkin onto the table. "I don't know. He's home every night, but he always smells like a perfume factory instead of a mechanic."

Maxine chewed a large bite of her sandwich and swallowed. "First time you catch him messing around, you kick his lazy butt out the door."

"I can't afford to, Mother. My job alone won't support me and the kids."

"They're his kids, too. Nail him for child support." Brandi

sighed, but Maxine continued. "You stick it out until he really decides to leave you for some other chick and then what? Your job still won't support you and the kids, *and* he'll be wiggling out of his fair share for those kids."

Brandi collected the kids' plates and cleaned up the crumbs they left behind. "I can't believe he'd really cheat on me, but what am I supposed to think when he smells like that?"

"I told you! Get rid of him. It's a big pond out there. Go find yourself a better fish. There's plenty to choose from."

"Oh, Mother, you don't understand."

"Really? Married and divorced three times. Tell me what I don't understand."

"Never mind." Trash in her hands, Brandi walked over to the patio door and slipped inside.

I remained silent, uncertain how to extricate myself from such a personal conversation. Without a trace of apology or embarrassment, Maxine looked at me and grunted.

"Happy Mother's Day."

Kim set aside plates for both Travis and Stan, but when they returned, Travis grabbed a sandwich and called down to the pond where Brandi was supervising the kids. "Boss called. He wants me to come in to work this afternoon." He stuffed half the sandwich in his mouth.

"On Sunday? Mother's Day?" Brandi trudged up the hill to the patio. "For how long?"

Chewing, Travis talked around the food in his mouth. "They didn't say."

"How are we supposed to get home if you take the truck?"

"Stan said he'd take you. Just ask him. I got to go." Travis raised his hand with the sandwich and called a thank you to Kim then ran to his truck. Hands on hips, Brandi stood staring at the driveway until the engine noise died away down the street. Her shoulders slumped as she called to Riley and Micah to gather their things so they could go home.

Ruby caught Brandi's hand as she walked past. "Pray for him, honey. Don't give up praying for him."

"Thank you, Ms. Ruby. I won't quit." Brandi's mouth curved into a smile that matched the sadness in her eyes. "I pray for him every day." She covered Ruby's hand with her other one. She sniffed and turned to go, her eyes blinking a rapid beat.

Anthony and his sister left shortly after Stan shuttled Brandi and her children home. Ruby and Jean retired to their rooms for a nap, but Maxine parked in front of the television to watch an afternoon Rangers game.

Kim called me into her office and closed the door. Dropping into her desk chair, she ran her fingers through the sides of her hair, pulling it away from her face. Eyes closed, she exhaled heavily.

"You look like you could use a nap, too." I took the chair closest to her desk.

Kim dropped her hands from her hair, and she opened her eyes. "I don't do naps. But I wanted to tell you how much I appreciated your help today, with the brunch and with Jean." She sat up straight and pulled herself close to her desk. "I was planning to hire someone else, but if Anthony can vouch for you, I'll take you on. I should warn you though, I can't pay much. How much were you expecting?"

"How much would I be doing for you?" I hadn't considered getting paid. The prospect of earning my keep appealed to me, but it would require my Social Security number and other things Anthony wanted kept secret.

"I'll take care of the meal planning and any nursing care, but cooking will be your primary responsibility. Some laundry and light cleaning. Mainly, I want you around in case I'm tied up when one of the ladies needs something—like today with Jean." Kim closed her eyes once again and shook her head, then continued. "I'll show you the medication schedule and go over the meds with you, but I don't expect you to be responsible for that. I'll also show you how to check Maxie's blood sugar. She's not very good about keeping an eye on it and watching her diet."

I pretended to consider her proposal. "I know Anthony kind of threw me on you with little notice. Why don't we make this a room and board arrangement?"

Kim pushed a folder aside, then moved it back. "I'd still need some kind of contract with you in case an inspector or anyone from the state showed up—to prove I'm not over my limit of three residents. You'd be acting as an aide."

"Where do I sign?"

Kim blew out a breath and smiled. "Let me draw up a contract, and we'll both sign it later this evening. I'll talk to Ruby and see if she'd mind sharing a room while you're here. I don't think it'll be any problem. Thank you, Lorraine. You are a Godsend."

If God sent me, I wish He'd have done so without taking away my husband and my home. I retrieved my phone from my purse and went out to the patio. The afternoon was warm, but comfortable, and I was hungry for some solitude. I pulled a patio chair over to a shady spot and sat down to text Anthony about my agreement with Kim.

While waiting for his reply, I studied the untended flowerbeds and planters around the house. Would Kim agree to let me spruce up the place, plant some flowers and maybe even start a small vegetable garden? Or maybe I shouldn't get too ambitious, considering I wasn't planning to be here long enough to harvest anything. But a few hours in a garden might be the very thing I needed to figure out where that memory card might be hiding.

Anthony replied to my text, happy to hear a deal had been worked out, but he cautioned me about giving out any personal information that might provide a clue to my whereabouts. We exchanged several messages back and forth before signing off. He'd be back tomorrow morning to take Ruby out for the day.

The scene before me, the yard and the beds, led me to thoughts of home. Had my lilac bushes survived the fire? What about the cherry tree on the side of the house that exploded into pink and white every spring? I imagined my low shrubs close against the house all shriveled and brown from the heat, everything else trampled by firefighters in their quest to put out the flames. Was it only two days ago I'd worked those beds, tended those shrubs? It seemed like ages, and yet a week before that, I kissed Roy good-bye for the last time. And that seemed like yesterday.

Up in the sky, a lone helium balloon floated—remnants of someone's celebration. Its string untethered, it moved aimlessly through space, carried along by whatever wind currents it encountered. How long would it float along with nothing, and no one, to anchor it in place?

I wished I knew.

CHAPTER 12

"Good morning, Ms. Jean. How are you today?" Anthony pulled up an extra chair and sat at the corner of the breakfast table beside Ruby. His resonant voice filled the lull of conversation. Jean cocked her head and gave him a quizzical look.

"I'm fine, thank you. Have we met before?"

Anthony's smile dimmed slightly and his gaze swept the rest of us at the table.

I touched Jean's arm. "We met Anthony yesterday at the Mother's Day lunch."

"I need a new brain." Jean pressed her fingers to her forehead.

Anthony's laugh rumbled. "I might-could use a new brain myself."

Looking at Anthony, Jean held her hand out in my direction. "Did you meet Elaine when you were here yesterday? She's new here."

"You mean Ms. Lorraine?" Anthony winked at me.

Jean looked at me, the furrows in her brows deepening. "No. You're Elaine, aren't you?" Her hand dropped to the table. Her fingers fiddled with the knife and spoon beside her plate, turning them over and over. She alternately licked her lips and pressed them tight together.

I placed my hand over hers. "Jean, you may call me Elaine if you'd like. No need to get upset. I go by either Elaine or Lorraine."

"Oh, okay." Keeping her head bowed, she blinked several times in rapid succession, then picked up her spoon and dipped it into the bowl of oatmeal in front of her. Anthony took up the conversation again.

"Maxine, you're looking beautiful this morning. More like a movie star every time I see you."

Maxine puckered her lipsticked mouth and blew him a kiss. "I love it when you're around. You need to visit more often."

Anthony patted Ruby's shoulder. "Mama tells me the same thing."

"Listen to your mama." Maxine pointed her fork at him.

Kim offered Anthony the last bit of oatmeal left in the pot, but he turned it down. "I'm saving my appetite for later. Taking Mama out on the town today."

When everyone finished eating, I cleared away the dishes and loaded them into the dishwasher. I'd signed the agreement with Kim last night, so after Anthony and Ruby left, Kim explained the medication schedule to me and demonstrated how to test Maxine's blood sugar.

"I doubt you'll ever need to do this, but it's good for you to know just in case." Kim applied the lancet device to Maxine's finger, then pressed out a drop of blood and caught it with the meter strip. "And don't let Maxie give you a hard time if I ever ask you to test her."

Maxine pressed a cotton ball to her finger. "Me give someone a hard time? When did that ever happen?"

Kim half-smiled. "When *doesn't* it happen?"

"Just making sure you earn what I'm paying you."

Kim recorded the blood sugar reading, then put everything back in her office cabinet and locked it with a key. "Do you have any questions?"

"Is there anything you need me to do right now?"

"It's Monday. I usually try to do laundry today. We'll need to strip the beds and put clean sheets on them before starting to launder the clothing."

I picked up a pen that lay on the corner of her desk and tapped it against the papers stacked there. "All right. In between loads, would you mind if I did a little work on the flower beds and planters?"

Kim laughed. "Anything you can do to make this place look better, I'm all for it. You'll find some tools in the detached garage. Oh, wait. It's probably locked." She separated the keys on her ring and twisted one off. "Here you go."

I stripped the beds and replaced the sheets with clean ones. As soon as I got the first load in the wash, I sorted through my clothes to find something appropriate for gardening. Maybe my brown capris wouldn't show much dirt. Too bad I hadn't bought a sun hat.

A search of the garage produced a rake, a hoe, and some hand tools, and I took them out to the planters by the front door. Antique rose bushes in full bloom provided the only color on this side of the house. The red petals clashed with the orange brick siding, but white impatiens or petunias around the base might soften the mismatch. A pallet or two of other colorful flowers at the ends of the planters would go a long way to lessen the dreary institutional look of the house.

Only a few strokes with the small hand rake made me wish for some garden gloves. A stiff old pair I'd found in the garage proved too clumsy. I took them off and tossed them aside before dragging my rake through a mound of loose dirt. Ants swarmed everywhere. I'd never seen such a hoard, rushing in every direction, climbing up my rake, onto my hand and—

"Ow!" I dropped the tool onto the mound and slapped at the ants surging over my hand, biting and stinging. I scrambled away as thousands of ants still poured from the mound.

Stan rounded the corner of the house, took one look at my hand, and dragged me by the wrist to the nearest spigot, swatting ants off my hand as we moved. He turned the water on and held my hand under the stream, spreading my fingers and brushing away every ant still clinging to my hand.

When he finally turned the water off and let go of my hand, angry red welts dotted my skin. An intense burning sensation brought tears to my eyes.

"Feels like I'm on fire. What are those nasty creatures?"

Stan ushered me to the front door. "You've never seen fire ants before?" He opened the door and called for Kim. As we entered, Jean, Ruby, and Maxine all looked up from the morning talk show that blared from the television. Stan once again took hold of my wrist to examine the bites.

Maxine turned from the television to watch us. "What happened to you?" Her tone wasn't exactly sympathetic.

"She got into some fire ants," Stan explained. "Where's Kim?"

"I'm right here." Kim came out from the wing of the house that comprised her private rooms. "What happened?" She examined my hand. "Let me get some Benadryl. Are you allergic to ant bites?"

"I have no idea. I've never been stung like this before." Extreme itching now accompanied the pain, and my fingers were feeling fat.

"She's beginning to swell," Kim said, spraying my hand with an anti-itch medicine. "Come into the kitchen, and let's get some ice on it."

"Are you feeling okay?" Stan kept hold of my elbow, removing his cap and setting it on the dining table as we walked to the kitchen. "No trouble breathing or anything?"

"No, but the swelling seems to be spreading up my hand to my wrist.

Stan traced his finger over the bites on the back of my hand and pressed his fingers into the puffy skin.

"She might need to go to a clinic." Stan looked at Kim. "It's her first time with fire ants."

Kim drew her head back as if having an Aha! moment. "You've never encountered fire ants before?"

"We don't have them up north."

Kim half-frowned. "I should've warned you before I let you go out and dig around in the flower beds. Dad, would you put out some bait and see if we can get rid of them before she does any more gardening?" She turned my hand over and back, counting the number of welts. "I agree. The way this is swelling up, she needs to have a doctor look at it. I can't even see all the bites anymore. Can you take her?"

Stan bobbed his head. "Sure. Let me run home and get my truck. I'll be right back." He grabbed his cap, exited the patio door, and hurried across the backyard.

My thoughts raced ahead. A doctor's office would require identification, like my Social Security number and insurance. Would I have time to call Anthony?

Maxine appeared in the kitchen. "Where's Stan going?"

"He's taking Lorraine to the urgent care clinic. I don't like the way she's swelling up." Kim wrapped an ice pack around my hand. "Maxie, would you mind going and getting her purse for her?" Kim put a glass of water in my hand and urged me to take an antihistamine pill.

Maxine backed out and returned with my purse. "Never seen

a purse in camouflage green before." She wrinkled her nose as if she'd bitten into a dill pickle.

Kim accompanied me out to the driveway to wait. When Stan arrived, she opened the door and helped me into the seat. "Keep that ice pack on your hand until you see the doctor. It'll help both the swelling and the itching." She waved and headed back inside.

Stan backed onto the street, apologizing for the ants in the planter. "I didn't think to treat the beds for ants because no one was planting anything. But that's no excuse, really. I should've treated the whole yard, including the planters and the beds."

He raised the windows and punched the A/C button, sending an initial whoosh of warm air onto my face. "So, tell me about yourself. You came here with Anthony. What did you do before you came to Waco?"

I wasn't ready for an interrogation. Hard to think with my hand on fire, but a chill settled on my shoulders that had nothing to do with the air conditioning.

"I...lost my husband." My throat closed up, and with my good hand, I dug through my purse for a tissue. Would I ever get past these sudden onslaughts of grief? Stan glanced my way.

"I'm sorry. Losing your mate is devastating. This happened recently?" The tenderness in his voice could only have come from experience. I remembered Anthony saying Kim's mom died from heart disease.

I swallowed the lump that cut off my breathing, nodded, and faced the side window. Dabbing my eyes behind my glasses, I cleared my throat, then tried my voice.

"I understand you're—?"

"I'm a widower, yes. My wife had a heart condition. She passed away almost ten years ago. I find the grief subsides, but never really leaves. It lurks in the shadows, waiting to attack when you least expect it."

Not the most comforting thought, but I appreciated his honesty. The ice pack slipped off my hand. I readjusted it, then stared out the window as we drove through the neighborhood. Older one-story homes with neat yards gave way to an armory with a military tank parked in front. We passed Little League fields and a children's park with a small Ferris wheel before entering more of a retail district. Feather flags called attention to a drug store, cell phone repair shop, nail salon and others in the strip shopping centers before we turned onto Waco Avenue. I asked Stan if he'd lived here long.

"Most of my adult life. I've pastored Good Hope Baptist here in Waco until retiring year before last. Kim says I haven't truly retired, but I no longer earn a regular paycheck. Occasionally, I sub for the new pastor or others around town, and I do a little counseling, mainly with my older parishioners who aren't as comfortable with the new, younger minister. But most of the time, I'm yard and maintenance man for Kim." He accelerated as the traffic thinned and a grin formed on his face. "One house call, and I can fix your toilet for now and your soul for eternity."

I chuckled. It was the first time I'd laughed since seeing that photo in the newspaper. Stan exited the highway and turned into the parking lot of an attractive building that listed several medical services. Once parked, Stan came around and helped me out of the truck, picking up my purse that had fallen on the floor.

"Don't think I've ever seen a purse in such an... interesting...color."

I swallowed and stuck my chin in the air. "It's the last gift my husband bought for me."

Pink tinged his tan cheeks. "The man had good taste."

I looked Stan in the eye. "Preachers aren't supposed to lie. You and I both know this is about the ugliest thing I ever hope to carry. I only keep it for the sentimental value. If he were still alive, I would've exchanged it before the end of the first day."

The corners of his mouth curved up despite his obvious attempts to quell the grin. "Yes, ma'am. I understand." Hand on my elbow, he directed me toward the door of the clinic.

Inside, he stood back while I checked in. The clerk questioned my refusal of any insurance claims, but I insisted on paying cash. I swallowed hard as I handed over a good chunk of the money I was supposed to live on for the next couple of weeks.

By the time they called me to the examining room, the ice pack had lost its chill, and that burning itch had returned to my hand. The doctor examined my hand, checked my respiration, and tried to give me another antihistamine. He recommended continuing doses as needed until the swelling went down, then wrote out a prescription for a cortisone cream to help with the itching. But filling a prescription required more information than I was willing to give, so before I returned to the waiting room, I folded the paper up and stuffed it in my purse.

Stan couldn't understand why the doctor hadn't done more than put a fresh ice pack on my hand, but I assured him I was satisfied with my treatment. His kind, gentle manner reminded me of Roy, and it felt odd to be alone with a man my age less than two weeks after Roy's death. Not that I had any romantic notions.

Unlike Maxine, I had no interest in looking for a new husband, though I did find myself enjoying Stan's company. His quiet confidence put me at ease, making it unnecessary to fill our drive time with forced conversation, and I found myself almost nodding off as we drove up the street to Kim's house.

Stan's cell phone rang. He answered and listened for a minute. "All right," he said, "I'm just pulling into Kim's place. I can be there in about twenty minutes." He said good-bye and slid the phone into his shirt pocket. "One of my former parishioners got himself into some trouble. I'll have to drop you off and go down to the jail."

"He called you instead of a lawyer?"

"No, that was his wife. It's not his first DUI ticket. If we can't get him to stop drinking, he'll lose his license. She's afraid he may be getting in deeper, mixing alcohol with prescription drugs."

Stan walked me to the front door, but left without stepping inside. I found Kim in the kitchen working on getting lunch ready and offered to help, but the antihistamine was taking a toll on my alertness.

"You look like you might fall asleep on your feet," Kim said. "Go sleep it off. I can take care of things here."

I mumbled an apology and shuffled off to Ruby's room. Yesterday, she'd insisted I share her room rather than sleep in the living room, so Kim transferred the linens to her couch. I lay down and slept the entire afternoon. The grogginess persisted during my appearance at the supper table. I managed to eat a few bites of Kim's Mexican lasagna, but on her orders, I crawled back into bed for the night. One text message from Anthony awaited me before I fell asleep.

> Sorry I missed you. Wanted to say goodbye. Leaving tomorrow. Need anything, let me know. Watch those fire ants. Should've warned you.

Leaving tomorrow? Tuesday? I thought he'd stick around at least until Thursday. The thought of being here, completely alone without any real identification, sent shivers through my body. Was that his purpose all along, to get me down here, out of the way, and abandon me? I pulled my thoughts together enough to reply.

Why are you leaving so soon?

Meeting a contact in Dallas PD re: drug trafficking case. Heading home from there.

My muddled brain struggled to connect Dallas to Chicago. I knew enough from Roy's work that illegal drugs traveled I-35 from Mexico to all points north. The interstate ran from the Mexican border right through Waco up to Dallas and continued all the way up to Minnesota. Of course, police departments from different cities often cooperated in various arenas, but wouldn't drugs be under the federal government's jurisdiction? My mind refused to go any further in such a thick fog. I fell asleep without sending a reply.

CHAPTER 13

Travis gave the socket wrench one more firm twist and pressed the button to lower the car to the floor. The vehicle descended until the tires flattened slightly under its weight. He still needed to get the paperwork to the front desk and clean up his tools before calling it quits for the day. He braced himself against Dustin's appeals to go out for drinks after work. If it were just some of the shop guys, he'd be all in, but it sounded like the invitation only included Dustin's girlfriend, Kaitlyn, and Lindsey from the front office.

The car's key slipped from his hand and he picked it up from the neatly painted floor. Almost clean enough to eat off of—a big change from the dingy, cramped independent garage where he'd worked without A/C or heat, choking on the dust and grime of old engines. This place paid better, too, even if he did get called in occasionally on his days off. There were worse things than making double time wages to fix the owner's car on Mother's Day. He owed his buddy, Dustin, for recommending him to the boss.

Travis dropped the key into a plastic page protector with the work order, deposited the envelope in the upright file slot for completed jobs, and put away his tools.

Dustin caught up to him on the way out to his truck. "Meet you at happy hour?"

"It's only Monday."

Dustin shrugged. "What's wrong with that? Better than waiting all the way 'til Friday."

Brandi's last words before he left for work this morning nagged as if she were standing beside him. Did she have to hassle him first thing in the morning? Of course, it wasn't much better when he got home at night. She'd deserve it if he walked out and never came back, but he couldn't do that to Riley and Micah. The pain of his parents' divorce when he was their age no longer seared his gut, but the ache never died out either. Still, he hated Brandi pushing him around.

"Yeah, I'll see ya there."

Dustin smiled and waved as he hopped into his late model Corvette. He must be quite a salesman to afford a car like that. A job on the sales floor appealed to him, but with the kids, he needed a guaranteed income. Working on commission was simply too risky and undependable.

Kaitlin and Lindsey motioned to them from the bar when he and Dustin entered the club. Kaitlin handed Dustin a drink and slid her arm around his waist, pulling him close for a kiss. Lindsey looked away, blowing cigarette smoke into the air while giving Travis a raised eyebrow and a seductive smile. Behind the front desk at work, she made an attractive first impression on customers. Her clothing choices emphasized her figure, and Travis had no doubt she'd received a multitude of requests for dates.

If he were single, he'd get in line, but he wasn't aiming for another entanglement. Besides, her perfume was strong enough to gag a fly at fifty feet. What did she do—bathe in it?

Maintaining a reasonable distance from her, Travis stepped up to the bar and ordered a beer. The television hanging behind the counter showed highlights from an auto race. He feigned interest, but Lindsey didn't take the hint.

"Glad you could make it tonight, Travis." She slid over next to him and leaned against his arm. "I hate feeling like a fifth wheel."

Travis glanced around looking for Dustin, but he and Kaitlin were nuzzling noses, gazing into each other's eyes with silly grins on their faces.

Lindsey's hand slipped along the inside of his arm and she whispered in his ear. "What do you say we go someplace quiet where we can talk and get to know each other better?"

Her perfume both intoxicated and suffocated him. He rotated his wedding band with his thumb, hoping to send a signal.

Lindsey covered his hand with hers while her other one slithered up the length of his arm and snaked around the back of his neck. Her breath brushed his hair as her lips touched his ear. "If she's not available, I am."

CHAPTER 14

The fog had cleared when I awoke Tuesday morning, but the burning itch on my hand tempted me to spend the day with my hand in the freezer. With the reduced swelling, I counted eleven welts between my fingers and on the back of my hand. Kim's anti-itch cream soothed it for a few minutes, but I preferred the numbness of an ice pack.

The doorbell rang early, before Maxine made it to the breakfast table. Kim asked me to put the rest of the food on the table and went to open the door.

"I'm sorry to be so early, but I need to talk to Mother." Brandi's heels beat a rapid staccato rhythm all the way back to Maxine's room.

"Oh Lord," Ruby whispered as I set the pancakes on the table. I stopped and bowed my head, thinking she was going to bless the meal. "This early in the morning, it can't be good." She and Jean exchanged knowing glances as the voices carried loud and clear from Maxine's room at the end of the hall.

"Well, Mother, you can't say I never listen to you. I kicked him out. He's gone."

"What'd he do this time?"

"He came home late smelling like he'd been in a perfume factory all day. It's that flaky woman that works the front desk at his new job. She's been hot after him since he started. But I won't stand for a man who cheats on me. I packed his bags and told him to get out."

Ruby lifted her voice. "Lord, we give you thanks for this food and the hands that prepared it."

The conversation carried along the hallway, growing louder as they neared the dining room until Brandi shushed her mother.

"We thank you for every good and perfect gift sent down from above, and we pray these things in the blessed name of your dear son, Jesus Christ. Amen."

Brandi peeked into the dining room. "Good morning, ladies. Sorry you had to hear all that. The kids are in the car, and I need to get to work. Mother, I'll talk to you about it later." She waved her fingers at us and left, the rat-tat of her heels on the floor receding until she exited the front door.

Maxine rolled up to her place at the end of the table and pulled her napkin off the plate. "I never did like that punk."

After breakfast, Ruby joined me in the laundry room, telling me all about her day out with Anthony while I sorted clothes for the washing machine. When she finished with that topic, she moved on to Brandi's troubles.

"I've been praying for her and young Travis for a while now," she said. "Money problems can destroy a marriage if the couple aren't equally yoked. Both working and trying to raise children makes it even harder."

"They seem like good parents, what I saw of them at the Mother's Day lunch." I tossed a pair of slacks into the pile for cold water wash.

Ruby agreed. "They do love those kids. That Travis is still part kid himself." She shook her head, an indulgent smile disappearing from her face a moment after it appeared. "Hate to see them break up. The kids'll suffer the most."

"I'm sure they can use all the prayers they can get." I measured the detergent and turned the dial on the machine to start the water flowing.

Ruby shuffled her walker an inch or two, then leaned heavily on it. "Are you a prayer warrior?"

"Me? Hardly." A short laugh escaped before I knew it. Disappointment etched Ruby's expression, and I touched her hand. "I admire people like you who are confident in their faith. I've just never found it to work for me. At least, not when I needed it."

Ruby stared at the piles of laundry on the floor, her chin making several side-to-side motions before she responded. "I'm sorry to hear that. Do you mind talking about it? I'm not meanin' to pry, but I'm always curious to know what happens when people feel that way."

I held a handful of white clothes over the suds, grief rising in me like the hot water in the washer's tub. A moment later, anger pushed it aside, and I fought for control as I faced Ruby. "I waited twelve years for an answer to prayer, not so much for my benefit, but for someone else's. When the answer finally came, it cost me my husband and my home." My voice shook and tears dampened my cheeks. I dropped the clothes into the wash and let the lid slam. "I don't understand why God lets terrible things happen to good people. He must be either incompetent or inadequate. Or nonexistent."

In the tense silence that followed my outburst, Ruby bowed her head and murmured, "Lord, to whom shall we go?" Then looking to me, she said, "Forgive me for asking."

The sight of Ruby's sagging shoulders filled me with remorse. None of what happened was her fault, but I'd dumped all my frustration on this sweet woman. I palmed the tears from my cheeks, took a deep breath, and gave her a light embrace.

"No, Ruby. Thank you for caring."

She squeezed back, then turned about face with her walker. "I wish my son hadn't left so soon, but maybe it's a good thing. I'm awfully tired after yesterday. Think I'll go to take a nap."

I followed her out of the laundry room, heading for the main part of the house. Maxine sat before the patio door, pushing it open.

"Good morning, Stan. How nice to see you." She welcomed him inside and used her wheelchair to corner him. A tight smile formed on his lips.

"Nice to see you too, Maxine."

"I was hoping you'd be by. You're just the person I need."

"Really?" Stan tried to dodge around the table, but Maxine caught his hand.

"I have a question about the Bible, and I know you could answer it for me. Can you sit down for a bit?"

Catching sight of me, Stan excused himself. "I'm afraid that will have to wait for another time, Maxie. I'm only here for a minute to see how Lorraine is doing." He gave Maxine's hand a pat and pushed her wheelchair back far enough to squeeze past her.

"How's your hand?" He hurried over, pushing his cap farther up on his head. I spread my fingers for his inspection. He winced. "I'll go put out the ant bait now, but I thought you could use these if you do any more gardening." He pulled a pair of soft leather gardening gloves from his back pocket and laid them in my hand.

"That's very thoughtful of you, Stan, but not at all necessary. I'd planned to buy a pair myself as soon as Kim takes us shopping." I thrust them back at him, but he refused.

"No, no. Please, take them. It's the least we can do."

His concern touched me, but behind him, Maxine looked as if she'd been slapped in the face. Glowering, she wheeled past us into the living room where she snatched up the remote and raised the volume on the television. Jean covered her ears and complained she couldn't read her magazine, but Maxine only raised the volume higher. Finally, Kim came out of her office and turned it down to a more reasonable level.

I stayed out of Maxine's way the rest of the morning, but the next time I entered the laundry room, Jean followed me. She closed the door and spoke in a hushed voice next to my ear as I transferred clothes to the dryer.

"You be careful around Maxie. She is *not* happy you were out with Billy yesterday, and she's pretty ticked off that he came to check on you today."

I frowned at her. "Billy? You mean Stan?"

Jean rolled her eyes. "No, Billy. You know. Billy Graham."

I chuckled, then realized she was serious. "I think you mean Stan Graham. Kim's dad?"

Her mouth pressed into a thin line. "You're just trying to confuse me. I know who I'm talking about, and his name is Billy. Just you watch yourself, and don't make Maxine jealous."

I waved my hand as if to brush the thought away. "Maxine has nothing to worry about. My husband passed away only a couple weeks ago. I'm certainly not looking to replace him." I pulled the wet clothes from the washer and dumped them into the dryer.

Jean inhaled sharply and put her hands to her chest. "That recent? Oh, I'm so sorry. It wouldn't matter to Maxie, though. She's been married and divorced three times, and she's looking for number four to take her out of here. Obviously, there aren't a lot of men around this place, so she's set her sights on Stan. He's a wonderful man, sweet and stable, but Maxie gets awfully jealous when she sees him paying attention to anyone but her."

"He's not interested in her, is he?" She didn't exactly seem like his type.

"Oh, no! But to her, anyone who gets near him is competition."

I sighed. Could life get any more complicated? Widowed. Homeless. Living under a false identity in a nursing home a thousand miles from anything familiar because someone wants me dead. And now I was the unwilling third point in a love triangle.

CHAPTER 15

His fingers drummed the desk, halting the moment his call was answered. He didn't bother with niceties.

"Find. That. Woman."

"The old lady? What about her? Her house is gone along with everything in it. Whatever evidence her old man had, it's burned to a crisp."

"Except she wasn't in the house." He took care to enunciate the last words. "And she hasn't surfaced anywhere. She's hiding. That tells me she knows the truth. She may even have the evidence with her."

"We've been watching her accounts like you said. Nothing. No activity. Nada. Not since late Friday, the night of the fire."

"Yes, and that transaction was a cash withdrawal recorded close to midnight. How many widows in their late fifties are out getting cash at midnight on a Friday while their house is burning?"

"Maybe she got mugged. Somebody already did a job on her and used her card."

"Then why was it only used once? Wouldn't you go back

again, take all the cash you can get? I'm telling you, she's out there somewhere. I'm putting out a news story on her, but I expect you to find her."

"But—"

"Now!"

"Yes, sir."

CHAPTER 16

"Mother, he's threatening to take the kids away from me."

Brandi's barely-hushed tone carried into the dining room where I sketched out a design for the larger flowerbeds. Across the table, Riley chewed her pencil and pretended to concentrate on her homework. I recognized the ploy from my years in the classroom.

"Riley, why don't you go outside and enjoy the nice day?"

"I can't. Mom says I have to do my homework." Her eyes shifted toward the voices coming from the living room. She rubbed the corner of her worksheet with her thumb.

"Did she say you have to do it right here? Micah's out there reading under the tree. Come on. Bring your books, and let's go sit at the table on the patio."

The girl hesitated, obviously reluctant to miss any part of the dramatic conversation. But she picked up her things and carried them through the open patio door.

"What are you working on?" I asked as we settled at one of the tables.

"Math." Her fingers waggled a pencil, tapping it against her cheek.

I laughed. "You make it sound like some kind of dreaded disease. I take it you don't like math."

She shook her head. "It's hard."

"What are you working on?"

"Long division."

"Would you like some help?"

"Are you good at math?"

"I used to teach it, a long time ago before you were born. My students were older than you, but some of them had a hard time with it, too. I challenged them to think of it as a game."

Riley's nose scrunched in disgust. "Doesn't sound like a very fun game."

"Let me ask you something. When you were here on Sunday, you and Micah played a game where you made up the rules yourselves. What happened when you forgot or broke a rule?"

"I didn't."

"But what if you had? What would've happened?"

"I'd be out, and Micah would've won."

"Exactly. Now, let's pretend math is a game. It has certain rules, and as long as you remember the rules and play within those rules, you win. But if you don't know the rules or forget them, you lose."

Riley tilted her head, her forehead creased in thought. "I kinda get it, I think."

"Why don't you show me what you're working on, and let's see if we can remember all the rules?"

She showed me her long division problems, and we reviewed all the rules involved in solving them. By the time she got to the last problems on the page, she was working them by herself. She finished and held her paper for me to see.

"I did it!"

I grabbed her hand and raised her arm up in the air. "You won! Good for you. See that? You can do this. But remember, those rules are important. Don't forget them."

"I won't." Riley glanced at the windows, and her smile and confidence drained away like water down a sink. "Mrs. Johnson, my mom said Dad's not coming home. Do you know where he is?"

My heart broke for the hurt in her small voice. "No, honey, I don't."

"Neither do I." She studied the windows. "I wish he'd come home. I miss him."

Ruby's earlier fatigue worsened into a stomach bug that evening. Thinking she might have caught something while she was out with Anthony yesterday, Kim moved me out to the living room again to limit my exposure. I mentioned it to Anthony during our nightly texting. His sister managed Ruby's care since she lived closer. But Wednesday morning, he asked about her.

She seems a little better, but very tired. She'll probably sleep most of the day.

OK let me know if anything changes.

By that evening, Ruby could sit up and drink some broth, but she went to sleep early. I'd changed into my nightgown and brushed my teeth when Kim gathered Jean, Maxine and me around the dining table to review good hand-washing technique and remind us to practice good hygiene.

The four of us chatted quietly about Ruby and various illnesses until a snappy little jingle sounded from the living room. We exchanged puzzled looks until I realized it was my new phone. I'd never heard it ring and couldn't imagine who might be calling me.

Only Anthony had this number, but he had always texted instead of calling. I retrieved the phone from my purse, expecting a telemarketer or a simple misdial. The display showed *Ann*, and I pressed the answer button.

"Hello?"

"Ms. Elaine, are you alone? Can you talk?" He sounded anxious. Not the booming, confident voice to which I was accustomed.

"Why, Ann, how nice to hear from you! It's been a long time."

A pause. "I take it you're not alone."

"You are so right, my dear, but it's good to hear your voice. Tell me what's been going on with you."

"Can you go somewhere else without attracting attention?"

"Oh, I understand perfectly, but go on." I covered the mouthpiece and caught the other ladies' attention. "It's an old friend of mine. I'll go out on the patio so I don't disturb anyone."

"Voice sounds awfully deep for a woman." Maxine narrowed her eyes at me. "Did you say Ann or Stan?"

I mouthed the word Ann, waved my fingers at her, and slipped out the door to the patio. Maybe Anthony had found the answer to our mystery. Had he discovered who killed Roy and kidnapped Jenny? Did he know who was trying to kill me?

Darkness shrouded the backyard now that the sun had set, but some well-placed floodlights illuminated the patio enough for me to find a chair away from the windows. Moths and June bugs flew erratic laps about the lights, occasionally leaving orbit to check out this human invading their evening ritual. The intermittent glow of lightning bugs added sparkle to the grassy lawn. A subtle fragrance of honeysuckle drifted over from the neighbor's yard. I picked my way across the lawn, shoes whispering through the grass, and found a seat on one of the oak branches that touched the ground.

"Okay, I'm out back by the oaks. The patio door's closed. What's going on?"

"Keep your voice down anyway, and guard your responses, especially your expressions in case anyone is watching."

"They'd have to use night goggles to see me out here. Besides, the curtains are drawn, and Maxine and Jean will soon be in their rooms trying to avoid your mother's virus. Out with it. Tell me what's happening."

He hesitated. "Your house...I'm so sorry, Ms. Elaine. It's a total loss. The only thing left standing is the front door frame and the outer brick walls."

The news shouldn't have surprised me. I'd seen the flames, and even from a distance, they'd looked voracious. But the reality punched me in the stomach. I doubled over and closed my eyes. An image of the house, hollow and blackened by soot, took shape behind my eyelids.

"Are you still there?"

With some effort, I straightened and took a deep breath. "Yes, I'm here. It's just hard to think about—"

"I understand. But it gets worse."

"What else?"

"Your next-door neighbor, Lauren, saw me drive in. She came across the street crying and all upset. I figured it was the fire, but she asked if I'd heard anything about the funeral."

"Funeral? Whose funeral?"

"Yours."

"My—but I'm not dead!"

"I know that, and you know that. Someone else knows it, but I'm guessing they've fed a story to the media that your body was found in the rubble after the fire. They claim the body was charred so badly it required dental records to identify you."

"Why would someone lie like that?" I pinched the neck of my nightgown, pulling it tight enough to choke myself.

"I think it's tied to whoever burned your house. They're wanting to destroy any records that might have been there."

"Well, I could've told them there was nothing there. Believe me, I looked. They just burned a perfectly good house for nothing." I stood and walked toward the massive trunk of the tree.

"They're probably afraid you know the truth, maybe trying to smoke you out in the open." Anthony's breath rasped through the phone. "There's one more thing. You ain't gonna like this."

"What is it?"

"It's about Roy."

"What about him? Did you find out who ran him off the road?"

He sucked in a huge breath. "They're blaming—they're saying Roy is responsible for your student's disappearance."

My mouth hung open, my tongue refusing to form a recognizable word. Knees trembling, I sank against the tree. Its rough bark bit into my arm and shoulder.

"Do you want to know more or not?"

I barely had enough strength to whisper, "There's more?"

"The news reports say he was a suspect all along. That's why he left the department. They say a recent find of solid evidence connected him, and he got wind of it and killed himself."

Impossible! My heart screamed the word while my head explored the possibility. Roy had always loved children. Not having any of our own severely disappointed him. He was off work the day Jenny disappeared, and he knew we were doing a field trip to the museum. But why would he kidnap Jenny? What would he have done with her? I didn't want to know.

His determination to solve the case—was it only a cover-up to make sure he didn't get caught? I pressed a fist against the rising nausea in my stomach. Suicide? No! There were witnesses. People saw another car force him off the road. The accident was no suicide. Roy was no child predator. How could I ever doubt—

"Ms. Elaine, you all right? You still there?"

"Lies. They're all lies."

"Of course they are. But whoever put them out obviously has connections with the news media, not to mention the emergency personnel who handled the fire."

Anger coursed through my veins, replacing my former weakness with renewed energy. I stood upright, peering into the darkness at the edge of the yard. "Who would dare try to discredit Roy?"

"He's a convenient target, because he's not around to defend himself. Neither are you if you died in the house fire."

"Then I need to come home. It's up to me to prove them wrong, to defend Roy's good name."

"I can't let you do that, Ms. Elaine."

"Why not? All I have to do is show up in person. That proves I didn't die in the fire—"

"And you become a visible target. You'll end up as dead as Roy."

"Well, I'm certainly not doing any good here. How am I supposed to resolve this mess from a thousand miles away?"

"Leave it to me. As long as I know you're safe, I can do the snooping and figure out who's behind this. Besides, you have nowhere to live. You told me you wouldn't endanger any friends by living with them."

"Couldn't I live with you?"

Anthony chuckled. "Patience, Ms. Elaine. Give me a little more time. We'll uncover who's behind it all. While I'm working on it up here, you be thinking about where Roy might have stashed that memory card. If we find that, we'll know who we're looking for."

CHAPTER 17

Dustin bounded through the door of his house, twirling keys around his index finger. He tossed a brown paper sack into his car. "I've got to drop something off for someone. I won't be gone long."

Travis held up his hand to stop him. "Hang on a minute." He pulled the battery out of his truck's engine. "Would you be able to run me up to get a battery? I think this one's about to die."

"Uh...yeah, sure, hop in."

Travis sank into the Corvette's passenger seat and set the battery on the floor between his feet. "Thanks, man. I really appreciate this. And thanks again for letting me crash at your place last night. Crazy how everything seems to be going wrong lately."

The tires squealed and left rubber on the pavement as Dustin accelerated and roared down the street. "So are you and Brandi splitting up?"

Travis shrugged. "Who knows?"

"Been almost ten years since high school. 'Bout time to trade 'er in for a newer model, if you ask me." A sly smile twisted Dustin's lips.

"Yeah, well, that newer model is the reason I'm on your couch." Travis frowned. "I'm not gonna do anything to risk losing my kids."

"Suit yourself."

"If Brandi doesn't change her mind soon, I'll look for a place of my own. Might have to find a second job or something to pay for it." He ran his hand along the seat's leather upholstery. "How long you been working to be able to afford this?"

Dustin chuckled. "Not as long as you'd think. I've got a little side business that makes good money."

"What kind of business?"

"You might call it a—a delivery service."

"A delivery service?" Travis laughed. "Maybe I should get into the delivery business if it pays this well."

Dustin shrugged, then smiled and nodded as the car bumped over the discount store's parking lot entrance. He stopped in front of the auto service door. "I'll come back and get you. Wait for me right here."

Travis pushed on the shop door and set his old battery on the counter. Maybe he should've waited until tomorrow. He could've checked his battery at work, if it still had enough juice to get him there in the morning.

The service writer tested it and showed him the result. Almost gone. Travis picked out a replacement, paid for it and went outside to wait for Dustin. A delivery service? Yeah, right. Something didn't add up. Either Dustin was in debt over his head or he'd found a way to make some really big bucks.

He couldn't begrudge the guy his success, though. Not when he'd been generous enough to offer him a place to crash on short notice, in addition to the job recommendation. Maybe Dustin would deal him in on this delivery business as well.

Travis checked the time on his phone. Almost thirty minutes had passed since Dustin dropped him off, and still no sign of the 'vette. He wandered farther out, his gaze sweeping the street in both directions then moving across the huge parking lot that spread out to his right. He turned back toward the automotive shop, his eye catching a spot of red at the far end of the lot. He squinted. Definitely a Corvette, but it couldn't be Dustin's. He never parked that close to other cars.

Travis watched. A low-riding Impala, its grill facing the opposite direction, sat close enough the drivers could practically reach out and open the other's door. It sure looked like Dustin's 'vette. Travis trotted back to where he'd set his battery on the ground, picked it up and made his way toward the two cars. The drivers exchanged what appeared to be brown paper bags.

Drugs? Is that Dustin's delivery service?

Of course. It all made sense. What else could bring in enough money to buy a fancy car like that? Travis halted, scanning the parking lot for security before hurrying to the car. He pounded on the window.

"Open up."

Dustin flinched, and then frowned as he worked the locks.

Travis pulled open the door and sank onto the seat, setting the battery on the floor. The driver in the Impala looked young, high school or early college age.

"I told you to wait." Annoyance laced Dustin's voice.

"I saw your car. Figured I'd save you a trip. This the delivery service you mentioned?"

Dustin muttered something, nodded to the other driver and revved his engine a couple times. Sirens erupted, at least two, and they seemed to come from different directions. Dustin checked the rearview mirror, cursed, slammed the car into gear and stomped on the accelerator. Travis braced one hand against the dash, the other on the door as Dustin spun the wheel right to avoid an unmarked cruiser pulling up in front of them. Another patrol car blocked their exit. They fishtailed, spinning a complete doughnut before coming to a stop inside a circle of police cars. Dustin spewed every cuss word in the book.

Travis swallowed hard and closed his eyes against the strobe of flashing red and white lights. His pulse threatened to explode in his head. This couldn't be happening. Not now. Not this. Brandi already thought he was cheating on her. This would send her over the top. He'd never see his kids again.

"Is everything all right, Lorraine?" Kim peeked at me from the kitchen when I closed and locked the patio door behind me.

"My stomach's a little queasy, but I think I'm all right." The very thought of someone blaming Roy for Jenny's disappearance roiled my stomach.

Kim held her wrist to my forehead. "No fever. You'd better get to bed and get some sleep. The night nurse will be here soon, if you start feeling worse." She waited until I had slipped under the light cover on the living room couch before dimming the overhead dining room light and turning off the rest of the lamps.

I closed my eyes, but my thoughts kept me awake long after the nurse arrived. Who was behind all this? Could it be that former client who tried to outsmart Roy to protect his illegal business dealings? Or maybe someone convicted because of Roy's investigation? Maybe it was that man whose wife got the huge divorce settlement after Roy uncovered his multiple affairs.

No, somehow, it all linked back to my discovery of Jenny's pendant and Roy solving the mystery of her disappearance. For the hundredth time, I chided myself for not pressing him harder to tell me whom he was meeting that day. But knowing the name wouldn't help without the evidence contained on that memory card. Since I alone knew of Roy's particular habit, the kidnapper had no reason to search for it. That must be why he was coming after me. Whoever it was believed I knew what the evidence proved. Anthony was right. I needed to figure out where Roy hid that thing. Find that and we'd have the answer to everything else.

I'd searched Roy's office. If he hid it anywhere else in the house, it was charred and melted by now. Anthony could get access to the car and check it out thoroughly. But if it wasn't there, and it wasn't burned to a crisp, where could it possibly be?

Disjointed images of fire and death filled my dreams that night and I woke with the same sour stomach I had when I went to bed. The smells emanating from the kitchen made it worse. I certainly wasn't earning my keep with a swollen hand and an unsettled stomach. While Ruby managed some soda crackers and a little gelatin at breakfast, I sipped a cup of chamomile tea.

Was it my upset stomach that brought forth more misgivings about Anthony? Doubts continued to niggle at the back of my mind, much as I hated to admit it. I still questioned the wisdom of giving him all my ID and credit cards. How could I possibly know whether or not he was telling me the truth? What if he's the man I should be running from?

I pulled back from considering such a thing. After the fire and losing Roy, the possibility of Anthony betraying me was too much to ponder.

Tom Jones's song, "What's New Pussycat," interrupted my thoughts.

Maxine wiped her fingers on a napkin, reached into the side pocket of her wheelchair, and pulled out her cell phone.

"Yeah, Brandi, whatcha need?" She listened then added, "Okay, well, I'm fine so far. Tell my baby girl I hope she feels better."

Clicking off, Maxine dropped the phone into the side pocket again. "Riley got sick last night after they got home. Brandi says a stomach bug's going around the school. She saw me giving her a sip from my soda can and wanted to warn me in case I start feeling sick."

"Nice of her to let us know." Kim picked up the breakfast dishes. "Must be the same thing Ruby had. I hope you're not getting it, Lorraine. Dad mentioned bringing over some flowers and mulch this morning if you feel up to working on the front beds again. But it can wait if you're not well enough."

A little dirt therapy sounded perfect for discovering whether my upset stomach was due to nervous anxiety after Anthony's call last night. The only problem was that with Stan around, I wouldn't have time to sort through all the crazy thoughts that had kept me awake half the night.

Then again, that wasn't the only problem. Maxine narrowed her eyes at me and pushed her chin out, her red lips turning down at the corners. Was she thinking of the gloves Stan bought for me? For a moment, she reminded me of those nasty fire ants. My hand was nearing its normal size again, but the fiery itch persisted.

An hour later, with tools assembled, I pulled Stan's gift onto my hands. The leather rubbed against the bites on my right hand, irritating and aggravating the itching. I tore the glove off and determined to use my bare right hand only when necessary. Stan pulled into the driveway as I stood back to assess where I'd left off. He backed up to the sidewalk, lowered the tailgate and unloaded bags of composted manure and mulch. Flats of petunias, portulaca, and zinnias lined the rest of the truck bed. The sight made me happier than if he'd given me a bouquet of roses.

"I figured your hand would still bother you, so let me do the heavy work," he said. "Once I get this compost worked in, you can lay out the flowers where you want them."

"No, sir!" I shook my finger in his face. "I'm out here to dig in the dirt and I'm not about to let you have all the fun." Stan grinned, tugged on his cap and tore into a bag of manure. We worked a couple of hours, finishing with a layer of mulch about the time the sun peeked over the roof and started heating up that side of the house. Bright pinks, reds and yellows added much cheer to the front entrance. Stan brushed himself off and removed his shoes while I went inside to prepare some cold drinks for us. Ruby, Jean, and Maxine looked up from the television as I poked my head into Kim's office on my way to the kitchen.

"Go take a look at the front entrance. Your dad did a wonderful job with the plantings."

"You're finished?" Kim rolled her chair back and stood up.

"Only with the front. Still a lot to do on the other beds and in back."

Kim rounded her desk and headed for the front door while I made my way into the kitchen. I filled two glasses with ice, adding water to one and sweet tea to the other. Maxine wheeled around the corner and blocked my way to the dining room.

"Excuse me, Maxine. I was just going to set these on the table. Can I fix you something to drink?"

She inched closer, nostrils flaring, voice low as it came through fiery red lips. "Quit flirting with Stan."

I set the glasses on the counter. "Maxine, you have nothing to worry about. I..."

"I ain't worried. You stay away from my man, you hear? He's mine."

"But—"

"No buts. Just stay away." She wheeled about, then held out one hand. "Give me the sweet tea."

"It's for Stan, but I can pour some for you—"

"I know it's for Stan. Give it to me!"

I placed the glass of tea in her hand, and she moved over to the table, waiting until Stan and Kim came through the front door. Her voice climbed a whole octave from the tone she'd used with me.

"Stan, honey, you must be thirsty after all that hard work. Come have some tea."

I stayed in the kitchen with my ice water while Maxine, Stan, and Kim chatted around the dining room table. No sense throwing fuel on that fire. A romantic relationship held no interest for me right now. My heart still belonged to Roy. I hadn't even had time to properly grieve his passing before being catapulted from my home into a whole new world.

Despite Maxine's animosity toward me, we were more alike than she realized. All of us—myself, Maxine, Ruby, Jean—we all mourned our loss of independence, no matter the reason. Kim worked hard to make this house feel like a home and family, but not one of us wanted to be here. Only Maxine and I held any hope of regaining our freedom and self-sufficiency. I suspected her past marital failures deepened the ache for a man to love her and take care of her. Were the red lipstick, platinum blonde hair, and brash manners a cry for someone to notice her, a plea for attention?

"What's new, pussycat?" Tom Jones again.

"Hey, Brandi." Maxine listened for a moment then said, "Wait, slow down. He what? Why?"

The alarm in her voice drew me out from the kitchen. Wrinkles lined Maxine's forehead, and her lips pulled into a deep frown.

"Tell him to walk. That's what he deserves...No! Let him figure it out." She argued back and forth with Brandi, then handed the phone to Stan. "She wants a favor. Tell her no."

Stan took the phone and listened. "Of course, Brandi. I'll be happy to go pick him up...I'm glad you called...I'll do what I can for him...No need. You're welcome."

"What's that all about?" Kim asked. The television noise ended abruptly. Apparently the phone call caught Jean's and Ruby's attention, too.

Maxine rolled her eyes. "Travis got himself arrested last night along with a friend who was dealing drugs. They're releasing him without charges, but he needs a ride back to where he left his truck. With Riley sick, Brandi can't leave, so she asked if Stan would go get him." She shoved the phone back into the pocket on her chair. "I say make him walk back to wherever he left his truck. Give him time to think about who he's hanging out with."

Stan set his glass on the table and fitted his ball cap on his head. "Well, I hate to drink and run, but it seems I have an important mission. Ladies, if you'll excuse me." He tugged on the brim of his cap and tossed a smile my way as he headed for the door.

"Thanks again for helping Lorraine with the flowers, Dad. They look great."

The flowers did look nice, but Maxine's scowl would've wilted every last one of them.

"Can I get my battery? It was on the floor of the car." Travis collected his keys, wallet and change at the desk of the county jail and stuffed them back in his pockets. The officer behind the desk tapped some computer keys.

"Car's impounded as evidence."

"So—what? I can't get my battery? It's not part of the car, had nothing to do with the drug deal." He waited, but got only an apathetic look from the officer. Travis clapped his hand on the counter. "I need that battery. How am I supposed to get to work without a battery in my truck?"

The officer shrugged. "Buy another battery and return this one later."

"How much later? I only have thirty days to return the thing."

The officer pursed his lips, shook his head, and stared at the screen.

Travis huffed. Stan put a hand on his shoulder and turned him toward the door. "Let's go get you a new battery, son." They walked out to Stan's beat up old truck. Travis yanked the door open and climbed in.

"Worst two days of my life." He slammed the door shut and clamped his jaw tight against the words he didn't dare use in the company of a preacher. Stan climbed into the driver's seat, started the engine, and drove away from the county jail building without a word. They were pulling into the store parking lot before Travis trusted himself to speak.

"Thanks for coming to get me, Stan. I owe you one."

"Not at all. Isn't that what friends are for?"

Travis sighed. "Yeah, I guess. But some friends..." He left it there as Stan parked and shut off the engine.

"Care to talk about it?"

Travis raked a hand through his hair then leaned his elbow on the open window. "I'm sure you heard about Brandi and me." He ran his thumbnail along the weather stripping.

Stan angled to face him, his back against the door. "I did, but I'd rather hear the straight scoop from you."

"Night before last, Brandi kicked me out. She thinks I'm having an affair."

"Are you?"

"No. I went out for drinks after work with Dustin and a couple of the girls from work. One of the girls hit on me. I admit I was tempted, especially since Brandi and I have been fighting a lot lately. But I didn't sleep with her, didn't even kiss her." He stared out the windshield then pulled his arm down to his side. "When Brandi insisted I leave, I called Dustin, and he let me sleep on his couch. Then last night, he said he had to run out for something, and I asked if he'd drop me by to get a new battery for my pickup. He said he had to make a delivery." Travis crooked his fingers in the air like quotation marks around the word delivery. He turned to face Stan. "How was I supposed to know he was delivering drugs?"

"How long have you known Dustin?"

"Long time. Never really close friends or anything, but we hung around some in high school. Kinda lost touch after we graduated. Then a couple weeks ago, I applied for that job at the car dealership. I never knew he worked there, but he saw me, put in a good word, and next thing I know, I've got the job." He shook his head. "I had no idea he was dealing."

"You aren't one of his customers?"

"Me?" Travis sat up straight. "No. I don't do that stuff. I mean, sometimes I drink more than I should, but I don't do the hard stuff." He pounded the door with the fleshy part of his fist. "Just our luck a couple of cops had the parking lot staked out to catch whoever's been breaking into cars. They saw the deal go down and that was it."

Stan ran his forefinger around the inner circle of the steering wheel. "Are you going back to Dustin's?"

"Yeah, I have to get my truck."

"I mean to stay. I have an extra bedroom you're welcome to use."

Travis dropped his gaze. "Thanks, but I think I'll stick with Dustin for now. If Brandi and I don't get back together soon, I'll look for a place of my own."

Stan opened his door. "All right then. Let's go find a battery and get your truck running again."

Travis stepped out, closed the door, and fell into step beside

Stan. Staying with a retired preacher sounded about as exciting as watching oil drip from a filter. But Stan was okay for a religious guy. If you made a mistake, he didn't point a finger to shame or embarrass you. Never made you feel like pond scum. If things didn't work out with Dustin, he might reconsider the older man's offer.

CHAPTER 18

"Maxine's blood sugar is rising."

Kim studied the chart where she recorded each of Maxine's readings. "Sometimes that indicates she's getting sick." She measured out the meds for each of the ladies, and I returned the containers to the cupboard in her office. "Stress can also make her sugar high."

"Maybe she's stressed because she thinks I'm trying to steal her boyfriend."

Kim cocked an eyebrow. "Dad?" I nodded, and she laughed. "Forgive me for asking, but are you trying to steal him? Wait, didn't you say you lost your husband fairly recently?"

"Two weeks—" I choked, and Kim drew me into a hug. "Two weeks ago, today." Her shoulder muffled my words.

"Oh, Lorraine. I'm so sorry." She pulled back and gave me an understanding look. "I'll tell Maxine to back off."

I tore a tissue from the box on her desk and dabbed my eyes. "I don't want to make trouble. She's as lonely as I am."

"I'll simply let her know your grief is too fresh to worry about finding someone else. Was your husband sick?"

I shook my head, and reminded myself to be careful about revealing too much. "No, it was an accident. A car accident."

Kim winced. "I'm so sorry, Lorraine. Is that how Anthony talked you into coming all the way down here? A change of scenery?"

I nodded, unwilling to get any closer to the truth.

From the living room, Maxine's voice rose over the noise of the television.

"What's up, Brandi? How's Riley?" She hesitated then continued. "Will you quit crying? I can't understand...What? He better not take those kids. They don't need a dad that gets arrested for...Yeah, well, if he's hanging around with pushers, he's probably using, too. I hope you threatened to have him thrown in jail again if he gets anywhere near them."

Kim caught my eye and whispered, "There's our answer to what's causing her stress." We both listened in on the last of the conversation.

"Well, bring them over here if you have to, but don't let him near them. And make sure the school knows he's not to have contact with them, or he's likely to try grabbing them some afternoon. Yeah, okay, tell Riley I'm glad she's feeling better. Hope Micah doesn't get it." Maxine said her good-byes and muttered to herself. Kim stepped out from the office.

"Problems?"

Maxine's top lip curled into a sneer. "That idiot she married is threatening to take the kids away from her." She dropped the phone into her side pocket. "They had a big fight about him getting arrested, and she told him she didn't want him around the kids." She called Travis a name that's generally not used in polite company.

Kim walked over to her and knelt on one knee beside Maxine. "How are you feeling?"

Maxine leaned back on her elbow. "How am I feeling? A heckuvalot better than Brandi is. I'd like to take that kid and—"

"Okay, calm down." Kim put her hand on Maxine's arm. "I'm asking because your blood sugar has been going up, and I'm guessing it's the stress over Brandi and Travis and the kids. We'll need to keep close watch on it, but it would help if you don't get too worked up over it."

"Who's worked up? I swear that jerk gives me a stomach-ache. An honest-to-goodness stomach-ache." She shook her head and rubbed her belly.

"All right, well, if you start feeling worse, you let me know." Kim patted her arm and rose.

"I'll be fine, but if he ever gets close to my grandkids—" She aimed the remote at the television and raised the volume.

Shortly before the night nurse arrived, Maxine hurled everything she'd eaten at supper, removing any doubts about the cause of her rise in blood sugar. I'd moved back in with Ruby, but the sounds from the hallway told me Maxine was keeping the night nurse busy. The gray half-circles under Kim's bloodshot eyes the next morning said she'd been awake for most of the night as well. Her shoulders drooped as she set out cold cereal and milk for breakfast. I offered to fix scrambled eggs.

"If you and Ruby and Jean want some, go right ahead." She shuffled down the hall to Maxine's room.

The other ladies were satisfied with cold cereal, so I added milk and orange juice to the table before sitting down to eat. Kim returned several minutes later and sank into her chair on the other side of the table.

"I think we're finally over the worst. Her blood sugar has leveled off." Elbows on the table, she rubbed her eyes in a circular motion. "At one point, I thought she'd be making a trip to the hospital. I had 9-1-1 punched into my phone and my finger on the call button." She yawned and dropped her hands to the table. "I need to let Brandi know, but I hate to disturb her so early on a Saturday now that Maxine is stable."

"Why don't you go lay down for an hour before you call Brandi?" I assured her I'd take care of the breakfast dishes and check in on Maxine every fifteen minutes or so. "I'll come get you if there's anything I'm not comfortable handling."

Kim waved one hand in refusal then appeared to reconsider. "Are you sure?" She looked at each of us with half-closed eyelids.

"Go on and get some sleep now," Ruby said. "We'll be fine."

Jean agreed. "You'll feel better with at least a short nap."

"Okay, just a few winks. Thanks." Kim pushed herself up from the table and headed for the door to her suite beyond the kitchen. "Don't bother knocking if you need something. Just come on in." With that, she closed the door, leaving it slightly ajar.

The three of us cleaned up the dishes and put the breakfast items away. As soon as we finished, Maxine called for Kim. I hurried to the door of her room.

She looked shrunken against the bedclothes. Her blonde hair was pulled back in a lopsided ponytail, dark shadows hung beneath her eyes, and her fair skin now looked pasty white. Her lips looked especially pallid without the usual coating of lipstick.

"Where's Kim?"

"She's resting for an hour or so. How can I help you?"

Maxine grunted and looked away. "I want something to drink, something with some taste." Her hand fluttered toward the glass of crushed ice on her nightstand.

"Kim left some ginger ale on the counter for you. Are you ready to try some soda crackers or gelatin?"

She moaned and rolled over, face to the wall. I hurried to the kitchen, filled a glass with ice and sugar-free ginger ale, and searched the cabinets for a straw. Before returning to her room, I detoured to find a pretty bloom from the flowerbed to brighten her room, if not her spirits. I opened the front door and found Brandi with her hand poised to knock.

"Well, that's service," she said. "Door opens before I even knock." Riley and Micah peered from behind their mother.

"Good morning," I said. "Kim was going to call you in a bit. Your mom's been sick all night."

Brandi's shoulders drooped. "Oh, no! Same thing Riley had?"

"Sounds like it."

"Is she awake? Can I see her?"

"I was just coming out to pick a flower to cheer her up before taking this to her room. Riley and Micah, why don't you each pick a couple flowers for your grandmother?" She might not appreciate me giving her a flower, but she'd love them from her grandkids.

Micah picked one petunia. Riley gathered the short stems of red, yellow, white and pink impatiens between her fingers and held them up for her mother's approval.

"Grandma Maxie will love that." Brandi accompanied me down the hall, warning the kids to stay in the doorway. They stopped and held out their flowers.

"Maxie, we picked these for you," Riley said. "Hope you feel better."

Maxine turned over, a wan smile on her face. "Thank you, darling. And Micah, too. That makes ol' Maxie feel better already." She offered the cup with the crushed ice as a vase for the flowers.

Brandi set the blooms in the cup and centered it on the nightstand by Maxine's bed. "I don't want to get too close, Mom. I can't afford to miss any more work, but I'm so sorry you're sick."

I stuck the straw in the ginger ale and set the glass on the nightstand beside the flowers.

Maxine grunted. "When will Kim be up?"

"Where is she?" Brandi asked.

"She's taking a quick nap. It's been a long night, for both her and your mom."

Brandi clicked her tongue against her teeth, glanced at the kids and told them to wait for her in the living room. When they were out of earshot, she confided, "I was hoping I could ask her about leaving the kids here this morning. They called me to work, just until noon since it's Saturday."

Maxine shifted in bed, took a sip of the ginger ale and frowned. "In case you haven't noticed, this is a nursing home, not a daycare."

Brandi grimaced and threw her hands up. "Oh, Mother, this is *not* a nursing home. One week in a real nursing home and you'd be begging Kim to let you live here. Besides, you're the one who pushed me to kick Travis out. Now what am I supposed to do? I can't afford to lose this job." She hitched her purse strap higher on her shoulder and looked at me. "What do you think, Lorraine? Too much of an imposition? Would Kim say no?"

I hesitated, uncomfortable making that decision without Kim's permission, but I hated to wake her so soon. "Let me see if Ruby and Jean would mind helping me watch the kids this morning." I started down the hall, but stopped when I reached Jean's room, listening in on a conversation between the two ladies and the children. It seemed rude to pose the question with Riley and Micah listening. The children were well-behaved, and they'd only be here until lunchtime. Kim might fire me for this, but I decided to let them stay. Between the three of us who were still on our feet—four if we counted Kim—we should be able to supervise two children for a few hours. As long as no one else came down with the stomach flu, we'd be fine.

I returned to Maxine's room and gave permission for the children to stay. Brandi released a breath.

"Thank you so much, Miss Lorraine. I didn't know what I was going to do with them." She blew a kiss to her mother. "Hope you're feeling better when I come back, Mom. Try to sleep. That's the best thing."

I encouraged Maxine to let me know of anything else she needed and followed Brandi out to the living room. She gave the kids last minute instructions.

"You be good and obey Miss Ruby, Miss Lorraine, and Miss Jean. And Miss Kim, too, when she gets up. I'll be back around lunchtime."

Riley pouted and crossed her arms. "Why can't we stay home with Daddy?"

"Daddy's not home, and he won't be for a while. Give me a kiss."

"Can we play outside?" Micah bounced on his tiptoes.

"As long as one of the ladies is willing to watch you. Stay in the backyard and don't go near the pond. Micah, I put a couple of your books in the bag here. I bet Miss Ruby would love to hear you read. And Riley, you've got some schoolwork to make up before Monday." Brandi thanked me once more and waved goodbye on her way out.

Riley sank onto the end of the couch. Her elbow hung over the armrest and she stared at the floor. Her right cheek moved as if she were sucking it in between her teeth. Micah sat beside her and shuffled his feet on the floor.

"We miss our dad," he said.

Ruby reached for his hand. "Let me say a prayer for your daddy. Dear Lord, we thank you for the earthly fathers you give us to watch over and care for us. You know where Riley and Micah's daddy is, and You are able to bring him back home. We ask you to watch over him, turn his steps toward home, and bless and comfort these precious children until he returns, keeping them in your care. Please, Lord Jesus. We love you and trust your care for us. We ask this in the name of your sweet son, our Lord Jesus Christ. Amen."

Micah raised his head and looked around the room as if searching for an idea.

"Can we watch TV?"

"I think we should go play outside for now, before it gets too hot," I said.

Ruby volunteered to stay inside and alert me if Maxine needed anything, so Jean and I accompanied the children outside. Micah ran over to the old oak branch where I'd sat the other night and climbed onto it, challenging Riley to walk its length like a balance beam. I retrieved an old deflated beach ball I'd seen in the detached garage and tried blowing it up. It didn't hold air for long, but Micah found a way to play with it anyway and each of the children took turns blowing whenever it needed to be inflated again. Thirty minutes later, Riley hopped onto the patio and collapsed into a chair.

"I'm thirsty." She pushed her bangs back from her face and pulled her hair off her neck. Micah joined her, keeping the beach ball bobbling in the air.

"Water or lemonade," I asked.

"Lemonade!"

I left them with Jean and hurried into the kitchen to defrost and mix up some lemonade. Ruby watched from one of the chairs at the dining room table.

"I haven't heard a thing out of Maxine," she said. "Do you think she's all right?"

"I'll go check on her in a minute. Would you like to move outside and enjoy some cold lemonade with Jean and the kids?"

Ruby got to her feet and maneuvered her walker through the patio door. I followed, carrying four plastic cups and the pitcher, then left the two ladies in charge of serving the lemonade.

I peeked into Maxine's room, noting the steady rise and fall of her chest in rhythmic breathing. Head drooping to one side, mouth slightly open, and the bedcovers pushed down to her waist, she didn't look nearly as intimidating as she usually did. I reached for the doorknob and pulled the door almost closed so Riley and Micah wouldn't disturb her when they came inside.

The insistent ring of the doorbell hurried my steps up the hall. I hoped that wasn't Micah's idea of fun. If he disturbed Maxine or Kim, we'd be having a serious talk. But a glance out the side window made me reconsider waking Kim.

Travis left off the doorbell and pounded his fist on the door. "I want my kids!"

I took a deep breath and opened the door halfway. "Hello, Travis."

"Where are they?"

A faint scent of alcohol touched my nostrils, and I tried to stall. "Your children? You mean Riley and Micah?"

"Who else would I mean? I know they're here. I watched Brandi drop 'em off." He peered around me into the house. "They're my kids, too. She has no right to keep them away from me."

His sullen look and his stance reminded me of the belligerent young teens I had taught so many years ago. I never let them bully me then, even when a growth spurt gave them a size advantage. I filled my lungs, straightened to my full height and looked him in the eye.

"I'm sorry, Travis, but the children can't see you right now." I moved to close the door, but his hand shot out and held it open. Though he couldn't see the children from here, if they started playing again, their shouts might echo from the backyard. I had to get rid of him as quickly as possible.

He leaned against the door jam, and his voice took on a pleading tone. "Look, I don't want to make trouble here, but I have a right to see my kids. I want them."

"I'm afraid you'll need to work that out with Brandi."

"They're mine!" He pounded a fist against the doorframe, and I jumped. But I recovered soon enough. Planting my palm on the center of his chest, I pushed him back and stepped outside, closing the door behind me.

"Children are not possessions to be fought over. Riley and Micah love both you and Brandi deeply, and they don't understand what has happened. If you're taking them merely to get back at Brandi, I suggest you rethink that plan. You may discover it's a lot more than you bargained for."

He sneered. "What do you mean?"

"If you take custody, you'll be responsible for getting them up and dressed every morning and feeding them breakfast."

"They can do that themselves."

"You'll have to drop them off at school, fix nutritious meals for them, make sure their clothes and bodies are washed and clean, help them with homework, make sure they get to bed early enough so they're not tired at school. Riley's been sick with stomach flu this week. How do you feel about cleaning up vomit? Are you patient enough to cater to them for several days until they're healthy again? You'll have to take time off work. And no more going out whenever you want or stopping off to have a drink after work."

Travis's intense gaze softened. He swallowed, and his arms went limp at his sides. "Riley's been sick? Is she okay now?" I nodded, and he backed away. He ran a hand through his hair, keeping his eyes on the ground. "I didn't really intend to take them. I only wanted to see them. I miss 'em."

I recalled the image of him last Sunday, striding alongside Brandi with a child hanging over each of his shoulders—Micah and Riley laughing and giggling in protest until he set them on the ground. At the time I'd thought, *There's a man who loves his children.* I stepped toward him and touched his arm. "I believe you."

Travis raised his head to look at me.

"I may be over-reaching my bounds here, but humor this old woman, if you will. I don't want to intrude on your relationship with Brandi, but if you care about those children, you'll do whatever it takes to work things out with her. It's none of my business what you're doing or why the two of you separated, but those two youngsters need both you and Brandi. Together. They should never have to hear their daddy got arrested or came home smelling of someone else's perfume."

Travis hung his head and turned his back to me. His shoulders moved up and down as he inhaled and exhaled. He looked around the yard, kicked at a bare spot in the lawn. I moved to his side, peered into his face.

"I speak from many years of experience as a teacher, seeing the effects on kids when their parents make bad choices. Travis," I waited for him to look at me. "Be the kind of dad you'd want for Riley and Micah. Be a daddy those kids can be proud of. I have a hunch if you do that, you'll be the kind of man Brandi welcomes home."

Excited shrieks and laughter erupted from the backyard. Travis lifted his head as Riley shouted, "You're it!" He took several slow steps toward his truck in the driveway then stopped, turned, and faced me.

"Tell 'em I said hey. And I love 'em. Will you tell them that?"

I nodded, and he continued toward his truck. He'd almost reached it when Riley raced around the corner of the house with Micah in hot pursuit. Seeing Travis, she skidded to a brief stop then launched herself at him.

"Daddy!"

Travis caught her with one arm and knelt to catch Micah with the other, hugging them close as the kids wrapped their arms around his neck and shoulders.

"Where have you been?"

"We've missed you."

"Are you coming home?"

The children plied Travis with questions as he loosened his hold and looked each one over, giving Micah's shirt a tug and brushing the hair away from Riley's face.

"I'll be home soon. I just came by to say I love you and I miss you."

"But why can't you come home?" Riley asked.

"I've got some things I need to do, but as soon as I finish, I'll be home. I promise." He stood and took their hands in his. "Come on and walk me to the truck."

I stiffened. He could easily throw the kids in the truck and take off with them. Then what would I do? How would I face Brandi? Or Maxine?

"Let's keep this a secret until I come home, okay? Don't tell Mommy I came to see you today. Can you do that?" The kids nodded. Travis picked up each one, gave them a final hug, and sent them off to play. Riley stayed beside the driveway, her chin quivering. Travis shot a glance toward me and climbed into his truck. The tires squealed as he backed into the street and pulled away, his arm out the window waving to Riley. She wiped her cheeks and ran to the street, waving until his truck disappeared around the corner.

CHAPTER 19

I racked my brain to figure out who might want the truth about Jenny's kidnapping to remain buried, and where Roy might have hidden that memory card. But I still came up with nothing. Today was Saturday, and I'd received no texts or voice messages from Anthony since his phone call Wednesday night. I hoped three days' silence meant he was having some success with our investigation.

Late that afternoon, I plugged the phone in and flipped it open to make sure it was charging. An alert indicated a voice message from Ann. I pressed the play button and held the phone to my ear. A hesitant, feminine voice spoke, and I pulled back to check the number. Definitely Anthony's number, but who was this speaking? I pressed play again and listened.

"Hello, this is Amanda Fisher. I'm not sure who I'm calling, but my dad is Anthony Fisher. He insisted I call this number from his phone and tell you he's—he's been arrested."

My breath caught in my throat. *Anthony? Arrested?*

Amanda sounded scared, confused. No wonder I hadn't recognized her voice. How lost she must feel with her daddy sitting in a jail cell. Why? And why didn't he let her know it was me? Surely, he trusted his own daughter. If I'd answered instead of voice mail picking up, we'd have recognized each other.

Amanda sniffled and continued. "I'm sorry. This–I'm just really stressed out. We're doing everything we can to get him out, but he's been charged with arson and murder. They say he set fire to the house across the street from us, killing Mrs. Sutterfeld, the woman who lived there." Her voice rose to a thin whine and ended with the sound of sobbing. After a couple quick breath intakes, she regained control. "Whoever you are, Daddy was adamant about leaving this message, so I hope you can help. Please."

I replayed the message to convince myself I'd heard correctly.

Anthony charged with burning my house, causing my death? I'd already played with this scenario. It was nonsense. He was with me at the symphony when the fire broke out.

But what if he'd used a timer so he'd have me as an alibi? Or was this voice message simply another ploy to gain my trust when in reality, he was the one I should be hiding from? I struggled to believe such a charge against Anthony, but if he did set the fire and was keeping me captive down here, I needed to cut all ties with him and find a way to prove his guilt.

On the other hand, if this voice mail was legitimate, I possessed the power to get his charges dismissed. All I had to do was return to Chicago, show up alive and verify that he was with me when the fire broke out. But if I did that, we'd be no further along in solving this mystery than we were now. In fact, we'd both become visible targets for whoever wanted Jenny's case suppressed.

Everything depended on that memory card. Was it gone for good, destroyed in the fire? Or had Roy hidden it somewhere else, some unusual place?

Head spinning with questions, I wandered out of the

bedroom into the living room. Somehow, I needed to learn what was really going on in Chicago. But how to do that without making my whereabouts known?

Maxine lay on the couch, a light blanket covering her from the waist down. It was good to see her well enough to show some interest in her Texas Rangers. From one of the armchairs across the room, Jean read a magazine and occasionally glanced at the game. I headed to the kitchen to help Kim prepare supper. At the dining room table, pen in hand, Ruby held a folded-up newspaper at arm's length, reading the clues to a crossword puzzle.

"Lorraine, you're just in time." Kim opened the refrigerator and pulled out some packages of lunchmeat. "I keep Saturday nights simple—sandwiches with a cooked vegetable and some fruit for dessert. If you'll take over the sandwiches, I'll steam the broccoli and cut up the fruit." The nap had done wonders for her.

I layered slices of ham and Swiss cheese onto several slices of bread, topped them with lettuce and another piece of bread, and set the cut halves on a tray. I put the mayonnaise and mustard on the table, stopping to study Ruby and her crossword puzzle. An idea tickled my brain.

The newspaper, of course! Everything Anthony and Amanda had told me should be in the news if it were true. No one would discover my whereabouts if I checked the online version of the Chicago Tribune. I'd know for certain whether Anthony deserved my trust if I saw the stories in black and white. But if he'd lied and the stories weren't in the paper...well, I'd cross that bridge when, and if, necessary.

Later that evening, I looked in on Kim in her office. A spreadsheet filled the screen of her computer, and I turned to leave until a more opportune time.

"Lorraine? Did you want something?"

I stopped and stepped back into the room. "I wanted to ask a favor, but it can wait. It looks like you're busy."

"Actually, I'm ready for a break. Ask away."

I nodded toward the monitor screen. "I wondered if I might use your computer to look up something online. It shouldn't take long, but I don't want to interrupt if you're working on something."

"I'm done with this. Just forgot to close it out." Kim clicked out of her pages and exited her account. "Here, you can use it now. Sign in as a guest and let me know when you're finished." She stood and offered me her chair before going out to the living room to chat with the other ladies.

I settled in, pulled up a new browser and typed "Chicago Tribune" in the search box. The webpage came up and I held my breath during a search for the word "police." One recent article described an officer being charged with civil rights violations after the release of a troubling video. Another reported a commendation. Several more searches using other key words uncovered nothing about Anthony's arrest.

My heart sank. I wanted to believe I could trust this man who'd been such a caring friend and neighbor to Roy and me.

Moving on, I typed "fire" into the search box. Four different stories told of fires in other locations, but none were my address. I tried another search phrase and found the story listed halfway down the page, a correction to a previous story.

"Correction: The body of an elderly woman first reported absent when her house burned last week was apparently found in the subsequent investigation. Elaine Sutterfeld, 58, was identified by dental records. Fire officials have not yet determined how the fire started, but state that it is suspicious."

One hit, one strike. One more story to go. I debated what to enter in the search box. Roy's name would likely pull up his obituary. To avoid that, I typed in "police detective." Up popped Roy's official Chicago PD picture. My fingers pressed hard against my quivering lips. The words blurred, and I waited for my eyes to clear before reading the account.

> "Former Chicago police detective, Roy M. Sutterfeld, has been linked to the disappearance of young Jenny Ortiz over twelve years ago. The case made headlines when the thirteen-year-old student disappeared from a field trip and was never found. At the time of her disappearance, the student was under the supervision of the suspect's wife, Mrs. Elaine Sutterfeld.
>
> "A source who was not authorized to speak because of the nature of the case says the former detective has been a person of interest since the disappearance, but police are not disclosing what evidence they have that points to his involvement. Sutterfeld was eventually dismissed from the force. No charges will be filed due to Sutterfeld's death in an auto accident last week."

I grabbed a tissue from the box on Kim's desk and wiped my eyes, then clicked on Roy's image to enlarge it. I lingered, drinking in every detail of his young handsome face. The photo dated back to his promotion to detective. My fingers reached to touch his cheek, connecting instead with the cool glass of the computer monitor. I had no pictures of him. They'd all burned in the fire.

"Kim," I called. "May I print one sheet?"

"Sure. Go right ahead."

I checked the printer for color copies, clicked on print, and closed out the browser. Like a teenager with a picture of her favorite rock star, I held the printed photo in my hands and kissed the image. Then clasping it to my heart, I exited Kim's office and hurried to my room, grateful that Ruby was elsewhere while I hid Roy's picture.

The time between climbing into bed and actually falling asleep always brought new waves of grief as unwelcome memories played across my mind. But tonight, with Roy's picture under my pillow, I recalled every moment of our married life. The scratch of his mustache on my upper lip when I kissed him, the way my shoulder fit beneath his arm when we snuggled on the couch to watch television, the sound of his voice and the way he alone called me Lainey, the safe feeling that came from knowing he was lying in bed beside me at night.

Loneliness smothered me, becoming an almost physical pain. Memories were both a blessing and a curse. They kept Roy's memory alive but deepened the awareness of his absence.

In the morning, leftover emotions from a vivid dream left me feeling as if I'd actually spent time with Roy. I dreamed he was helping me remove a large stone from the backyard flowerbed. When he lifted one side, he disturbed a fire ant mound. The ants swarmed over him, and I complained that Stan hadn't treated the beds as he'd promised. Roy assured me the ants didn't bother him, even though I could see little red welts popping up on his arms and hands. He brushed the ants off and tried to lift a different corner of the stone. This time, a snake darted out and bit him.

Somehow, I knew this was a venomous one, even though I'm ignorant when it comes to snakes. I searched my pockets for my phone to call 9-1-1 until I remembered Anthony had taken my phone. I yelled for help, hoping someone in the house or even a neighbor might respond, but no one answered. As Roy lay there dying, he kept repeating, "Be strong, Lainey. Be strong."

Sunday morning, Ruby insisted church clothes weren't necessary at Brother Stan's church. She persuaded me to accompany her and Jean and Stan to worship services while Kim stayed home with Maxine. I listened to the sermon long enough to hear the story of a woman who offered her tent as a hiding place to the commander of an enemy army. She was credited with saving Israel by driving a tent stake through the commander's head after he fell asleep. It wasn't the most comforting story I might've heard, especially after my dream.

The vividness of that dream was probably the reason I mistakenly thrilled to the sight of a man who looked like Roy from behind. My heart shouted *That's him!* only to plummet to my heels when the gentleman turned, and I saw his face was nothing like Roy's. All the way home, I gripped my olive-drab purse, running my fingers over it as if I were a child stroking a security blanket.

Stan ushered the three of us out of the van and up to the front door. Before I went inside, he touched my elbow.

"Are you ready to do some more work on the flower beds?"

I swallowed the reproach on the tip of my tongue for not treating the beds as he'd promised, and reminded myself that was only a dream. Actually, I was looking forward to working on the beds this afternoon, but I'd hoped to do so alone. I needed some solitary time to think. "How about tomorrow? You could pick up some flowers in the morning on your way over."

Stan glanced down and rubbed the toe of his shoe against the sidewalk. "I believe you have a much better eye for color and style. May I pick you up before I go so you can pick out what you think would look best?"

I hesitated, not wanting any more trouble with Maxine. "I guess that would be all right." After stepping inside the door, I turned back to him. "Would you mind making another stop while we're out? I've been needing a few things, and with Ruby and Maxine sick, I've had no way to get to the store."

A smile brightened his face. "Of course. What time shall I come by?"

We agreed on eight-thirty the next morning.

"Dad?" Kim called. "You want to stay for lunch?"

Stan accepted the invitation. I groaned silently. Had Kim talked with Maxine yet? I feared she might need to speak with her father as well. But thankfully, I didn't have to endure any of Maxine's black looks. Instead of eating with the rest of us, she ordered crackers and gelatin served in her room.

I helped Kim clean up lunch, Stan went home for his Sunday afternoon nap, and Ruby excused herself for a nap as well. Kim attended to some paperwork in her office, leaving Jean and me to ourselves.

"Would you care to watch a movie?" Jean asked. My mind was already on weeding and cleaning up the flowerbed.

"Maybe another time. I need to work on that bed in the backyard. Stan is picking up some flowers for it tomorrow, and I'd like to have it ready for planting."

Jean placed the remote on the TV stand. "Mind if I join you? I really should get outside and enjoy these nice days before summer comes and it gets too hot."

Would I never get time alone to think? I couldn't refuse Jean without sounding rude, and the last thing I wanted to do was hurt her feelings. I changed my clothes, gathered my tools from the garage, and knelt beside the large oval-shaped bed opposite the old oaks.

Grass runners scaled the brick edging in several spots, spreading throughout the bed in every direction. Thistles and dandelions grew in the middle, along with several broadleaf and vining weeds. Jean dragged a patio chair over while I assessed what needed to be done.

"Looks like a lot of work." She shielded her eyes from the early afternoon sun. "Does it all need to be done today?"

"As much as I can." I stood and pulled my rake over the weeds, tugging through the tangle to break up their root systems. "Wish I had a tiller. It'd save me a lot of time and energy." Jean eased onto her knees at the far edge and tugged on some of the grass runners. "Watch for ants. You don't want this." I held up my hand, still sporting several pimple-looking bumps.

"I forgot about that." She jerked back and slid onto her chair. "What about you? Where are the gloves Stan bought for you?"

I stopped raking. "I forgot all about them. I haven't wanted to wear one on this hand because it irritates the bites and makes them itch worse. But with Ruby and Maxine sick, I completely forgot about the gloves." I flexed and squeezed my hand, testing the sensitivity of the bites. "Maybe I could tolerate a glove today."

"You want me to get them for you?"

"Would you?"

"Are they in your room or the garage?" Jean headed toward the house.

"I think I left them in the garage. Look on the shelf opposite the door you enter. The light switch is on your left when you walk in."

I watched until she entered the garage before working the rake again. Jean had been mostly lucid the last couple of days, but Kim warned she could make perfect sense one minute and talk gibberish the next. How does one cope with a mind that's no longer dependable, sending you off in an unpredictable direction without a moment's notice? I dug the rake deeper into the ground and dragged it through the bed, dislodging several vines and one thistle by its roots.

Jean, Maxine, Ruby—all of them were here because a doctor

had declared them incompetent to fully care for themselves. I didn't yet share their loss of independence, but I understood very well the shame of incompetence.

The words rang in my ears as fresh as if I were standing in that personnel office a month after Jenny disappeared. The circumstances dictated administrative leave as standard procedure. Even my termination didn't come as a total surprise, but the derisive, condescending tone of the personnel director made me feel like little more than a rebellious student.

Incompetent. Irresponsible. Teachers simply don't lose their students.

I dug and tore at the vines that cluttered the bed. Oh, how I missed Roy. He'd held me steady when Jenny disappeared, looking at the problem from every possible angle. I needed his level-headed guidance, not to mention a good dose of his confidence.

But Roy wasn't here. And if Anthony was sitting in a Chicago jail cell, he couldn't help me either. I stopped and leaned on the rake's handle, biting back tears. With no one to confide in, I'd never felt so alone, so incompetent, so irresponsible. Roy always told me the director's assessment was wrong, but if I'd been responsible, I'd have demanded to know whom Roy was seeing and where they were meeting.

Actually, a responsible person would've insisted Roy turn the evidence over to police rather than meet with the suspect. And if I'd been at all competent, I would've learned the details of the case before he left.

A competent, responsible teacher would've kept Jenny safe. She should've been alive today, maybe with children of her own.

I dropped the rake handle, letting it fall into the grass next to the brick edging and eased onto my knees to pull at the grass runners around the edging. An ant scurried across a brick, and I suddenly remembered Jean. What was taking her so long? Had she not found the gloves where I said they'd be? I turned the rake over and pressed the tines into the ground to avoid any accidents, then got to my feet and headed for the garage.

"Jean?" No answer. Maybe she couldn't hear well inside the garage. The walk-in door to the garage stood open. "Jean?" I stepped inside. "Are you in here?"

Still no answer. I peered around the room, peeked behind the riding mower and in between large garbage cans, a weed whacker and the dusty accumulation of decades. My gloves were missing from the shelf, so Jean must have been here. Maybe she went inside for something.

I turned off the light, closed the door and made my way to the patio. Slipping inside, I hurried down the hall to Jean's room, calling her name softly so as not to waken Ruby or Maxine. Her bed was made. A few items lay scattered across her dresser, but no Jean. The bathroom door stood open, and after checking inside, I hurried up the hall to Kim's office. She looked up as I entered.

"Has Jean been in here?"

Kim shook her head. "I haven't seen her. Wasn't she with you?"

"She was, but I forgot my gloves. She offered to get them out of the garage for me. The gloves are gone, and so is Jean. I can't find her."

Kim rose, pushing back her chair. "You've checked her room?"

"Yes, and the bathroom."

"What about the other rooms, yours and Maxine's?"

"No, I didn't think to check there."

"I'll look in on them. You go outside and make sure she's not out there looking for you." Kim strode down the hall as I once again exited the patio door. A visual scan of the backyard failed to turn up any sign of her, so I circled to the front of the house, calling her name.

Kim met me at the front door, worry lines creasing her forehead.

"She's not in the house."

"And she's not out here."

"I'm calling Dad. He can drive the streets and look for her." Kim whirled toward her office then reached into her pocket to retrieve her cell phone instead. She punched a number and waited. We listened as the ringing continued until a mechanical voice announced that this number was not available. Kim growled. "Come on, Dad, answer your phone." Her eyes darted up and down the street and she walked out to the curb. "Dad, it's Kim. We have an emergency. Call me."

CHAPTER 20

Where is that woman?

From the window of his fifteenth-floor office, he looked out at the labyrinth of Chicago's city streets and buildings.

Where is she hiding? According to his men, there'd still been no activity on any of her accounts since that last withdrawal the night of the fire. But he refused to believe she'd somehow met an untimely death by some other means.

Her prolonged absence all but proved she knew his secret. And as long as her whereabouts remained unknown, he risked exposure. Had she entered some kind of witness protection program? Was she working with authorities right now, spilling all the evidence on him that her fool husband had collected? He never should have let him leave this office.

If he'd been smart—his brothers would say competent—he'd have ordered an immediate hit on her. His incompetence had led to this ultimate game of hide and seek. Fortunately, Jack and Lester weren't around to taunt him.

He poured himself a drink and swallowed it in one gulp, gritting his teeth as the burn slid down his throat. It galled him to be paying for one careless mistake more than a decade later. He'd known many girls since then, some more memorable than others in making him feel like a man—successful, confident, in control.

Ironically, he'd never taken his pleasure with the one causing him so much trouble. He'd taken only her necklace from her, in a silly moment of sentimental weakness. But the token had served him well in building a feeling of belonging and secret privilege in his girls.

Too bad Tiana broke the rule. But with her out of the way and the uproar about her surprising overdose quieting down, he could focus all his energy on finding that Sutterfeld woman.

His gaze swept the cityscape once more. Several streets over, dust and debris filled the air around an imploded building. Trucks from several media outlets were parked on surrounding streets, reporters filming the event for the evening news.

Planting those news stories hadn't flushed the woman out of hiding, but the cop's arrest should get results. The officer knew something, he was sure of it, but they could only hold him for so long without presenting evidence to the formal charges. Time was running out.

I'll find you, Elaine Sutterfeld—if it's the last thing I do.

CHAPTER 21

Minutes passed as slowly as Chicago's rush hour traffic in a construction zone while they waited for news from Stan. He'd gone out to drive the neighborhood as soon as he heard.

Kim paced through the house, stopping at the end of each lap to peer out the front door. Maxine demanded we help her into her wheelchair so she could join Ruby and me in the living room.

Ruby sat with her eyes closed in one of the upright armchairs. I assumed she was praying since she'd already taken a nap.

Was this how Jenny disappeared? Had I been so preoccupied with other students I never noticed she was missing? I chided myself now for being too focused on my own worries to notice Jean hadn't returned. I could've asked her to hold my tools while I retrieved the gloves, should've at least kept her within sight. Kim had every right to dissolve our agreement and toss me out on the street.

I decided to follow Ruby's lead and offer a silent prayer for Jean's safe return, adding a confession of guilt for being irresponsible while she was under my supervision.

Kim's cell phone rang and she pressed it to her ear.

"You found her? Oh, thank God. Where is she?" Kim's shoulders relaxed. She pressed a hand to her mouth. "Okay, bring her home. Thank you, Dad." She disconnected and heaved a sigh that seemed to come all the way from her toes. "Jean is safe. Dad found her walking up the street about ten blocks away."

Ruby clapped her hands to her cheeks and looked up to the ceiling. "Hallelujah. Thank you, Jesus."

"Amen to that, sister." Maxine pounded her palm on her wheelchair's armrest.

I exhaled and whispered a prayer of thanks to Ruby's God for watching over Jean. Maybe I should pack my few belongings and leave before Kim had a chance to send me away. But where would I go?

Chicago, of course. I'd prove Anthony wasn't guilty of murder. In the light of day, everything seemed so obvious. I felt silly for not trusting him. Anthony knew I hadn't died in the fire, but he didn't have the connections to plant that sort of news story. Whoever did likely must have connections in the police and fire departments, too—connections that put Anthony in jail on suspicion of arson and murder without a shred of evidence. This trip to Texas had been a waste of time. I'd never find the answers to my questions down here. I needed to get back to Chicago.

But how? I barely had enough cash to pay for a one-way flight if I could find one of those cheap fares. But those were usually only available months in advance. I'd need a credit card to make a reservation unless I showed up at the counter in person. That meant transportation to Dallas, which would require more money.

I remembered seeing a bus station sign along the freeway when we drove into town. A bus ticket wouldn't require a credit card and my false ID shouldn't be a problem either. But I'd still need money for a taxi ride to the bus station and for transportation when I arrived in Chicago.

No telling how long it might take to get Anthony out of jail and recover my cards from him. Where would I stay? Poor Lauren might die of fright if I showed up on her doorstep when she believed me dead.

At the rumble of Stan's truck, Kim threw the front door wide open and rushed out to meet Jean. Maxine wheeled herself to the door. Ruby and I stayed back until everyone came inside.

Jean's cheeks were flushed and beads of sweat dotted her upper lip. I fixed a glass of ice water and brought it from the kitchen, placing it in her garden-gloved hands.

"Why, thank you," she gushed. "This is a lovely party. Do you know who the guest of honor is?"

I took hold of her arm and leaned close to whisper, "My dear, I believe it's you."

Monday morning, Kim still had made no mention of my error, but she appeared to keep a closer watch on Jean. Along with letting Jean get away, Travis's visit weighed on me. I decided not to mention it to anyone. Maxine and Brandi would only get stirred up and anxious, and they probably wouldn't believe me if I told them he could've easily thrown the kids in his truck and left but chose not to. I kept my fingers crossed that Riley and Micah knew how to keep a secret.

Kim agreed to let me accompany Stan to the nursery. Purse in hand, I knocked on Maxine's door before leaving. She pulled the door open and wheeled back.

"Yeah, whaddya want?"

Her brusque manner hadn't suffered any damage from her

illness. She still appeared weaker than normal, but her red lipstick did wonders to brighten her pale complexion.

"Stan will be over to help plant flowers later this morning. I thought you'd like to know so you can rest now and be ready for him later."

Maxine backed away an inch and cocked her head at me, as if I were offering her a deal on waterfront property in Arizona.

"I'm leaving in a few minutes to shop for flowers to plant in that large bed out back. Do you have a favorite I could look for?" I already had the layout of the bed planned, but thought it would be fun to include favorites of the ladies. Maxine stared at me a moment longer before answering.

"Roses. I like roses."

"Red ones?"

"Yeah. How'd you know?"

"Lucky guess. The hybrid roses require a lot of care, but maybe I can get one or two bush-types that bloom longer. Would that be okay?" She nodded, still looking sideways at me. "All right then. I expect to be back in an hour or so. 'Bye." I closed her door and walked out to Stan's truck.

"How's Jean doing this morning?" Stan asked as he backed down the driveway and headed out of the neighborhood.

"She seems better. She doesn't remember her little jaunt yesterday, but Kim is worried about her. If she's starting to wander, she needs to be in a more secure facility."

Stan winced. "I'd hate to see that."

"Does she have any children? I noticed she didn't have any guests for the Mother's Day lunch."

"She has three, all grown with children of their own. Her son is the only one who's geographically close. He's in Dallas, comes down about every other month or so, but he runs his own business, and it keeps him pretty busy. One daughter lives in New Mexico, the other one is out east somewhere."

"What about a husband?"

"I believe he passed away a few years ago. Prostate cancer, if I remember correctly."

I tsk'd and shook my head. "Such a shame. If she has to go into memory care, maybe her son will find a place in Dallas. Seems like having her closer would benefit both of them."

"I agree, but he wanted her to remain in familiar surroundings as long as possible."

At the nursery, we found a rose bush for Maxine. With a name like "Unconditional Love," I thought it was perfect. Jean had asked for zinnias and Ruby liked the portulaca we planted in the front. Stan pointed out an esperanza plant, saying it was a Texas native whose yellow bell-shaped blooms brightened summer days when most other plants wilted in the heat. I agreed to try it, and picked out a few vincas and pentas to round out the colors. Stan paid for them and we loaded everything into the back of the truck.

He slammed the tailgate shut. "You still want to do some shopping?"

"If you don't mind. It won't take long."

He helped me into the truck, climbed into the driver's seat and started the engine. "Where to?"

Minutes later, he dropped me off in front of a large discount store, promising to watch for me when I exited. I headed first to the shoe section to find a simple pair of sneakers for gardening. A sun hat, some slacks for Sundays, and another top or two would make my wardrobe last a bit longer between laundry days. While calculating the cost of my purchases, I thought to check and see how much cash I had left. I pulled out my wallet, and a business card fluttered to the floor.

I stooped to pick it up and checked the name. Ted Owens. He'd given it to me at Roy's funeral, but I'd forgotten all about it. I stuffed it back in my purse, his concern for me warming my heart. By now, he'd learned of the fire, and probably believed me dead.

And yet—I pulled the card out again. There was his office phone number. He'd gotten me out of one bad situation years ago. More recently, after Roy's death, he'd offered help more than once. Could this be my ticket home?

Anthony's stern caution about not contacting anyone rang in my ears, but he was no help to me while sitting in a jail cell. I shoved the card and my wallet back in my purse, hung my slacks and tops on the dressing room's discard rack and headed for the front door. More clothes weren't necessary if I were going home in a day or two, although I still needed a sun hat for working outside today.

Detouring to the accessories section, I picked up a wide-brimmed hat and checked my appearance in the nearby full-length mirror. The hat looked fine, but what caught my attention in the mirror's reflection was a smart-looking tan leather handbag on the shelf behind me. Exactly the kind I had in mind when I'd blurted out to Roy my desire for a new purse. I looked the purse over, examining every pocket and zipper section. Even the length of the strap on my shoulder was just right.

Reluctantly, I set it back on the shelf. Somehow, carrying a different purse felt disloyal to Roy's memory. I turned away and caught a glimpse of my reflection in the mirror, that ugly green purse hanging on my arm. A moment later, I'd grabbed the leather purse and was hurrying to check out. This pea-green purse would always be my connection to Roy, but from now on, I'd treat it like a child's much-loved blanket or stuffed animal that stays at home on the bed. Roy's last gift would be relegated to private comfort.

Travis slowed and made a right turn into the second park entrance. He drove past two other parked cars and backed into the farthest slot, facing the lake. Earlier heavy rains at the end of April had raised the reservoir level to flood stage. Marinas and most parks around the perimeter of the lake were underwater, including the lowest section of Woodway Park. Several yards from where he sat, gentle waves lapped at the grassy slope while behind him, the terrain rose high enough to maintain a playground and a few disc golf stations above the high-water level.

His hand dove into the paper bag beside him and came up with the last of the French fries whose aroma filled the cab of his truck in spite of the open windows. He should've ordered the supersized fries along with the drink. Savoring the last bit of salty flavor, he dug deeper into the bag and withdrew a double cheeseburger. The line at the drive-thru and the time it took to drive over here had eaten up half his lunch break already. But with everything on his mind, he needed this getaway.

He'd made a mistake going over to see the kids on Saturday. Riley's tears as he drove away stuck in his mind like a lug nut rusted on its post. When he looked back and saw her still waving from the curb, he'd nearly called Brandi right then and begged her to let him come home. But that wouldn't have solved anything. Given a day or two, they'd be right back where they were now with her nagging, suspicious of everything he did, and him feeling like a failure. Marrying her had been a mistake. No, the mistake had come earlier, when he allowed his physical needs to overpower everything else. He'd tried hard to wriggle out of the consequences until Granny got hold of him.

If she's good enough to get naked with, she oughta be good enough to wear your name.

He'd given Brandi his name, but starting marriage as a couple of headstrong teenagers made for a rough time. What surprised him the most was how much he loved being a dad. Teaching

Riley to dance the Texas two-step, wrestling with Micah—being their hero for no other reason than the fact he was their dad.

Had Brandi ever considered him a hero? Ha! Not likely. But had he ever given her reason to? Had he ever acted like a hero for her?

That new lady at Maxine's place reminded him a lot of Granny. At first, he'd resented her. She was a bossy old woman sticking her nose where it didn't belong. But the way she challenged him to "be the kind of dad you want for Riley and Micah," that was just the kind of thing Granny would've said.

Was divorce an option for him and Brandi? They were both young enough to find someone else. Brandi was good-looking and had enough personality to attract plenty of other guys. He imagined the kids calling some other guy Dad, and pounded his fist onto the dashboard. *He* was their dad. He had no intention of giving up that position to anyone else. He'd do what the old lady said, be the kind of dad he wanted for his kids. Even if it meant staying married to Brandi. Once upon a time, he'd been crazy about her, and he was pretty sure she cared about him. Maybe they could work things out, get back to where they started.

Travis stuffed the last bites of the cheeseburger into the bag and gulped half of his soda. The lake reflected the sky's deep blue today instead of the usual brown from river sediment flowing into the reservoir. Sunlight shimmered on the surface, broken only by a couple of kayakers enjoying the placid ride in the absence of motorboats. He scrunched the fast food bag into a tight ball, and managed to sink it into a garbage can on his way out. Score two.

Lindsey pulled into her parking spot as he got out of his truck. She swooped close, her perfume stealing every molecule of oxygen for several feet in each direction.

"Missed you at lunch. Where'd you go?" She pressed against his side.

"I had an errand to run." Travis held the door open for her, trying not to inhale.

"Can I interest you in supper at my place tonight? We can throw some steaks on the grill." Her long hair brushed soft against his arm as she walked, and she aimed a dazzling smile at him. Steak on the grill sounded a whole lot better than a frozen pizza.

"Yeah, okay. What time?"

"Is seven o'clock too late?"

"No, that'll give me time to get home and clean up. I'll see you then."

"Don't be late," she sing-songed as she continued down the hall, hips swaying with every step.

This'll be the last time, he told himself. He'd level with her. Though her interest flattered him, he really wasn't available. She'd be better off chasing someone else.

Riley's tearful image came to mind. He couldn't get it out of his head, despite all the work orders that came after lunch. Between oil changes, maintenance checks and tire rotations, she was always there, standing on the curb waving.

His supersized lunch drink drove him to the restroom at break. Dustin was on his way out, but held the door open and followed Travis back in.

"I hear you're having steak for supper tonight."

"News travels fast."

Dustin leaned against the sink, arms crossed over his chest. "Just wondering—are you still interested in a piece of my delivery business?"

Travis raised his eyes to meet his friend's gaze.

Dustin shifted, his hands sliding into his trouser pockets. "I think I could cut you in if, you know, if you still want a piece of the action. You can make some good money. Buy your way back into Brandi's favor. Or pay for a divorce." His mouth curved into a smug grin. He shifted his stance and once again crossed his arms.

A drug dealer. Dustin had gotten out of jail almost as quick as Travis, thanks to his supplier. And he hadn't shown any remorse. He had laughed it off, like it was all a game. But it was a dangerous game that got kids hooked and wouldn't let go. Would Riley or Micah be the kid in the other car someday?

Travis scrubbed his hands under the water and tore off a couple paper towels to sop up the moisture. *Be the kind of dad your kids will be proud of.* He crumpled the paper towels and dropped them in the trashcan next to Dustin.

"I'm not interested." Travis pulled the door open and exited the bathroom. Explain to Micah his dad was a drug peddler? Never. It bothered him to even think of admitting he lived with a drug dealer.

And Riley. How could he look his little girl in the eye and admit to having dinner with another woman besides her mother? Especially when the other woman's intent was perfectly clear.

The rest of what the lady at the home said came back to him as he returned to the shop. She said if he became the kind of dad his kids were proud of, he'd likely be the kind of man Brandi would welcome home.

Travis mulled over Lindsey's invitation the rest of the afternoon, and by quitting time, he'd made a decision. He packed up his tools and approached the shop supervisor.

"Sorry for such short notice, but I won't be back. I've got some personal issues to work out. I'll drop off a written resignation letter tomorrow."

"What? You're supposed to give two weeks' notice, y'know."

Yeah, he knew, but this was more important. Travis ignored the man's annoyance and headed for the front desk. Lindsey finished up with a customer and turned a bright smile his way.

He leaned over the counter and lowered his voice so only she could hear.

"I've changed my mind. I won't be coming for dinner...or anything else. I'm not coming back here. So long, Lindsey." He touched two fingers to his forehead in a mock salute and left her with her mouth hanging open.

Travis gunned the engine as he exited the lot. Ten minutes later, he pulled up to the curb outside Dustin's house. Now what? He needed to make some life changes if he intended to go home and live with his wife and kids again. Staying with Dustin was no longer an option, but he had no job to pay rent. He'd start looking for something else tomorrow. Even though his stint with the dealership was short-lived, it might open a few doors. But first, he needed a place to stay tonight.

He pulled up a name in his contacts list and thumbed the call button, waiting through three rings before someone answered.

"Hello, Travis. What's up?"

"Hey, Stan. Is that offer to use your spare bedroom still open?"

CHAPTER 22

Kim handed out glasses of ice water, then walked around the newly planted flowerbed for inspection. Stan, Jean and I welcomed the cold beverage and stood by, awaiting her approval.

"I love the splash of color. Wish we'd done this a long time ago." She completed her circle tour.

"It's beautiful. I just love those moss roses." Ruby leaned on her walker at the edge of the patio. Beside her, Maxine kept an eye on Stan and me.

We'd spent the last half of the morning cleaning out the rest of the weeds and thistles, then breaking up and amending the soil. We didn't actually start planting until after lunch, but with Jean's help, all the plants we'd purchased were in the ground. My sun hat proved a wise purchase with the temperature nearing ninety degrees.

Maxine replied to Ruby's comment. "Roses are a girl's best friend."

"A little of each of us," Ruby said. "Our favorite flowers to remind us to bloom where we're planted."

I took a long drink, enjoying the cool feel of the water in my mouth. The heat and physical labor had tired me out, but a look at my watch told me it was nearly time to start supper. I asked Kim to give me a few minutes to wash up and I'd be ready to help her. My purse and bags lay on my bed where I'd dropped them after returning from shopping with Stan. I remembered Ted's card, and while I changed clothes, I rehearsed what to say when I called him.

Hello, Ted. This is Elaine Sutterfeld and the reports of my death have been greatly exaggerated.

Hello, Ted. I don't want to give you a heart attack, but this is Elaine Sutterfeld.

Ted, I thought you should know that Elaine Sutterfeld is very much alive, and I could use your help.

Maybe it would be better to explain the situation to his receptionist and let her break the news to him.

I slipped my phone and Ted's business card into my pocket and checked the kitchen. Kim wasn't there yet, so despite the heat, I stole out to the backyard and perched on the branch where I'd last heard from Anthony. A welcome, light breeze lifted the hair from the back of my neck as I punched Ted's number into my phone. I took a deep breath and pressed the call button, still undecided what to say when he answered. His phone rang once, twice, three times. A woman's voice answered.

"Judge Owens's office. How may I help you?"

"I'd like—" I cleared my throat and tried again. "Excuse me. I wondered if I might speak with the judge."

"May I ask who's calling?"

"Lorraine Johnson. I'd like to speak with him about a favor he offered me." I decided using my alias might soften the blow, give me time to prepare him for the surprise of learning I was alive.

"Are you a personal acquaintance of Judge Owens?"

"Oh, yes, we go way back—thirty, forty years."

"All right, thank you, Ms. Johnson. Let me see if the Judge is available." She put me on hold. A classical music selection filled my ear as I imagined Ted declaring he didn't know anyone by that name, certainly no one of longstanding acquaintance. But eventually, his voice replaced Mozart's music.

"This is Judge Owens. May I help you?"

My heart pounded so hard I could barely speak.

"Ted..." My voice failed. Hearing him brought back all the pain, all the memories of my last week and a half in Chicago.

"Am I speaking with Lorraine Johnson?"

"No, this is Elaine. Elaine Sutterfeld. I didn't die in the fire at my house and–"

"Elaine? Is it...it's really you?"

"Yes, it's me. I'm living under an assumed name. It seems someone is after me, maybe even trying to kill me."

"Thank God, you're alive. I couldn't believe it when I heard about your house burning down. Where are you?"

"I'm in Texas."

"Texas?"

"Waco, to be exact. And I need help to get back to Chicago."

"How did you end up in Waco, Texas?"

"It's a long story. I'll fill you in later, but I must ask a favor of you."

"Anything. What do you need?"

"My neighbor, Anthony Fisher, has been arrested and jailed. They say he's responsible for the fire and for my death. But he was with me when the fire started, and as you can tell, I'm very much alive. I need to get back to Chicago to prove he's innocent. Can you help me?"

"I'll do anything you ask."

"I need a loan. I don't have access to my bank or credit cards here. Would you please buy a plane ticket for me from Dallas? I'll pay you back as soon as I get access to my accounts."

"I'll do better than that, Elaine. I'll come down and personally escort you back to Chicago."

"Oh, that's not necessary."

"On the contrary. I'd never forgive myself if I didn't take care of Roy's widow. I have a few loose ends to tie up tonight, but I'll leave as early as I can get a flight out tomorrow. You'll be home in Chicago by tomorrow night."

Relief surged through me as I gave him Kim's address and my phone number. He promised to let me know what time to expect him tomorrow. I closed the phone, exhaled, and felt the tension of the last two weeks drain away. I was going home. Not only that, but I'd finally have a familiar ally. No more pretending to be someone I was not.

And that was another problem. How would I explain myself to Kim and the other ladies? I didn't relish the thought of confessing my deception. Though at times it seemed I'd been here for months, I'd arrived only a little more than a week ago. Such a short time to grow so fond of Ruby and Jean and Kim. And yes, even Maxine. How could I admit I'd been deceiving them all along?

Ruby shuffled into the room shortly before bedtime. She halted, then laughed and covered her mouth with her hand.

"I forgot I have a roommate. For a minute there, I thought I was in the wrong room."

"I'm sorry I've inconvenienced you. You'll have your room to yourself again soon."

Ruby backed up to the bed until her calves touched the frame and eased herself down to the mattress. "Oh, I don't mind having a roommate. Reminds me of sharing a room with my sisters when I was young." Her light blue nightgown made an attractive contrast against her dark skin and gray hair. She looked down, her brows pinched and lips pressed together.

"Is something wrong? You look worried."

"I am worried, but I don't rightly know if something's wrong or not. Anthony didn't call this weekend. He's so good about calling, and I love hearing his voice. But the last time I heard from him was to let me know he made it home. I hope nothing's wrong, but I worry about him. He's a policeman, you know, up there in Chicago."

So, Amanda hadn't notified her grandmother about Anthony's arrest. I didn't blame her. She probably didn't want to upset Ruby if they could get the charges dropped. But what could I say to her?

"It's natural to worry, but surely someone would have notified you if anything was wrong, don't you think?"

Ruby blinked and bobbed her head. "I suppose you're right. He'll probably call one of these days and tell me he worked a double shift or something." She sighed and muttered the phrase I'd heard her say in the laundry room.

"What did you say?"

Ruby's chin dipped. She shuffled her feet. "Oh, it's just something I say to remind myself who's in charge."

"What's the saying?"

"Lord, to whom shall we go?"

"What does that mean?"

"In the Bible, when many of Jesus' followers turned away from him, he asked his twelve chosen disciples if they wanted to leave, too. Peter answered by asking who else they could go to since he was the Messiah and had the words of eternal life." Ruby shrugged and stretched out her legs. "Whenever I get to worrying and doubting, I use that to remind myself who has the ultimate answers."

I sat down in a chair next to the bed. "Interesting. And does He always give you answers?"

"Oh, no." Ruby laughed. "I'm not looking for answers. It reminds me to keep trusting Him."

"Why? Why trust God if he doesn't answer you?"

She thought a moment, gazing at the floor. "I guess because if you take God out of it, there's only ourselves left. And we don't have the answers. If we did, we'd have solved all our problems by now. It's like Peter said, where else can we go?"

Ruby seemed so sure of her faith. I wondered if I could ever accept that line of reasoning. She eyed the straps for my new handbag sticking out of the plastic shopping bag on my bed. "You get yourself a new purse?"

I pulled it out for Ruby's inspection, slipping the strap over my shoulder and modeling it.

"That army green one was a gift from my husband, his last gift before he died. He never forgot our anniversary or my birthday, but the gifts he picked out—" I rolled my eyes. "If there'd been a reality show for ugly gifts, he'd have easily made it into the final round."

Ruby chuckled. "You're lucky he remembered at all. My Charles couldn't remember his own birthday, much less any other special dates. One year, he even missed Christmas. Thought it was the twenty-sixth."

We laughed, and I sat down again to transfer the contents from one purse to the other. Wallet, tissues, phone, comb, lipstick, nail file, hand lotion, ibuprofen, and house keys. I dangled the useless keys in the air, tempted to toss them in the garbage. For now, I laid them on the bed.

Everything fit into the new purse with room to spare, and the separate pockets kept it all organized. I ran my fingers around the interior of the old purse, checking to make sure I hadn't missed anything. My fingers caught on a little something at the bottom near one corner. I held the purse open to the light to peer inside.

"What's wrong?" Ruby leaned toward me, blocking the light.

I stood and angled the purse to better see the inside. "There's something at the bottom, but it feels like it's underneath the lining."

"Probably one of those security tags."

I chuckled. "As if someone would steal anything this ugly?" Ruby laughed. My fingers traced a thin, square shape that moved wherever I pushed it. I tipped my head to peek inside again and noticed a small tear in the lining. Had my keys done that in the short time I'd had the purse? Examining the hole, I noted there were no ragged edges, no loose, fraying threads like I'd expect from an accidental tear. This looked more like a clean cut right along the seam.

Could it be?

I poked my finger through the hole, splitting the seam wider until two fingers fit into the opening. Ruby looked on as I shook the purse and tipped it this way and that to move the item closer to the opening. My fingers grazed the coarse outer cloth until at last, I managed to clamp the thing between my fingers. Carefully, I withdrew a cream-colored memory card.

Ruby squinted at it. "What in the world is that?"

It's gold, my dear. The treasure hunt is over.

I hated waiting until morning to see what was on this tiny bit of technology, but I didn't have much choice. Kim's computer was the only one in the house, and she was working late tonight, some kind of paperwork required for the home. I could wait until she went to bed, but that meant an awkward explanation to the night nurse about why I needed to use Kim's computer at such a late hour. I consoled myself with knowing I had the evidence right here in my hands.

While Ruby was in the bathroom, I snatched up my phone to call Anthony. It rang twice before I remembered he couldn't answer, and I cut off the call. Should I leave a voice mail? I stared at the phone in my hand. With no other numbers in my phone, I had no choice but to leave a message and hope Amanda would find it. I tapped the message icon.

Got your msg. Tell your dad I found the evidence.

I closed the phone and climbed into bed, holding the card tight in my hand, afraid it might disappear if I let go. But I couldn't hold it all night. I slid the thin little treasure inside my pillow then changed my mind and fished it out again. The ugly, pea-green purse hung on the arm of the couch by my head. I slipped the memory card back into its hiding place between the lining and the shell. Then I laid the purse beside my pillow. Ruby would understand the presumed sentiment if she noticed me sleeping with Roy's last gift by my pillow.

Contentment settled over me soft as a blanket. I nestled my head into the pillow, ecstatic over finding Roy's evidence. Once I had a chance to view the contents of the memory card, I'd turn it over to Anthony, and Jenny's case would finally be resolved. I closed my eyes to sleep, but a moment later, a sudden realization brought me wide awake.

If Roy hid that card where he knew I'd eventually find it, he was fully aware of the possibility he might not make it home.

Questions tumbled over me, one after another. Where had Roy gone that morning? Why did he take such a risk? What transpired during his interview with the suspect? I stifled the tears and sniffles until I heard Ruby snoring. Then giving myself over to grief for my husband, I wondered about the man he'd met on the last morning of his life. Who had decreed my husband must die because of what he knew?

That little square in my purse carried the answers. I toyed with the idea of sneaking into Kim's office during the night. But even if I managed to dodge the night nurse, I'd have to log out of Kim's account, and I didn't know her password to get back in when I finished. She'd know someone had used the computer without her authorization.

Dawn's light had barely touched the window above the couch when I rose, washed, and managed to get dressed without waking Ruby. I slipped the memory card into my pants pocket and went to see if the office was occupied. Kim sat at her desk, staring at the computer monitor with a frown on her face. She mumbled something, then noticed me standing in the doorway.

"Good morning, Lorraine. Can I ask you to fix breakfast this morning? I've got an appointment at 10:00 with Jean's son."

"Is this about her wandering?"

Kim threaded her fingers through her thick, auburn hair, pulling it away from her face. "I'm afraid so. I can't be responsible for her if she decides to take a hike. I'm not set up for that type of care." She bit the corner of her lip and looked back at the computer screen, clicking over to a different page. "I'll probably be tied up all morning. Do you mind getting breakfast ready? I laid everything out for you. You'll see it on the counter."

In the kitchen, I found everything as Kim said—eggs to scramble, cooked bacon to heat in the oven, cantaloupe to cut into pieces and mix with blueberries, and oatmeal in case anyone preferred hot cereal. The coffee was hot and ready to serve, so I poured a cup for myself and set to work. By the time the other ladies wandered in, the table was set and breakfast prepared.

"Where's Kim?" Maxine helped herself to several slices of bacon.

"I'm here." Kim called from her office. "Just working on something. I asked Lorraine to handle breakfast for me."

Maxine grunted and chewed a strip of bacon. I still sensed a thin air of suspicion toward me, but her antagonism had lost its edge since I alerted her to Stan's afternoon visit yesterday. Ruby included a prayer for Anthony's safety in her table grace. I wondered if Jean knew about the upcoming meeting with her son.

After the breakfast items were all cleaned and put away, I found a text message from Ted. He expected to arrive around 4:30, barring any delays. That should allow me plenty of time to view the contents of the memory card.

Jean's face showed surprise when her son walked in the door. He greeted her with a hug and a kiss, then turned to greet Maxine and Ruby. Jean introduced me to him and mentioned my efforts with the flowers outside.

"Take him out and show him what you did yesterday, Jean." Kim walked them to the patio door and accompanied them to the planter. No sooner had they stepped off the patio than Maxine cornered me.

"What's going on?"

Ruby shuffled over to me as well. "Is this because she wandered off?"

I pressed my lips together, uncertain how much Kim wanted to reveal. "Yes, it has something to do with Jean's little jaunt the other day, but I really don't know what's being discussed."

They came back inside and held a closed-door session in Kim's office. Since I was leaving on such short notice, I decided a little dusting and cleaning might help Kim out. She deserved a much earlier warning, but I resolved to talk with her as soon as she finished with Jean and her son. Maybe then I could use her computer one last time.

The office door opened. Jean murmured to her son, then walked to her room without making eye contact with any of us. Deep lines framed her mouth and eyes. She returned with her purse and, keeping her gaze to the floor, she and her son exited through the front door. Kim leaned against the frame of her office doorway, one hand covering her mouth. Maxine muted the television.

"Are you kicking her out?"

Kim scowled. "No, I'm not kicking her out. Just preparing for the inevitable. I wanted them to explore their options now while Jean is still capable of making decisions." She ran a hand through her hair then turned and walked into her office and closed the door again. Now was not the time to disclose my plans for an imminent departure.

Kim made a brief appearance at lunchtime, long enough to get a sandwich and return to her office. Maxine watched soap operas on television while Ruby studied her Bible at the dining room table. I went outside to pull the weeds poking up in the front planters. Plucking a dead head from one of the flowers, I debated whether to pack my things now or wait until later. With so few clothes and belongings, it wouldn't take any time to throw them all in a bag. I checked my pocket to reassure myself the smooth plastic square was still there. Maybe Ted could make sure it got to the proper, trusted authorities. No sense waiting for Anthony's release.

About mid-afternoon, Jean and her son returned and again took counsel with Kim behind closed doors. When at last the door finally opened, they all wore smiles as they came out to the living room. Jean's son gave her a long hug, whispered in her ear, and kissed her on each cheek. He shook hands with Kim and promised to return in two weeks. Kim and Jean hugged as well, but as soon as her son left, Jean retired to her room.

Muting the television again, Maxine aimed an icy glare at Kim.

"Is she staying?"

"Yes, she's staying. For now." Kim swiped moisture from the corner of her eye. "I'm sorry I've been holed up in my office all day. What's happening out here?" She sank onto the couch and leaned back, stretching her legs.

Maxine turned back to the television. "The Enterprise is being invaded by some kind of virus–"

"That's not what I meant, Maxine. Have you checked your sugar?" Kim pointed a finger at her.

"Of course. Lorraine checked it after lunch and again a few minutes ago when I finished my snack."

"I made a note of it," I said. "We'll just need to transfer it to your log sheet."

Kim mouthed the words *thank you,* then turned to Ruby who sat in a chair next to the couch. "Ms. Ruby, how are you doing today?"

Ruby clapped her hands together. "I'm jus' fine now. The good Lord answered my prayers for Jean."

"I should've known you were praying for us." Kim reached for one of Ruby's hands and squeezed it. "Thank you, dear lady." She got to her feet. "Well, enough playing for today. Guess I'd better start supper."

My watch showed 4:00. Ted would be here soon. I followed Kim into the kitchen where she thanked me again for managing everything. "I don't know what I would've done without you."

I swallowed and wiped my suddenly moist hands on my pants. "Actually, I need to talk to you about that. But first, would you mind if I used your computer once more?"

Kim pulled a prepared casserole out of the refrigerator. "Sure. Just log out first."

I pushed the door most of the way closed and sat down at Kim's desk. Clicking out of her account, I opened the guest account and inserted the memory card into the port. When the pages came up, I skimmed through the initial investigation to the most recent interviews and Roy's conclusion at the end of the report. My stomach clenched, and I stifled a cry.

The man ultimately responsible for Jenny's disappearance and death, the one who likely ordered Roy's death, was none other than Judge Ted Owens. And he was coming for me.

CHAPTER 23

Trembling, I sucked air back into my lungs. The time on the computer showed I had maybe fifteen to twenty minutes before Ted arrived. I needed to leave now, before he arrived. My hand shook so badly I tried three times to remove the card from the computer and get out of the browser. I stood and exited through the door that opened to the living room.

Maxine glanced at me, then turned back to the TV as I hurried to my room to pack. No time now to explain my sudden departure to Kim or the others. I hated leaving without a proper good-bye, but at least it would save me the trouble of explaining everything. Later, I'd write them a note of apology, maybe even come back for a visit and beg their forgiveness.

I stuffed the few clothes from my dresser into yesterday's shopping bag. My toiletries would stay behind. They could easily be purchased along the way. Was the memory card safest in my pocket or hidden in the purse? I pulled it out and stashed it once more inside the torn lining, making sure it was well down on the bottom, away from the hole. After gathering my bag, two purses and my jacket, I took one last look around the room. Roy's picture! I grabbed it from my pillow but couldn't decide where to stash it that wouldn't require folding. A bump at the door pushed it open and Maxine peered at the bags, purses and jacket on my arm. I hurried to slide Roy's picture down along the side of one bag and faced Maxine.

"Where are you going?" She sneered, looking at me through squinty eyes. Her wheelchair blocked my exit. I tried to push past her, but she held firm. "What's your hurry?"

"It's a long story, Maxine, and I don't have time to tell you right now. Please let me by."

"You've been awfully nice to me, letting me know when Stan will be here. Making sure I know what you're doing when you're with him. I want to know why."

"Because I know you care for him, and I'm not interested in that kind of a relationship." I checked my watch—4:25. Ted would be here any minute. "I really need to leave. Please. He'll be here—"

"Who? Who'll be here? You aren't rushing out to meet Stan, are you?"

"No, not Stan. It's not anyone you'd know." I nudged her wheelchair, but she pushed back.

"I don't believe you. I think you're meeting Stan. Maybe the two of you are eloping, keeping it a secret so ol' Maxie doesn't get wind of it. You were being nice just to throw me off."

"Maxine, you can have Stan. I don't care. Just let me out." I shoved her chair backward, creating enough of a gap that I could squeeze through.

And that's when the doorbell rang.

"Lorraine? There's a gentleman here to see you."

Maxine's eyes widened at Kim's announcement. She

wheeled backward, allowing me plenty of room. I dropped my purse and bags on the floor and walked up the hall, feeling like a Death Row inmate heading for the execution room. Every step grew heavier than the last.

Kim shifted a wooden mixing spoon to her left hand and welcomed Ted with a handshake while Ruby and Jean looked on.

"You're a friend of Lorraine's? Come on in. I'm Kim Caraway."

Ted stepped inside and flashed his handsome smile at each of the ladies. Charming, like a snake. Why hadn't I seen that before? His face lit up when he saw me.

"Lorraine, it's so good to see you again."

"Hello, Ted." My greeting fell flat. I stood rooted to the floor on the opposite side of the living room, my hands clasped tight to mask their trembling.

"Well, I'll be—" From behind me, Maxie spoke under her breath, ending with a profanity. Rolling past me, she raced to the door to offer her own welcome.

"Shame on you, Lorraine! Where have you been hiding such a handsome piece of manhood?" Maxine took his hand in both of hers. "Welcome, Good-lookin'. How long can you stay?"

Ted chuckled and shot a glance at Kim, then me. "I'm afraid I wasn't planning to stay. I'm only here long enough to pick up Ela —uh, Lorraine."

Kim tipped her head as she looked at me. "You didn't tell me you were going out for dinner, Lorraine."

Ted answered. "Dinner? No, I'm taking her back to Chicago. Isn't that what you wanted, Lorraine?"

"Are you leaving us so soon?" Kim asked. "Why didn't you say something? I guess I didn't give you much chance today, did I?"

All eyes turned toward me. My cheeks burned, and words stuck in my throat.

Kim closed the door, and turned back to Ted. "But since you're here, won't you please stay for supper and give us a chance to say our goodbyes to Lorraine?"

Ted eyed me with some puzzlement, and I repeated Kim's invitation.

"Yes, please do stay for supper if you have time." Though being in this man's presence turned my stomach, I'd do anything to avoid leaving with him.

For once, I appreciated Maxine's efforts to monopolize a man's attention. She and the others drew him to a seat in the living room, plying him with questions about how we knew each other. My stomach twisted into a knot, tighter and tighter.

He knew all about Jenny's death when he offered to defend me. Was he motivated by a guilty conscience? More likely, he was covering his tracks. Who'd suspect the defense attorney himself was guilty of the crime?

Kim turned down my offer to help with supper, urging me instead to enjoy Ted's company. I sat as far from him as possible. But that meant I couldn't avoid looking at him. His duplicity cost me a career I loved, deprived Jenny's parents of the chance to see their daughter grow and mature into a young woman. They'd suffered more than a decade of grief, never knowing what happened to her. Could I believe this man was cold-blooded enough to order the murder of his boyhood friend?

His power and connections would've easily allowed him to plant the false news stories, as well as arrange the arrest of an honest police officer. Had Anthony gotten too close to the truth? And what about the break-in and fire at my house? I doubted Ted had actually set the fire, but he must have known it would make his Saturday visit unnecessary. Was his attendance at Roy's memorial service merely a convenient alibi during the break-in?

While Jean and Maxine kept up a steady conversation with Ted, Ruby caught my eye and held my gaze for a long moment.

Did she sense something amiss? Folding her hands in her lap, she closed her eyes and appeared to nod off for a short nap. But I knew exactly what she was doing. And I'd never been more grateful.

Finally, I excused myself and fled into the kitchen where Kim was taking the casserole out of the oven. As I pulled the plates from the cupboard, Kim reminded me I didn't need to help her. I set the stack of plates down, braced my hands against the counter, and took a deep breath.

"Kim, I haven't been completely honest with you about my background. There's much I haven't told you, but I need your help. I can't go back to Chicago with that man. I'll explain everything once he's gone, but please trust me in this. If I leave with him, my life is in danger."

I choked down a few bites of supper, and tried to ignore Kim's worried glances. Ruby also occasionally studied me with uncertainty. Ted laughed and charmed Maxine and Jean until a quick knock interrupted. Everyone's attention turned to the front door, which opened and closed before Kim could get up from the table.

"It's just us," Brandi called. A skittering of shoes on the wood floor and Riley and Micah appeared. They each gave Maxine a hug, and Brandi stopped beside her mother's wheelchair, flapping her hand at Kim to stay seated.

"We've eaten. I thought we all needed a visit to the Sonic drive-in tonight." Noticing Ted, she said, "And who is this? I don't believe we've met."

"Ted Owens. And you are?" He rose and clasped Brandi's hand.

"Brandi Bullard. I'm Maxine's daughter. And this is Riley

and Micah. Can you kids say hello?" The children murmured their greetings.

"You have beautiful children."

I cringed at the way Ted's gaze lingered on Riley. Micah leaned into Brandi.

"Mom, can we watch TV?"

"No. Go outside and run off some energy." Brandi opened the patio door and shooed them outside while Kim cleared away the dishes.

"You're just in time to say goodbye to Lorraine," Maxine said.

Brandi brought one hand to her hip and raised a single eyebrow at me. "You're leaving? Isn't this kind of sudden?"

Ted checked his watch, wiped his mouth and set his napkin aside. "It is getting late and, as much as I've enjoyed my time with you ladies and this delicious meal, we need to get going if we hope to make it back to Chicago at a decent hour." He stood and turned my way. "Lorraine, why don't you get your luggage, and we'll say good-bye?"

I swallowed hard and fiddled with the unused silverware beside my plate. One glance at Ted sent a shiver down my spine. Everything in me wanted to run to my room and lock myself in, but instead I stood and faced Ted.

"I'm very sorry to have imposed on you this way, Ted, but I've changed my mind. I really can't leave after all. Forgive me, but you'll have to return to Chicago by yourself."

An uncertain laugh escaped his lips. "I—I don't understand. Yesterday, you were desperate to get home."

Roy's voice from my dream rang in my head. *Be strong, Lainey.*

I straightened my back, squared my shoulders.

"I've had a change of plans. I will return home, but not with you." My pulse throbbed. My mouth went so dry the simple act of swallowing became a challenge.

Ted's jaw twitched. Rage sparked in his eyes, but he extinguished it and pasted a smile on his face. "I cancelled everything on my schedule and paid for your return fare. And now you're backing out? I never expected this of you, Lorraine." He emphasized my name. There was no affection it it nor in the way his gaze locked with mine. He lifted his head and looked down his nose at me. "I must ask you to come with me as planned." His polite tone was anything but inviting.

The tension between us grew, and the others watched in silence, their expressions clearly confused by the drama playing out before them.

I raised my chin and forced myself to meet his gaze. "I am terribly sorry. This is embarrassing, but I'm more than willing to reimburse you for the cost of the plane fare. That is, as soon as I return. You see, I have an agreement with Kim and I need to finish out my contract with her." I looked to Kim, and she nodded her agreement but added nothing to the conversation.

A vein pulsed in Ted's neck. His chest expanded as he drew in a long breath. Then his posture relaxed, and again that fake smile spread across his face.

"All right then. If that's the way you want it. I'll see if I can get a refund on your ticket. You'll be hearing from me." He thanked Kim for the meal and offered to see himself out.

The door opened, then closed just short of a slam. Riley's playful screams and Micah's laughter lent an odd contrast to the tension that gripped the room. Kim's thoughtful gaze swept over the other ladies and settled on me. She crooked a finger at me and started for her office.

"We need to talk."

I moved to follow her, but Maxine blocked my way.

"Not so fast. Something smells fishy here, and it ain't the food. I want to know what's going on."

The immediate crisis over, my strength evaporated and I

collapsed back into my chair. "You all deserve an explanation. I'm tired of hiding the truth, tired of lying and pretending to be someone I'm not. After hearing my explanation, if you wish, I'll leave without argument."

Kim cleared the rest of the supper dishes, and I helped put the food away. Brandi went out to check on the children. Riley took a running jump onto the patio and gave her mother a breathless report.

"We were playing tag, but we're tired. So now we're playing hide and seek. Micah's hiding first."

Brandi reminded her to be careful about getting too close to the pond. "We're just talking grown-up so y'all can keep playing." She closed the door part way and took the seat Ted had vacated only minutes before. At last, Kim took her seat. She folded her hands on the table and gave me a look that said, *This had better be good.*

"All right, I think we're ready, Lorraine."

I spread my palms on the table. "To start with, I'm not Lorraine Johnson. My real name is Elaine Sutterfeld. Twelve years ago, I taught junior high school in Chicago until one of my students disappeared from a field trip. She was never found." I told them everything—how Ted and Roy grew up together, Ted's offer to defend me pro bono, and Roy's dismissal from the police force, all the way up to Anthony's decision to bring me here, and his first troubling phone call.

Ruby leaned forward.

"Why didn't you ask Anthony to take you back to Chicago?"

How could I tell her about his arrest without worrying her? I'd have to trust our friendship and her faith. I reached out and took her thin hand in mine.

"Ruby, I'm sorry to have kept this from you. Amanda, your granddaughter, left a tearful message on my phone Saturday night saying her father had been arrested and was being held on suspicion of arson and first-degree murder."

Ruby jerked backward as if she'd been slapped. Her dark eyes showed plenty of white. "Arson? Murder? Not my Anthony."

"Of course not. I don't believe it either, any more than I believe my Roy had anything to do with the kidnapping. Judge Ted Owens is a powerful figure in Chicago politics with many people indebted to him. I believe his connections in the media and the police allowed him to plant misinformation intended to draw me out. He's afraid I know the truth my husband uncovered. When the news stories didn't work, he used my connection with Anthony and had him arrested on false charges.

"Until this afternoon, I had no idea Ted was behind all this. I trusted him because of his connection to Roy and his willingness to defend me years ago. Ted's was the only phone number I had besides Anthony's. I trusted him to help me get back to Chicago, to go back and prove I'm still alive for Anthony's sake. But Ruby, last night when I found that memory card in my purse, I knew Roy had hidden it there intending for me to find it. That card contains all the evidence Roy collected to convict Ted." I looked at Kim. "That's what I was viewing on your computer before supper. It's why I asked you to help me avoid leaving with Ted. I have no doubt he intends to harm me."

Kim sucked in a breath. "Let me think about this. It may be that Dad and I can help you get back to Chicago, but let me talk to him. Do you still have the memory card?"

"I put it back in my purse."

"May I see it? I'd like to verify what you've told us."

I retrieved the purse from my bedroom and brought it back to the table. Micah appeared at the patio door.

"Mom? Riley's not playing fair. She won't come out when I call her."

Brandi got up from the table and stepped outside with Micah.

"Riley? It's time to come out. Micah doesn't want to play anymore."

No response.

"See? She's hiding somewhere. She won't come out."

"Did you check the front yard? Maybe she can't hear us from back here." Brandi and Micah stepped off the patio and headed around the side of the house.

The little bit of supper I'd managed to swallow rose in my throat. I set the purse on the table and hurried out front. Kim and Jean followed. Brandi stood on the curb holding Micah's hand, scrutinizing the house and property from one side to the other for any sign of her daughter. The sun still had a couple hours before it set, so it shouldn't be hard to find her. If she were hiding.

"Riley?" Brandi called. "We're not playing anymore. This isn't funny. Come out here right now."

Kim checked behind bushes and unlocked the detached garage, just in case. From the end of the driveway, I peered up and down the block, scrutinizing the cars parked along the side of the street. At home, Ted was known to drive a black Lincoln, or rather his chauffeur drove it. What kind of car would he rent? Had he come alone or with his driver?

Brandi's mouth set in a firm line. Her eyes held a fiery look as we gathered at the front door. She pulled her cell phone from her pocket, punched in a number and held the phone to her ear. "He's going to pay for this, I swear."

CHAPTER 24

"Travis, this is not funny. You bring Riley back here right now." Travis's voice jabbered through Brandi's phone. "Don't you dare lie to me. How do you think Micah feels?" She let go of Micah's hand and moved away from us. "Why should I believe you? You threatened to take them away from me." Her hand went to her hip. "Where are you now?" She whirled and looked at Kim. "Stan's? What are you doing there? I don't believe you. Let me talk to him."

Brandi crossed an arm over her stomach, catching her hand between her other elbow and her ribs. "Stan? Is Travis really with you at your house? What's he doing there? Since when? Is Riley over there with you? No, I don't know where she is. She and Micah were playing hide and seek outside. Micah came in complaining that she wouldn't come out when he called. We've looked all over for her. Okay. Thanks." She clicked off and tapped the phone against her cheek. A v-shaped wrinkle formed between her eyebrows, and she stepped closer to Kim. "Did you know Travis is staying with your dad?"

Kim shook her head. "How long has he been there?"

"Since last night. They're coming over to help us look for Riley."

Kim ushered us inside where Maxine blocked our progress into the living room.

"Did you find her?"

"She won't come out, Maxie." Micah went over and slipped his arm under Maxine's, hugging hers tight. Maxine guided him around to her lap and wrapped her arms around him. But at the sound of Travis's voice at the patio door, the boy burst from her embrace, ran to the door, and leaped into his dad's arms. His tan skinny legs encircled Travis's waist, arms tight around his neck. The rest of us moved to the dining room and gathered about the table.

Holding the boy close, Travis approached Brandi and reached out to her. She took his hand and gradually leaned into his side as Kim filled them in on Riley's disappearance.

"Have you called the police?" Travis asked.

Kim shook her head. "Not yet. We wanted to be sure she wasn't just hiding."

"How long do we wait? It's not like Riley not to come when she's called."

Stan cut in. "When was the last time anyone saw her?"

Brandi looked at me. "Wasn't it right after your friend left?"

My face burned. I groped for words, but what could I say? I feared the worst.

A faint musical tune sounded from my purse, the same ringtone I'd heard the other night. Maybe Anthony had been released from jail. I hurried to grab the phone from my purse.

"Anthony?"

A deep chuckle answered. "No, Elaine. He can't help you. Or Riley."

My knees buckled. "What have you done with her?"

"Nothing. At least, not yet. Although, she is a pretty little thing."

"I'm calling the police."

His voice hardened. "Do that and you will never see the girl alive again."

"How do I know you have her?"

"Oh, I don't think it's necessary to convince you. As soon as you discovered she was missing, you knew I had her."

"What do you want, Ted? Bring her back and I'll do whatever you say."

"That's what I like to hear. Now listen carefully, because you don't want to be responsible for another child's disappearance."

I ground my teeth. "*You* were responsible for Jenny's disappearance, not me. Don't you dare hurt Riley."

"I don't think you're in any position to tell me what to do." He paused. "Now listen carefully. I want you to walk out the front door, go to the street and turn left. Keep walking. Do not call the police, and don't let any of your friends call them either. The less they know about me, the better off they'll be. Do you understand?"

A terrifying image came to mind—of Maxine, Jean and Ruby trying to escape a house fire. "Yes, I understand."

"Good. I'll see you in a few minutes." He cut off the call.

Kim and the others gathered around me, bombarding me with questions as I flipped my phone shut.

"He has her?"

"Who is he?"

"Where are they?"

"What does he want?"

I raised my hand for quiet. "Judge Ted Owens has Riley. He's using her to coerce me into coming with him."

Brandi gasped and hid her tears in Travis's shoulder.

Maxine swore. "That man touches one hair on my baby's head, and I'll..." She vowed to deprive him of his manhood.

How had it come to this? Another child endangered on account of me. My stomach clenched, and a sour taste filled my mouth.

Be strong, Lainey.

"I'm calling the police." Kim took out her phone, but I grabbed her hand.

"No! He threatened to hurt Riley if we call them."

Maxine rolled toward me like a wolf advancing on its prey, her voice a low growl. "You could've prevented this."

"Maxie—" Kim tried to step in, but Maxine pushed her aside.

"You lied to our faces and put my baby girl in danger. Maybe it wasn't your fault twelve years ago, but it is now. If you'd had the backbone to stay and fight this chester, Riley would still be here with us. But you ran away and hid, riding your own little whimper wagon. So now what? You gonna stay in your private pity party and let everyone else suffer?"

"Maxine, that's enough." Stan cut her off.

She clamped her fire engine red lips tight, but the flames in her eyes still scorched. She was right. Jenny's disappearance cost me not only my job, but my reputation as well, insuring I'd never teach again. Roy did his best to shield me from the negative publicity, the awful personal attacks, but I withdrew into my grief, spinning a cocoon that shut out friends who genuinely wanted to help. I'd been so absorbed in my loss that I retreated, willing to let Roy, Anthony, and even Ted fight the battle for me. Where was the confidence I'd once relied on to regularly face down twenty or more seventh-graders?

Stan's warm hand on my shoulder brought me out of my reverie.

I raised my eyes to his. "It's me Ted wants. He thinks if he gets rid of me, there'll be no one to testify against him. He doesn't know about this." I dug the memory card out of my purse and held it up. "It's all here, the evidence needed to convict him."

Kim reached for it. "Let's get it to the police."

"There's no time. If we have any hope of getting Riley back safe and sound, I have to do what he says. And this might become a valuable bargaining chip." I dropped it back into the lining of the purse. "Maxine is right. I can't tell you how deeply I regret involving all of you in my personal troubles. Brandi, Travis, Maxine, you have no reason to trust me, but I give you my word I'll do whatever it takes to get Riley back to you. I'd willingly give my life for hers."

Uneasy glances skipped between the faces I'd grown to love in such a short time. Stan took my hands in his. "Are you sure you want to do this, Lorraine?"

The kindness in his eyes nearly broke my resolve, but I steeled myself for what lay ahead. "As sure as my name is really Elaine Sutterfeld. They can tell you my story." I pulled my hands away and scooped up that ugly green purse before meeting his gaze again. "I'd greatly appreciate your prayers, Stan. And yours, Ruby."

She reached for my hand and squeezed it. Jean did the same, but Kim and the others hung back.

"Wait ten or fifteen minutes after I leave. Then call the police. If they want any kind of corroboration, have them contact Anthony in the Cook County jail."

In the living room, I stopped and looked back once more. "Forgive me for bringing this on all of you. I am so very sorry." I marched to the front door and walked out to meet Ted.

From the back seat of the car, Ted squinted at the windshield. The sun's angle through the tree branches created a momentary, blinding spotlight, and he turned away, offering the girl a reassuring smile and a pat on her bare knee. She quivered and jerked away. Understandable, considering the tape over her mouth and around her wrists. With a whimper, she squeezed closer to the door, knees together, elbows tucked tight against her stomach, shoulders hunched forward.

In the driver's seat, Capone leaned forward, arms resting on top of the steering wheel. He'd earned the nickname because of his first name, Al, and the scar across his cheek. Ted trusted no one more than Capone, and none knew him and his tastes better than Al. He'd flown in last night ahead of Ted to rent a car and scout the territory.

"Is that her?" Capone lifted a forefinger to indicate the direction.

Ted shielded his eyes from the sun. "Yeah, that's her. Any shadows?"

"Not so far."

"Pull up to the corner, but if anyone's following her, keep going and we'll catch her on the next block."

The girl sniffled and lifted her head to peer out the window as the car rolled forward. When she saw Elaine approach the intersection, she grew antsy. Tears raced down her cheeks and her muffled cries increased.

Capone inched the car ahead, stopping when Ted's window was even with the sidewalk. "Looks clear. I don't see any movement behind her."

"Lower the window." Ted slid his arm around Riley's neck, clamping her to his chest, and pointed a gun at her head. Elaine's face blanched at the sight.

"Get in the car. Don't try anything, or she gets hurt."

My heart stopped cold at the terror in Riley's eyes, the gun at her head and her mouth taped shut. My knees nearly gave out, though I felt certain Ted had staged the scene expressly to shock and weaken me. Stumbling to the car, I wondered if I'd made an impossible promise to Riley's family. I yanked open the back door and slid in next to Riley, dropping my purse to the floor. The driver jumped out and opened the door behind him, allowing Ted to exit, then slammed it shut.

I cradled Riley next to me. Strands of honey-brown hair hung over her face, some of it glued to her cheeks by tears. She buried her head against my shoulder, violent sobs shaking her body. Her bound hands clutched mine.

The driver returned to his seat, and Ted took the front passenger seat, twisting to peer at Riley and me.

"What have you done to her?" I ground the words out through clenched teeth.

"I simply offered her a drink of root beer. She was thirsty after playing tag." He lifted a bottle of soda from the cup holder then replaced it. "By the way, the child locks are engaged so forget about trying to escape."

I cupped Riley's head against my chest and glared at him. "You've got me. Now let her go."

"Not so fast." Ted pointed the gun at me. "Put your hands out, wrists together." His driver adjusted his seat, turned, and wrapped duct tape several times around my wrists. Finished, he settled back into his seat and tucked the roll of tape into a black bag. Ted lowered the gun.

"All right, Capone. Let's move it."

Capone? I guessed it was a nickname, but the threat wasn't lost on me. The man had a stocky build like the Chicago gangster, but his head was shaved like Mr. Clean. A long scar ran diagonally across his right cheek, and every time he glanced in the rearview mirror, I knew I never wanted to meet those eyes in a dark alley. Or anywhere else.

Riley's tears subsided, but her little body still trembled. I comforted her as best I could with my wrists bound. Removing the tape from her mouth might help calm her down, so I began to pick at it. Ted reached back and grabbed my arm.

"Leave it."

"Why? The windows are up. We can't get out. There's no reason to gag the poor child."

His eyes narrowed to slits. He gripped my arm tight enough to bruise it and held up one index finger. "One chance. If she blows it, the tape goes back on and stays on."

Pain shot up and down my arm, but I refused to flinch, gritting my teeth until he released me. I reached again for Riley's cheek, but she pushed my hand away. Her slender fingernails scraped at the edges of the tape, easing it away bit by bit from her mouth and chin. When the last stickum let loose, she sucked in a huge breath, gulped twice and wiped her cheeks with the backs of her hands. Snuggling into my side, she whined.

"I don't feel good. I want my mom."

"Shh. I'm here with you for now. Put your head in my lap and rest." She scooted onto her side and laid her head on my legs. Once more, her hands found mine, and our fingers intertwined.

Through the window, I recognized the nursery where Stan and I had picked out flowers a few days ago. I might have been able to find my way back to the home from there, but with the many turns the driver made, I lost all sense of direction. Except for the cursory glimpse of restaurants and businesses lining the freeway the night I arrived with Anthony, my jaunts around Waco had been limited to the urgent care clinic, Stan's church, the nursery, and the discount store.

Ted eyed Riley and spoke to his driver. "Maybe I should take the girl back to Chicago. I could pass her off as my granddaughter at the airport." The man shrugged, and Riley pressed into me with a whimper.

"You'll never get away with it." I covered Riley's ear as best I could and kept my voice low. A smirk curled Ted's lips.

"On the contrary, it would be very simple. Capone drops us off at the airport. He returns the rental car when he's finished and flies home. The car's in his name. No one will connect us. And if they ever discover your body, no one will know who you are or where you're from. I must remember to thank Officer Fisher for his thoughtfulness in confiscating your ID and bankcards. It makes everything so much simpler. Of course, I might reconsider if you'd be willing to turn over any evidence Roy collected."

I nudged my purse under the seat with my toe, not yet ready to bargain. "You burned the evidence, remember? When you torched my house."

Ted studied me, his mouth settling in a firm line. His eyes, always so warm and kind in the past now reflected an icy hostility. I forced myself to meet his gaze and not flinch.

"All right, Elaine. If that's how you want to play—" He lowered his gaze to Riley. Her fingers had loosened their grip as we talked, and her eyes were closed, her breathing slow and even.

"Riley?" I shook her shoulders, lifted her head. No response.

"Care for some root beer?" Ted held up the beverage bottle. His smug grin sent a challenge.

"What did you put in it?"

"Nothing dangerous. Just enough to keep her quiet until we're finished." He tipped the bottle toward me. "You might want a little yourself. Trust me, you'll be much more comfortable."

I swiped at the bottle to knock it out of his hand, but he jerked it away. "I'll never trust you again, Ted Owens."

"Suit yourself."

The names on street signs as we traveled through town meant nothing to me, though I tried to commit them to memory. But with nothing in my experience to connect them, one slipped away as soon as another took its place until I saw the familiar blue and red shield for Interstate 35. On the opposite side of the freeway loomed the stadium Anthony and I had passed on our way into town hardly more than a week ago.

Capone drove under the I-35 overpass and alongside the Baylor University campus with its stately red brick buildings. We passed the athletic facilities, a domed structure, and various apartment buildings that probably housed students. Another mile or two went by before we left Waco behind in the setting sun. No more than two cars met us along the road, and I noted little activity at any of the farms we passed. Barbed wire stretched between fence posts that looked like they'd been cut from tree limbs, not the uniform kind I was used to seeing in Illinois. Here and there, a plastic shopping bag had snagged on the barbed wire, and discarded beer cans nestled in the tall grass that grew beside the road.

I shuddered as we passed a deserted office building, its entry door covered with plywood panels. Broken windows stared like vacant eyes. We slowed, and I wondered if Ted planned to leave me here, but instead we drove farther on to another intersection.

"I regret Roy's demise," Ted said as we turned off the paved road. "He left me no choice. My reputation and everything I've achieved would've been ruined. You must understand, I have no intention of spending the rest of my life in prison."

"So you killed him. Your friend since youth was nothing more than an obstacle in your path." Good thing Riley was unconscious. This distasteful conversation wasn't meant for young ears.

Ted twisted around and looked me in the eye. "I don't kill people, Elaine."

"You're a liar as well as a killer."

"I was in my office when Roy met with his unfortunate accident."

"What about Jenny Ortiz?"

"Do you really believe I would've defended you if I'd killed the girl?"

"Oh, that was a brilliant move, wasn't it? Who would ever suspect the defense attorney's guilt in the very case he's arguing?"

"I've never killed anyone."

"Maybe not with your own hands, but you ordered their deaths. Both Roy and Jenny would be here today if not for you."

The car bounced over ruts and potholes, tires crunching on the crushed gravel. We passed one farmhouse with a car parked outside its garage. Once the sun went down, the darkness out here would be as thick as tar, a stark contrast to the lights of Chicago. The streetlights around Kim's place were fewer and dimmer than on my street back home. At first, it felt scary, disconcerting. But I'd grown to appreciate the lack of artificial light. Maybe I could somehow use it to my advantage.

We followed the road through two more turns before it dead-ended into what had once been a driveway, now overgrown with grass and weeds that scraped the underside of the car. Two parallel tracks showed signs of a recent visitor, and I guessed Capone and maybe Ted had been out here earlier today. An old clapboard-style farmhouse stood to one side, its white paint now dingy gray. The porch roof sagged toward a broken support column. Two shutters still clung haphazardly to the window frames, but the windows looked as vacant the ones on the office building.

Capone parked behind a barn that looked in worse shape than the house. The middle section of the roof had collapsed, and the whole structure leaned to one side. The paint had long since peeled away, leaving the siding with a weathered look the color of storm clouds. In front of us, two posts were all that remained of a livestock pen.

Capone exited the car. Ted aimed his gun at me as the rear

door opened and Capone pulled Riley away from me. She slipped from my bound hands before I knew what was happening.

"No! You can't have her." I lurched across the seat as Capone dragged Riley from the car. Ted cocked his pistol.

"Let her go, Elaine. I'm warning you."

I glanced at Ted. "Go ahead and shoot. You've taken everything else I care about—my student, my life work, my husband, my home. You might as well take my life, too." I stopped to catch my breath and remembered his earlier boast that he'd never killed anyone. Was he nothing more than a coward after all?

"Pull the trigger, Ted. I dare you."

Before Capone could close the door, I kicked it wide open. The edge caught his thigh, and his dark, menacing eyes nearly froze my heart. He slammed the door shut, hefted Riley over his shoulder, and strode toward the house. I pounded my fists on the window.

"Bring her back!" I thought of Maxine, Brandi, and Travis. How would I ever face them again if I let anything happen to Riley?

CHAPTER 25

"Don't worry. You'll be joining her soon." Ted lowered the gun and leaned against his seat. "I never touched her, if that makes you feel any better."

I watched Capone disappear around the back of the house with Riley over his shoulder. "I'm not worried about how I feel. This is about her."

"I was talking about Jenny. Although the same is true for Riley."

My stomach turned at the mere sound of Riley's name coming from his mouth. But if he was willing to talk about Jenny, I had a list of questions over a decade long.

"How did Jenny end up with you? I doubt you were at the mall where my class stopped for lunch."

Ted stared at the field that lay before us, though I suspected he was seeing something other than the innocent fireflies that darted here and there among the tall grasses.

"A couple of my boys were out looking for candidates and noticed her at the museum. They made contact and followed her to the mall. One flirted with her, and she responded. It wasn't hard to lure her out to their van where they could throw her inside and drive away without any cause for concern. She and I were chatting, getting acquainted when the news about her hit the television."

"Why did you have to kill her?"

"I didn't kill her. She simply died of a drug overdose." Ted scanned the property and checked the direction Capone had gone. "She had a pretty good idea why she was there. With all that publicity, I knew there'd be an investigation if I let her go. She could've identified me."

"You're still responsible for her death. Where is she? Why wasn't she ever found?"

Ted sighed and rubbed his forehead. "Helen and I were having the backyard landscaped at the time. I fired the contractor and brought in my boys to finish it." He turned from the windshield to look at me. "I think you'd approve of her resting place."

Approve? He was more twisted than I thought. Before my next question, I choked back the vomit rising in my throat.

"How much did Helen know?"

"Nothing." Ted shook his head and fingered the gun. "She had her suspicions about me. That's why we divorced. But she knew nothing about Jenny."

"And the necklace with the pendant—why keep it?"

He raised an eyebrow at me. "Unique, isn't it? Only a tiny tweak changed it to my initials. It's been exceptionally useful in my subsequent relationships."

I remembered the photo in the newspaper, the way the bowl of the J appeared to be missing. He'd changed the "J" to a "T" and used it as his personal badge to identify victims as his property.

A gunshot ripped the air, taking my breath with it and bringing Ted to full alert.

"Riley! Oh no, no, no!" I tore at the handle to open the door, sat back and kicked it with my heels. It didn't budge. I pounded the window and looked around for something I could use to break it.

Ted snatched up his gun and climbed out of the car as Capone rounded the corner of the house. "What was that for?"

"Rattlesnake." Capone held up the carcass of a snake no less than four feet long. He approached the car, tossing the snake into the tall grass, weeds, and thistles that had taken over the yard through years of neglect.

I shrank from the door and leaned my head against the back-rest. One moment of terror had drained the strength from my limbs and sent my heart and lungs into panic. But Riley was still alive, at least for now. Before I had time to recover, Ted opened my door.

"Your turn. Out." He waved the gun, motioning me out of the car. I stopped to retrieve my purse from under the seat then stepped out. Ted grabbed the purse. "You won't need this where you're going."

I tried to snatch it back, but he tossed it to Capone. The driver's dark expression repelled me, but I had to get the purse back.

"See what's in it," Ted ordered.

Capone opened the purse and peered inside, shook it, then pulled out my keys and dangled them on one thick forefinger.

"Empty. Except for these."

Ted pinned me with a disbelieving gaze. "No woman only carries keys in her purse."

"Unless she buys a new handbag and transfers everything over to the new one," I explained. "Since I no longer have a house or car to unlock, I left the keys in the old purse."

"Then why did you grab this instead of the new one when you left? Could it be there's something else in there?" Ted took the purse from Capone and inspected the inside. "The lining is torn."

"The keys poked a hole. It got worse as I used it, and I haven't taken the time to sew it up." Ted shook it and squeezed the fabric. I held my breath, praying he wouldn't feel the memory card in there.

"You didn't answer my question. If everything is in your new purse, why take this one?"

I hunched my shoulders in what I hoped was a careless shrug. "Sentimental reasons. It's the last gift Roy gave me. I didn't think I'd need lipstick, cough drops, or an emery board when I left to meet you."

Ted considered that for a moment then held it out for Capone to drop the keys in, and tossed it to me. "We're wasting time. Let's go."

We followed in Capone's tracks through the weedy yard. The trail led to an old well. Its concrete casing rose a few feet above the ground, edges cracked and chipped. Off to one side lay the broken remnants of the well's cover. Riley's limp form lay on a large panel of plywood. She looked like a child's rag doll that had been tossed aside. Suspicious of Capone's snake display, I dropped to my knees beside her and felt for a pulse. Her blood thumped beneath my fingers, and warm air from her nostrils puffed across my hand.

Capone lifted her and carried her to the edge of the well. Her head flopped to the side, one arm dangled loose. He held her suspended above the well and looked to Ted. "Now?"

"Wait!" I jumped up and clutched Ted's arm. "Don't put her down there. She's done nothing wrong. Leave me, if you must, but if you have any decency at all, let her go."

Ted jerked his arm from my hands. "Don't worry. You're next. You'll have all the time in the world to rescue her."

My breath burst from my lungs as if he'd punched me. How

could I save Riley and return her to her family from the bottom of a well? I spotted my purse on the ground where I'd dropped it to check on Riley.

"Wait. I have the evidence. It's yours. Just don't hurt her." I snatched up the purse, fumbled with the clasp and tore at the lining, my fingers searching for the card.

Ted tore the purse from my hands and pitched it into the grass. "I'm not playing games anymore." He waved the gun toward the well, but I resisted, searching his eyes for any hint of compassion.

"You don't need to do this, Ted. You're successful, well-respected. Please—"

"Yes, and I plan to keep it that way. Drop her, Capone."

"No!" I spun just in time to see Riley disappear, heard the thunk of her head against the wall and the splash. I leaned over the edge. "Riley!" The water and probably a soft sediment bottom cushioned her descent, but already blood oozed from her head where the rough concrete scraped away some of her hair. My throat closed as she slowly slipped underwater.

"Your turn, Elaine. Jump in and save the child. It's what you've wanted to do ever since Jenny disappeared."

"I thought you didn't kill people." With a coldness I'd never have believed, Ted raised the barrel of his gun, tipped it toward Capone, and smiled.

"I don't, but he does."

Capone aimed his gun at Riley's sinking form. Even a poorly aimed bullet would likely ricochet into her body. She sank farther, the water now covering her nose.

I had no choice. I jumped into the well.

"What about my little girl?" Travis's fist hit the table with enough force to bounce the napkin holder. "How long do we have to wait for someone to get out there and look for this guy?"

"You need to get out there and find my grand-baby," Maxine added.

The police officer standing closest held out both palms. "Sir, ma'am, you need to calm down. I understand your impatience—"

"Do you? Has some pervert ever kidnapped your daughter?"

The officer stepped back and rested one hand on his Taser. Brandi's hands wrapped around Travis's arm urging him away from the table. He expelled a breath through his nostrils and turned, raking his hair with his fingers. He locked them together behind his neck as the other cop spoke.

"I know it feels like it's taking forever, but we already have several cars searching the immediate vicinity, setting up a perimeter. The more information we gather, the better our chances of finding him and rescuing your little girl."

"He left twenty minutes ago. You really think he's hanging around here? While you're gathering information, he could be raping my grand-baby." Maxine glared, her face nearly as red as her lipstick. The officer held her gaze, his mouth set in a firm line.

The second officer tapped a pen against his notepad. "We've got a description of the suspect. Did anyone see the car he was driving?"

"I did." Stan cleared his throat. "It was a mid-size SUV, a Durango or maybe an Explorer. Dark blue."

"License number?"

"I wasn't close enough for that." Stan's shoulders sagged.

"Where'd you see it?"

"One block over. When Lorraine—"

"Elaine," Jean whispered. Stan blinked several times before he continued.

"When she left, I followed. She told us he'd threatened to

hurt Riley if we called the police. I cut around behind the houses."

"Did you see her get into the car?"

"She got into the back seat. As she approached, the window came down. She seemed to falter, but she opened the door and got in. There were at least two men, one in front and one in back. The driver got out and opened the back door. Then another man got out of the back and moved to the front passenger seat. They sat there for a minute or two, then made a sharp left turn and sped away."

"Did you get a good look at them? Were there other people in the car?"

Stan thought a moment. "There was definitely someone in the passenger seat. I think Lorraine saw something through the open window that made her stumble a bit. And if they had Riley plus the two men, that would be at least four including Lorraine."

"Elaine." Jean covered her mouth with her hands.

Maxine cursed and rolled her chair back. "What are we waiting for? Do I need to go out and look for this creep myself?"

"No, ma'am. I'm going to call it in right now." The officer finished writing on his notepad and headed for the door. "I'll come back after I finish." Both officers left.

Without a word, Kim moved to the window and stared outside at the patio, forehead creased with wrinkles. Ruby's eyes were closed, but she had taken one of Jean's hands in hers. Head bowed, Jean peeked up at each of them in turn. Brandi moved to stand beside her mother.

"This is my fault," Kim said. "I accepted her story based on Anthony's recommendation. I never bothered to have her background checked. How could I have been so lacking in judgment?" She rubbed her arms up and down.

Ruby opened her eyes. "Weren't nobody's fault, but that man's. Lorraine, Elaine, whatever you call her, she'd'a never had to come here if he hadn't set her house on fire and killed her husband. She's only trying to find justice for a little girl that's been needing it for twelve years. Lord, have mercy."

Brandi hugged her shoulders, never taking her gaze off Kim. "If we believe what she said about him setting fire to her house, is it possible he'd come back and do something here if he suspects Lorraine told us everything? Travis and Stan are close, but a fire here could get out of control before they ever knew it. I think you need to hire a guard, at least at night when it's dark."

Kim glanced in the direction of the door. "I'll ask the officers. Maybe some of the off-duty guys would be interested in earning some extra cash."

"Ruby has the right idea." Stan pulled his hands from his pockets. "We need to pray. Join me?" He reached for Jean's hand and extended his other toward Maxine.

She regarded it for a moment then raised her gaze to his and gingerly placed her hand on his palm. Brandi took her mother's hand on the other side, and Travis, Kim, and Ruby completed the circle.

Stan bowed his head. "Our Father in heaven, we humbly beg your intervention in this frightening situation. The enemy, our adversary, has stolen two of our loved ones, and though we have no knowledge of where they might be, we know, Lord, that they are not hidden from your sight. Because You see them, we ask you to watch over them, cover them with your mighty hand and protect them from any and all evil that would threaten to harm or even destroy them."

Brandi sniffled, and Travis squeezed her hand, pulling her close under his arm.

"Lord, in your mercy and by your grace, lead the police to Riley and Lorraine."

"Elaine," whispered Jean.

Stan corrected himself and continued. "Make their whereabouts known. Lead your instruments of righteousness to the place where they may be found. And grant us, if you will, the peace beyond earthly understanding you have promised for your children.

"Lord, our trust is in you no matter what happens, for no one else holds the keys to life and death. We cry out to you for little Riley and for Lorrai—uh, Elaine. Answer us, O Lord, according to your will through the precious name of your Son, Jesus Christ. Amen."

The front door opened and shut. Firm footsteps approached from the living room, and the officer rejoined them in the dining room. "All right. We've got patrols doing a perimeter search for any type of similar vehicle. We've issued an Amber Alert and we'll get photos of your little girl on the news networks." He laid several business cards on the table. "We'll let you know if we get any hits, but if you happen to hear anything from them or think of something else, call me. Leave a message if I don't answer. I'll get it." A grim twist to his mouth added to his grave expression. "We're going to find your little girl, and your friend. If there's anything at all you think might be helpful, let me know. Any questions?"

Kim escorted him to the front door, asking about the possibility of hiring security to watch the house.

Micah called from Maxine's room. "Mom, can I come out now?"

"Yes, you may."

Micah ran up the hallway, skirted Maxine's chair, and pitched himself toward Travis. "Have they found Riley yet?"

"No, son, she's still missing." Travis hugged the boy to his chest, breathing in the sweaty smell of his son and savoring the feel of Micah's head on his shoulder.

Brandi patted her son's back. "I suppose we should get him home. It's getting late."

"But it's not dark yet," Micah objected.

Travis faced Brandi. "Are you okay staying alone?" She hesitated, and he added, "I'm not trying to weasel my way back. I know I've done some stupid things lately. But I want to clean up my act and be the kind of dad my kids need. I just thought you might want someone else around tonight. I'll sleep on the couch."

Brandi's eyes watered, and she nodded her agreement.

CHAPTER 26

I barely had time to lift Riley's head above the blood-stained water before darkness enveloped us.

Ted and Capone fitted the plywood panel over the top of the opening and, judging by the sound, weighted it down with the remaining section of the concrete cover.

Not much to see at the bottom of a well, but if I'd paid closer attention to what the walls looked like, I might've discovered a way for us to climb out. The few slivers and dabs of light that initially peeked in along the worn, chipped edge of the well faded quickly, leaving me in total darkness, unable to see my hand in front of my face.

The cool water soothed the raw scrape on my arm. Though not quite icy, the chilly water posed a distinct possibility of hypothermia if we stayed here too long.

I cried out. "Help! Help me." My voice echoed off the walls. How could I attract attention when there was no telling if anyone was even up there?

By some miracle, I'd avoided landing on Riley. She'd sputtered and coughed when I first pulled her from the water, but still offered no other response. Three feet of water and the mucky bottom kept me mostly injury free, though my left knee and ankle ached. I tried tugging my feet from the yogurt-like consistency of the mud, and the pain in my ankle almost doubled me over.

At least the chill of the water should keep any swelling to a minimum, but I'd need to avoid putting weight on it. How was I going to keep Riley above water while balancing on one good leg? When I stayed still, the water level settled around my waist, too deep to sit in.

I lifted her arms and ducked my head up underneath so her arms draped over my shoulders. Her bound wrists would keep her from falling away, and by shifting her to my back, I could brace myself with my good leg, sandwiching her between my body and the wall. This required a great deal of effort and hopping around, but it worked. It would also keep her head slightly higher than mine if I should slip down.

Breathing hard, I used my teeth to tear at the tape around my wrists. I needed my hands free so that if, or when, Riley awoke, I'd be better able to comfort her. Maybe together we could figure a way out of here. Part of me wanted her to remain unconscious to spare her the trauma of this nightmare. But it would help if she were able to support her own weight.

I guessed the temperature of the water was somewhere below seventy-five degrees. We both needed vigorous movement if we had any hope of warding off hypothermia. Already, my legs were beginning to feel numb.

"Riley? Riley, can you wake up?" I slid my cold fingers along her arms, reaching back to touch her face and neck. She reacted by squirming away, bunching her shoulders in an effort to protect her neck. "It'll be very dark when you open your eyes. You won't be able to see anything, and I can't see you. You'll have to tell me if you're awake."

She mumbled something about a bathroom. To this point, I

hadn't worried about bacteria and other hazards. This well once provided fresh water to the farmhouse, and there was no odor down here. But by now, the water held blood contamination, and I didn't relish the idea of sitting in our own waste. Without clean water, we faced dehydration in addition to hypothermia. We had to find a way out of here.

"Where are we?" Riley's voice was small and weak.

"We're in a well, a deep, dark hole. But I'm here with you."

"I'm cold." She shivered.

"We need to jump around and move to warm up. Are you awake enough to do that?" She responded by tightening her arms around my neck and circling her legs about my hips. Her head tipped further sideways and her breathing soon lapsed into the slow regular pattern of unconscious sleep.

If nothing else, the water buoyed some of Riley's weight, but she was growing heavy. I shivered, and tried to adjust our position without jarring my leg, tried not to think about the possibility of being here in this cold tomb all night. The farmstead was abandoned. No one had a reason to come down to the end of the road, to enter the house or wander around the backyard.

Ruby's pet phrase seemed to fit the situation perfectly. I spoke it out loud.

"Lord, to whom shall we go?" There was more to it, something about words and life, but it wasn't clear in my mind. Ruby believed God answered prayers, and I had no doubt she was praying for Riley and me even now. Maybe He'd answer this time.

I shifted Riley a bit higher on my back. Both of us shivered uncontrollably. By now, Kim should've contacted the police. Had Stan and Travis joined the search? How I regretted bringing all this trouble on my friends.

Interesting. I hadn't used that term, friends, in such a long time. In my guilt and shame over losing a student, I'd erected a wall that isolated me from people whose company I'd once enjoyed. Within the confines of that wall, I'd indulged myself in the pity Maxine had clearly recognized. I'd believed the accusations of those who called me incompetent and irresponsible, and willingly jumped down that deep, dark hole of self-pity and condemnation. And there I had stayed for twelve long years.

Teaching had been my purpose in life for as long as I could remember. I loved the energy in a classroom, loved watching a student's face light up when a concept suddenly made sense. I didn't need any awards or thank-you notes from former students to know I was good at my job. I knew it in my heart by the confidence and excitement I felt when I stood before a classroom full of students. But deep in that dark well, I'd given up hope of ever teaching again, of finding answers, of uncovering the truth.

Now, as I shivered in a literal deep, dark hole, I vowed not to give up this time. Not with Riley's life at stake. Not with the promise I made to her parents and Maxine. I would not give up, despite the chattering of my teeth and the constant shivering.

"Hey! Is anybody up there? We're in the well. Can you help us?"

God, where else can I go? We have no other hope.

Travis rolled onto his side, searching for a more comfortable position on the couch. He punched his pillow, but it wasn't the furniture keeping him awake. Where was Riley? What was that scumbag doing to her? Thinking about it made him want to puke.

Micah, asleep on the love seat, stirred but didn't wake. Too scared to stay in his own room, he'd insisted on sleeping out here "with Daddy." Travis drank in the sight of his son and wondered if he'd have another chance to watch his daughter dream as well.

He checked his phone on the coffee table for messages. The time showed 1:16 a.m., but nothing from either Stan or the police.

Travis switched to lying on his back then decided there was no use staring at the dark ceiling. He got up and started the coffee maker in the dim glow of light from the stove hood. Brandi appeared as he was pouring the first cup. She sank into a chair, propped her elbows on the table and covered her face with her hands. Travis set the cup in front of her and poured another for himself. Judging by the tangles in her blonde hair and the dark circles under her eyes, she was as restless as he.

"I keep wondering where he's taken her, imagining how scared she must be, even if Lorraine is with her." Brandi folded her arms on the table and dropped her head onto them. "Dear God, I hope she's okay."

Travis reached across the table and covered her hand with his. "Thanks for letting me stay here tonight. It's where I should've been all along. This would never have happened if I hadn't—"

Brandi raised her head and looked at him through bloodshot eyes. She pulled her hand away and held both palms out. "Travis, I can't deal with us right now, not with Riley missing. Once they find her, then we can figure out what's happening with us."

"Can I just say something?" Travis wrapped his hands around the coffee cup and waited for her response. She slumped back in her chair and gave a brief nod. "No matter what happens with Riley, I'm not going to rush you. I've been talking with Stan about us, about me." He swallowed hard. "I'm sorry for the things I've done that hurt you. I was wrong, about a lot of stuff. I thought I only cared about the kids. But this thing with Riley has made me realize how much I care about you, too. I want to be here for both you and the kids. It's what I signed up for when I married you." Brandi's eyes widened as he spoke. "It's okay if you don't want me back yet. I need to earn your trust, I get that. But I want you to know I intend to be the kind of dad my kids are proud of, the kind of man you want to have around."

She looked fully awake now, sitting straight in her chair, her mouth open. Before she could say anything, his phone buzzed. Travis hustled to grab it from the coffee table. "Stan? What's up?"

"How soon can you be ready to go?"

"As soon as I throw on a shirt and some pants. Have they found her?"

"Not yet. I'm on my way. Watch for me." He clicked off, and Brandi popped up from the table.

"What did he say? Have they found her?"

"He said not yet." Travis shook his head. "But he's picking me up in a few minutes." He grabbed his jeans from the end of the couch and teetered as he aimed one foot and then the other into the legs. He ducked into his t-shirt and pulled it down over his shoulders and stomach.

"You're inside out." Brandi tugged on the tag in back.

"Don't worry about it. No one will notice in the dark. I need to get outside and watch for Stan."

She followed him to the door. "Call me as soon as you know anything."

"I will." He halted at the open door, looked at Brandi and pecked her on the cheek before hurrying out. The door closed behind him, and he waited for the clunk of the lock moving into place before hustling over to the driveway. He edged past his truck that sat next to Brandi's car. In the distance, a screech owl warbled its eerie call in the cool darkness. Travis paced in front of the house. What had they found? Where was Stan taking him?

The curtain in the front window moved, and Brandi peeked out to see if he was still waiting. He hadn't meant to make his little speech just yet, but the time seemed right. He wanted her to know his intentions, the first step in regaining her trust and respect. Too bad there hadn't been time to get her reaction. But then again, they'd have plenty of time to talk after Riley was home and safe.

Headlights careened down the street, coming to a stop at the curb beside him. He hopped into the pickup, and braced himself as Stan made a sharp 3-point turn.

"A former parishioner called and asked me to go with him to bail his grandson out of jail," Stan said. "The boy's parents are separated and his dad's not around much. The young man and a few of his friends found an abandoned farmhouse out east of town and thought it looked like a good place to consume a case of beer. Sheriff got wind of it and hauled them in. "

Stan stepped on the gas to beat a yellow light and they raced through an intersection. "While we were getting him checked out, I overheard one of the girls who'd been out there. She was trying to convince the officers the old farmhouse was haunted. Said she heard a child crying out there. Could be a drug-induced fantasy, although the kids said they were only drinking. Maybe just some feral cats, but I thought we should check it out."

I could no longer feel my toes. The numbness was working its way up my legs to the rest of my body. The shivering had stopped, but I knew that wasn't a good sign.

Riley moved in and out of consciousness. Between the drug Ted had used on her and the cold, she had a hard time staying awake. Most of the time, she was too groggy to realize the seriousness of our predicament. But she knew she was uncomfortable, and she wanted her mom and dad. I let her cry, joining her at times, until her speech grew sluggish, her thoughts disconnected. Despite every effort to keep her awake, she lost consciousness again.

I yawned and rubbed her slender arms, trying to generate

enough warmth to keep us alive. I couldn't afford to fall asleep, though I'd been awake nearly twenty-four hours. How long would it be before sunlight slipped through the cracks at the top of the well?

Disjointed fragments of Ruby's favorite Bible stories flitted through my head. Someone had been thrown down a cistern like us, but was it David or Daniel? Did Jonah go into the belly of a lion's den?

I shook my head and tried to pull my thoughts together. They'd all been rescued, some in ordinary ways and others by supernatural circumstances. Did God do miracles anymore? I wish I could ask someone. Roy might know. I'll remember to ask him when he gets home. He must be working late tonight. I'll just close my eyes for a little catnap until he comes home.

"You know how to find this place?" Travis peered into the darkness, his elbow hanging out the window of Stan's pickup. The overnight temps were still in the sixties, and a breeze that slid up the sleeve of his t-shirt drifted down to cool his ribs.

"My friend's grandson didn't know the address, but he gave me pretty good directions. We'll see." Stan turned off the paved road and flicked his brights on. Rabbits scurried into the brush along the side of the road, and at one point, a skunk ambled across their path. Stan hit the brakes and waited until it disappeared into the field.

Travis snapped his fingers. "I didn't think to bring a flashlight."

"There should be one under the seat." The truck bumped over a pothole and Stan swerved to avoid the worst of the road's hazards. "I keep a headlamp in the glove box, too. Comes in handy when I'm working on the engine."

Travis felt around under the seat, then opened the glove box and pulled out the headlamp. He turned it on and leaned over, aiming it beneath the seat. A heavy-duty flashlight lay just beyond his reach. He'd have to wait until they stopped. Soon, the car's headlights illuminated a dilapidated house and barn. "How'd they find these kids way out here?"

Stan pulled into what was once a driveway and followed multiple tracks in the tall grass where cars had parked earlier. "That last place we passed a mile or two back? The owner called it in. Said he'd noticed a vehicle drive back here earlier. When it left a while later, he figured maybe a realtor was showing the property to someone. But during the night, he got up to use the bathroom and noticed headlights on the road. Watched them drive past his place and keep going. Figured nothing good was going on this time of night, so he called it in."

Stan shut off the engine, but left the headlights shining.

"The kids said they were in the house, but let's check the barn first."

Travis hopped out and retrieved the flashlight. "You think that guy Ted might be here with them?"

"If he is, he kept well-hidden when all the teenagers were here. He coulda simply claimed it was his property and run them off." Stan shut the truck's door.

Travis offered him first choice of light sources, and he took the headlamp, fitting it onto his head. Travis played the flashlight over the ground in front of them. Rattlers and copperheads probably wouldn't be out until the sun came up, but he didn't want to mistakenly step on one. He and Stan reached the open doorway and peeked inside. Their lights bobbed over a pile of roof timbers jumbled about the middle of the floor.

"Riley? It's Daddy. Are you in here?" Travis held his breath and waited for an answer.

"Lorraine? If you can hear us, make some noise. We're here to help." Stan took a few steps inside, moving his head to sweep the corners with his headlamp. An owl swooped from one of the rafters, but the only sound was a lonely coyote in the distance.

"You think that's what the girl heard?"

Stan shrugged his shoulders and wagged his head.

"Riley? Where are you, baby girl?" The barn, the darkness, the shabbiness of it all was beginning to creep him out. As much as he wanted to find Riley, he hated to think she might be stuck in a place like this, scared out of her mind.

They turned toward the house, which wasn't in much better shape. Most of the shutters were missing, though a few still hung crooked at the broken windows. He and Stan tested every step onto the sagging porch before putting their full weight on it. No wonder kids thought it was haunted, especially if they heard voices.

The front door had been boarded up, but Travis climbed through one of the broken windows and shined the flashlight around the dirty room. Colorful graffiti screamed vulgarities from the walls. Everything from beer and soda cans to a stained and torn mattress littered the floor. An odor of urine pierced his nostrils. In the corner, a torn girly magazine lay on its pages. He tried not to imagine what went on here. When he connected Riley to those thoughts, his stomach threatened an all-out revolt.

Stan followed him through the window and moved into a hallway, checking the other rooms on the first floor. Travis beamed his flashlight up the stairway and tried the first step.

"Be careful," Stan warned before disappearing into another room. Travis grunted and put his foot on the next step.

"Riley? Are you up there? Anywhere?" The third step cracked beneath his weight and he moved closer to the wall where the boards would be stronger. Something, most likely a rat or a mouse, scurried across the top of the stairway.

"Riley, it's Daddy." A couple of the rooms upstairs contained soiled mattresses and more beer cans. This must be a popular hangout for teenagers pretending to be adults. He wasn't so old he couldn't remember a few parties from his own youth. The farmer up the road was right. Nothing good ever happened at those gatherings.

In the last bedroom on the second floor, he stood at the window and played his flashlight across the overgrown backyard. A couple of trails—one from the house and one from the side—led to a chunk of concrete lying on top of a piece of plywood. An old well someone had covered to keep animals from falling into it. Beyond and to the side, something lay in the grass, but he couldn't quite make out what it was. Didn't look like an animal.

Travis walked through the rooms again, checking every closet, knocking on the walls and calling for Riley, but getting no answer. He met up with Stan in the kitchen at the back of the house, and together, they moved out to the back steps. Low clouds hid the moon and stars, but reflected the lights of Waco to the west.

Travis exhaled his disappointment. "Guess it was either some cats or the drugs. I really hoped—"

"I'm sorry, Travis." Stan removed his headlamp, and held it in his hands, flashing it over the weedy yard. "Maybe I should've come out here by myself instead of getting your hopes up."

"No, I'm glad you called. It helps to have something to do while we wait for word, even it turns out to be a false lead."

"How's Brandi managing?"

"Rough. I don't think either one of us slept. I promised to call and let her know if we found anything." He stood still, listening for any unusual sound.

Stan put his hand on Travis's shoulder. "Ready to go?"

Travis took one more look around and exhaled. "Yeah, I guess so." He followed Stan through the door, then halted. "Did you hear that?"

Stan stopped. "What?"

Travis tipped his head, straining to hear the noise again. "It might've been what the girl was saying about a kid crying." He listened. Was his imagination playing tricks on him? Did he want to hear Riley so badly his mind conjured up memories of her cries? He stood still for several minutes but heard nothing. "Guess I'm just hearing things. Or maybe it was an owl. We can go if you want."

Stan led the way through the house, down from the porch and out to the truck, its headlights illuminating the front yard so well they both snapped off their portable lights. Stan climbed into the driver's seat and started the engine.

Travis stood frozen by the open door. He held up an index finger to Stan. "One second. I want to take another look out back."

"Want me to come with you?"

"Nah, it's probably nothing. You can wait here." Travis slammed the door and followed the track through the grass to the backyard. Stan inched the truck along behind him, lighting the way deeper into the deserted yard. When Travis reached the back, the path led straight to the old well. He walked up to it and listened, shining his flashlight on the grove of trees that surrounded the house on two sides. A pair of tiny red eyes stared back at him from between two trees, but he wasn't interested in a 'possum.

He whispered Riley's name, then spoke it out loud.

"Riley? It's Daddy. Can you hear me?" He waited in silence, then turned toward the truck. His flashlight splashed across the grass, bringing into focus the item he'd seen from upstairs. A purse. He picked it up, and recognition shot through his brain. He waved his arm at Stan and aimed his light at the purse.

"They're here!"

Stan cut the motor, jumped out of the truck, and ran toward

Travis. He grabbed the purse, opened it, and pulled out the set of keys.

"It's her purse, all right, but it looks like they took most everything." He scanned the immediate area lit by the headlights. "If they're not here, at least we know they've been here."

Heart hammering his chest, Travis moved the beam of his flashlight over the tops of the grass and tried not to imagine Riley's lifeless body dumped out there somewhere.

"What about the well?" Stan dropped the purse and lifted a corner of the plywood cover. "The wood looks new compared to everything else around this place."

Travis spotlighted the top of the well. The large panel barely covered the well opening on two sides. What looked like part of the original concrete well cover lay atop the rectangular board, insuring no easy removal by man or beast. Travis met Stan's gaze, and they both reached for the chunk of concrete.

"Wait a minute." Stan held up a cautionary hand. "We need to think about this. If they're down there, we sure don't want to risk dropping this thing on them."

Together, they pushed, pulled, and shoved the panel far enough aside to see into the well. Travis directed his flashlight down the hole. His breath caught in his throat.

"Riley!"

CHAPTER 27

A portable light tower turned the night to noon, at least in the immediate confines of the backyard. Mechanical voices crackling from radios mingled with urgent commands from the rescue crew. Two ropes dangled from a tripod secured on top of the well casing. Another rope attached to an air monitor hung over the side of the well.

"What's taking so long?" Travis paced the length of the fire truck under the watchful eye of a sheriff's deputy. His interference and insistence on rescue first, safety later had gotten him banished from the front line of action, unlike Stan who had been allowed to remain at the well.

A sheriff's deputy had planted himself at the corner of the ladder truck, leaving just enough room for Travis to see over his shoulder. The deputy glanced at his shoes and touched a finger to his earphone. "They're getting ready to go down now," he said. "They'll need you to stay out of the way until they get your little girl into the ambulance and stabilized."

Standing almost face-to-face with a law officer wasn't the most comfortable position, especially after his recent arrest. But no way would he miss seeing Riley brought out of that well. Brandi would be here any minute, after she left Micah with Kim.

Strapped into a harness, the EMT stepped off the platform and gradually sank from view. Travis had nearly jumped into the well himself when he saw Riley and the woman down there. Lucky for him, Stan stopped him or they'd have had to rescue him, too. They'd found nothing in the barn or the house with which to lower one of them down the well, and without a ladder or rope, the risk of landing on either Riley or Lorraine was too great, not to mention having no way to bring them back up.

Minutes seemed to pass like years until at last, a humpback figure rose from the well. The rescuer stepped down from the platform with Riley draped over one shoulder in a classic fireman's carry. While others removed the harness, Riley's head flopped gently against his back. Her wrists appeared bound, and strands of her hair hung in wet clumps. Water dripped onto the ground.

Travis's eyes filled. His breath came in shallow spurts, and he leaned into the officer. Every cell in his body urged him toward his daughter, but firm hands held him back.

"Don't rush them. Give them room to get her into the ambulance. Then you can go see her."

Stan approached the EMT, took Riley's hands and sandwiched them between his before hurrying over to Travis.

"Her pulse is weak, but she's alive. They suspect hypothermia. Won't know anything else until they can warm her up."

Travis sagged against the side of the ladder truck. He reached for Stan and pulled him into a hug. "Thank you," he croaked into the man's ear. "Pray? Please."

"Our dear heavenly Father, thank you for sparing Riley's life thus far. You have been Jehovah Roi, the God who sees, and you are Jehovah Rapha, our Lord who heals. Though Riley and Lorraine were hidden from view, you saw them, and you led us to them. We ask you now to revive little Riley and Lorraine. Bring them back to us in restored health and vigor. In the name of Jesus Christ, our Lord and Savior. Amen."

"Thank you," Travis rasped. "Thank you." He let go and pressed a knuckle to his eye. He sniffed to clear his nose. "What about Lorraine?"

"They're bringing her up next, if you'll excuse me."

"Yeah, yeah. Go." Travis waved his fingers through the air, and Stan hurried over to where a second EMT was stepping into the harness. From the corner of his eye, Travis caught sight of headlights racing up the road beyond the barn. Probably Brandi, since no flashing lights accompanied the vehicle. He winced, imagining what all those bumps and potholes were doing to her alignment, but under the circumstances, he'd have driven the same way. He headed toward the driveway to meet her.

The deputy called after him. "Where're you going?"

"I think that's my wife."

The deputy watched the headlights, hooked his thumbs in his belt, and nodded. Travis hurried to the driveway entrance where police cruisers formed a haphazard barricade. Brandi's car skidded to a stop on the shoulder, and she jumped out, leaving the door to swing closed on its own. An officer stopped her, but he let her pass when Travis hollered. "She's alive! They've got her in the ambulance. Come on." He clasped her hand on the run and led her back to his time-out spot.

"You can see her now." The deputy motioned them toward the ambulance.

Blankets covered Riley's body, and an IV bag already dripped fluid into her arm. The binding on her wrists had been removed. Her tanned complexion had turned ghostly white, her lips and fingernails a striking shade of purple. Brandi and Travis crowded in beside the gurney, and the technician handed Brandi a plastic bag of clothing. "We had to remove her wet clothes to get her warmed up. She's got heat packs in her groin and armpits to encourage warming."

Travis took her hand in his, startled at the icy coldness of her skin.

Brandi's voice trembled. "Will she be all right?"

"We won't know for sure until she wakes up, but children usually bounce back pretty well. With hypothermia, the body systematically shuts itself down, drawing blood away from extremities and then peripheral organs to protect the brain and the vital organs. As long as the heart keeps pumping the way hers is, we can usually bring them back up to normal function again. Once she's awake, the hospital will check her coordination and her cognitive skills."

"Which hospital?" Travis asked.

The technician named the hospital. He checked Riley's vital signs and the IV in her arm. "Okay, we're about ready to transport. Are either of you riding with us?"

Travis took one look at Brandi's red-rimmed eyes. "You ride with her. I'll drive your car and meet you there."

Brandi rolled her lips in, obviously struggling to control her emotions. They climbed out of the ambulance, and she hugged him before getting into the front seat.

"Thank you for being here."

"I'll see you there. Be right behind you." Travis closed the door and stood back as the rear doors were secured. The lights swirled, the engine revved up, and the vehicle ambled out of the driveway through an opening between the squad cars. He followed it out to Brandi's car, then turned around and jogged back to the well. Riley was safe and in good hands. He'd follow as soon as he checked on Stan.

I must be nearing the end of the tunnel, but the light is too bright to see anything. At least I'm not shivering anymore. But whose voices are those? They're talking too fast. I can't understand them. Are they talking to me? No, someone named Lorraine. Maybe she's farther back in the tunnel.

Strange. I seem to be in motion, but I can't feel my arms and legs at all. Are they still there? I open my eyes and catch a glimpse of Roy. At last I can tell him I found Jenny. She was right here with me a minute ago, but she's disappeared. I can't find her.

No, her name is Jenny. And why do you keep calling me Lorraine?

I open my eyes again, but this time I'm spinning on a merry-go-round. So dizzy.

Stop. Let me off.

The voices grow distant, except for one or two. But what's that humming noise? Wait, did I bring my purse? Can't forget that. Roy would be disappointed.

Stabbing. Needles and pins. All over my feet, legs, arms, hands. Why? Oh, it hurts.

"Lorraine, can you hear me?"

I struggle to make my tongue cooperate. "I'm...Elaine."

"Elaine, yes. That's good."

"Roy?"

"No, I'm Stan."

"Why so many needles? It hurts."

A different voice. "That's your body warming up. You're going to feel that for a while yet. You're in moderate hypothermia, so it'll take time to get you warmed up again. You'll be more comfortable when we get to the hospital."

I don't recognize that voice. "Hurts."

"Yes, I'm sorry. Rest now. Sleep if you can."

Cold. Bone-chilling, uncontrollable, shivering cold. The pins and needles were mostly gone. An IV dripped something into the vein on my left hand. I hoped it was something for the pain because my leg was throbbing along with my head. A gauze bandage covered part of my left shoulder. My legs itched, but scratching didn't help. The itch seemed to come from inside, under the skin.

I pulled the covers tight around me and snuggled deep, longing for my comforter at home. A nurse brought in some broth. She raised the head of my bed, but I didn't want to take my arms from the covers. She bent the top of the straw and held it to my mouth. The broth tasted good. Warm. I drank it in small sips, and when it was finished, I fell back to sleep.

Stan was in the room when I woke again. He fed me more broth and told me how concerned Kim and the others were about me. They'd sent the flowers sitting on my tray table.

"What happened to Riley?"

Stan paused and tipped his head sideways. "You don't remember? You and Riley were at the bottom of an abandoned well. Not sure how long you'd been there, but it was at least five, six hours before we found you. Do you remember how you got down there?"

My confusion faded, and I remembered the well, jumping into it, trying to keep Riley from sinking into the cold water. I remembered Capone's intimidating eyes, and Ted.

"I remember. What about Riley? Is she—"

"She's fine. Or at least she will be. She's in another room. Travis and Brandi are with her."

That was good news. I relaxed, but only until I recalled Ted tossing my purse into the grass. I couldn't lose it. Not now. "What about my purse? The one from Roy?"

Stan pulled out the drawer beside my bed and withdrew the pea-green handbag.

"We found it in the grass near the well. I'm sorry, though. It looks like they took everything except your keys."

"We?" I shoved aside the warm blankets and grabbed the purse from his hands. My fingers, still stiff and cold, searched the lining for the memory card.

"Travis and I. He noticed it beside the well. That's how we found you. Figured you must be close, or at least had been in the area. Everyone wants to know what happened, but the police are first in line whenever you feel up to it."

My fingers touched the little square shape, and with some difficulty, I drew out the memory card.

Stan raised an eyebrow and studied it. "Is that the memory card?"

"The police will want to see what's on this before they question me." Stan reached for the card, but I held it back. "Tell them to bring a laptop. And hurry." I yawned.

"Are you sure you're up to talking with them?"

I nodded and closed my eyes. "Wake me up when they get here."

My ankle wasn't broken, just badly sprained. Once the effects of hypothermia subsided, I had to learn how to hobble around on crutches before they'd release me from the hospital. On Friday, the third day since being rescued, a familiar voice announced my dismissal. "Ms. Elaine, you ready to get out of here? There's a whole lotta people waitin' to see you."

"Anthony. When did— What— How did you get here?"

He chuckled, that deep sound I loved, and moved aside while a nurse angled a wheelchair close to where I sat beside the bed. "Chief never believed the charges against me. He started working on getting them dismissed as soon as he heard I was in jail. But ever since the Waco PD sent along the information from Roy's memory card and their interview with you, I've been a free man."

"What about Ted?"

"Chicago police want to do their own interview before they make any moves. They sent me down here to escort you back to Chicago." He handed me my driver's license, bank card and credit cards. "You'll probably need these, unless you want to stay here mopping floors and emptying bedpans to pay off your bill."

Before we left, I asked Anthony to take me to Riley's room. I hadn't seen her since our rescue, and wanted to reassure myself she was all right.

Balloon bouquets and stuffed animals decorated her hospital room. Brandi sat on one side of the bed, Travis on the other. No doubt Riley was enjoying the attention from both mom and dad.

"How soon does our girl get to go home?" Anthony asked.

"As soon as we get the discharge papers. That's what we're waiting for." Brandi smoothed her daughter's hair down the back of her head, then rose to take my hand. "Lorraine." She stopped and grimaced. "I mean, Elaine. I'll never get used to calling you by a different name. Anyway, thank you for all you did to keep Riley safe and alive. We can't thank you enough."

"Nonsense. If it wasn't for me, she wouldn't have been in trouble in the first place." I waved my fingers at Riley. "We made it, didn't we?"

She nodded and hid her face in the soft fur of a big, golden teddy bear held tight in her arms.

"I'm so glad you're feeling better. I know your mom and dad and grandma will be so happy to have you home again. I bet Micah's missing you, too."

Riley's eyes cut to Brandi, and she grinned. I thanked Travis for his part in finding us. He came around the bed and squatted next to my wheelchair. "I need to thank you for talking some sense into me that day I came by. I didn't like hearing it." He hung his head, and his shoulders rose and fell twice before he continued. "But I needed it. And I'm gonna do what you said. I'm gonna be the daddy my kids need, and hopefully, the husband Brandi needs and wants."

I patted him on the back. He stood and gave me a quick hug. Brandi observed us with a curious look, and the questions started as soon as I was out in the hall.

"What did she say to you? Did you come by the house? When was that?"

Anthony explained our plans on the way to Kim's. "The doc said you'd be okay to travel. We got us a long day ahead. Kim and the ladies wanted to say good-bye, but we need to grab your stuff and get on the road to Dallas. The police want to interview you the moment we get into Chicago. Is that going to be too much for you?"

"I'll do whatever I have to do. I want that man behind bars."

You'd have thought I'd finished a marathon the way Kim and the others cheered when I hobbled through the front door. Maxine took one look at the splint on my ankle, and declared, "Will you look at that? Between the two of us, we've got a full pair of legs."

Still a bit weak, I sank onto the nearest chair and crooked a finger, motioning for Maxine to come close. She appeared wary, but I needed to tell her something.

"You told me what I needed to hear to get me out of my self-pity. Now let me return the favor. Embrace Travis. He's learning to be a man, a daddy, and a husband. Encourage him and Brandi. I don't think you'll regret it."

She leaned away and blew air through those red lips. "We'll see about that." She wheeled back and started to turn, then stopped. "Hey, you kept your word about bringing Riley back to us." She pointed a thumb at the ceiling. Her eyes filled, and she made a quick about-face.

Jean moved in and bent over to give me a hug. "I'm so glad you're back, Lorraine."

"My name's Elaine. Remember?"

Jean backed up, her eyebrows drawing together. "Elaine?"

"Yes. Like your sister?"

She pondered that for a moment. "I don't think I have a sister, do I?"

"Of course you have sisters," Maxine bellowed. "Who do you think we are?"

I squeezed her hands. "Jean, you call me anything you like, as long as it's decent." We both giggled, and she made way for Ruby to shuffle her walker alongside my chair. Ruby and I held tight to each other's hands.

"I was praying for you and Riley the whole time, asking Jesus to please show the men where you were hidden."

"I knew that, Ruby, and I admit it was a comforting thought. He answered your prayers."

She bobbed her head. "I wisht He'd'a done it sooner, but He doesn't always answer us right off the bat. Sometimes, we have to sweat and suffer a little."

"Why would He do that? When He has the power to rescue, why wait until people are half-dead before He steps in? What's the point of making us suffer?" Maybe I should've asked Stan that question, but it seemed to fit the moment. The question felt urgent.

"Our suffering isn't the point. It's our faith. Sometimes, He leaves us in that rough spot until He has our attention. Most times, we won't look up until there's nothing more to see at the bottom. Other times, He wants to give us a different perspective of His power or make us stronger by the things we've gone through. Tragedy and suffering themselves are never the point. To survive hard times, you have to get to know Him so well that there's no doubt He's as trustworthy in trouble as he is in good times."

"Then I guess I have a long way to go. But that verse you quoted, 'Lord, to whom shall we go?' The bottom of the well helped me understand that question. So maybe I'm heading in the right direction." She let go of my hands with a nod and a satisfied pat.

I flexed my leg to ease the pain in my ankle. Kim came from the hall, carrying my bags and my new purse. She handed them all to Anthony.

"I hate to see you go," she said. "Are you sure you're up for so much traveling today? You could always stay the night. I'd even put you in my room so you wouldn't have to sleep on the couch."

"Thank you, but I have a mission to fulfill, for my husband and for a young girl who should be alive today." Kim leaned in and gave me a hug. "I never thought I'd say this when Anthony brought me to your door a couple weeks ago, but I'm sorry to be leaving. You and the ladies here welcomed me, made me feel at home, and you've become dear friends in a very short time."

Kim hugged me again, tighter this time. "Please let us know how it all turns out. We'll be praying for you. And come back and see us. We'll figure out a place for you, a real place, if you ever want to stay."

Anxious to get to the airport, Anthony helped me up and stayed by my side out to the car. Stan ran ahead to open doors and steadied me as I plopped into the car seat and maneuvered my leg into the car to avoid banging my ankle. At last, I pulled the seat belt across and released a relieved sigh. Stan squatted beside me and pushed his cap back.

"I'm sorry to see you go," he said. "Would you mind if I called? Or maybe came to visit sometime?"

"It would be a pleasure to see you again, Stan, but I must be honest. My husband has only been gone two weeks. I haven't had time to grieve, and at this point, I'm not the least bit interested in another relationship. I can't say whether I ever will be. I'll leave it to you if you still want to stay in contact."

"I understand completely. I'll be in touch." He stood, shut my door, and waved.

"Godspeed to you both."

CHAPTER 28

Sirens blared in the street below Ted's office, their sound muted by a misty fog that had hung around all day, blanketing the traffic and congestion below. He settled into his executive chair and swiveled to face the desk. The meeting with the mayor had gone well. He'd apologized for missing their scheduled Tuesday conference. After receiving Elaine's call Monday night, Ted cancelled everything on his week's schedule. Fortunately, his assistant had smoothed things over, and today the mayor assured him there'd be plenty of funding for his anti-gang initiative.

He pulled the pendant and cord from his drawer and let it dangle from his hand. The girl in Texas was still a bit young now, but in three or four years... He imagined the pendant hanging around her neck. Too bad he had to leave her there in that old well. But, he had neither time nor reason for regrets. The girl he'd met last night was every bit as beautiful and enticing. The shy innocence of girls that age was so alluring, so appealing. So exciting.

A knock at the door made him drop the pendant into his desk

and shove the drawer closed. He'd forgotten about Patrice leaving early today. That's why she wasn't at her desk when he came in.

He stood, but before he could step from behind his desk, the door swung open, and the Superintendent of Police entered, followed by two officers. His stomach knotted at the look of business on the man's face.

"Welcome, gentlemen. What can I do for you?"

The Superintendent marched straight to his desk and held up some papers. "Your Honor, I'm sorry to say this is not a social visit. I have here a warrant for your arrest. You have the right to remain silent..."

One of the other officers came around the desk, pulled his hands together behind his back, and secured handcuffs on his wrists. Ted recognized him—the man whose arrest he himself had arranged. The officer's steely gaze did nothing for the sweat beginning to drench his shirt.

"Is this some kind of joke? I don't understand."

A movement at the door caught Ted's eye, and his mouth went dry. Lunch soured in his stomach. He clenched his teeth and ground out, "What are you doing here?"

Elaine Sutterfeld limped into the room on crutches. "You thought I'd be dead by now. But we aren't always what we seem, are we, Judge?"

Ted tore his attention away from her and focused on the Superintendent. "What are the charges against me?"

"It says here conspiracy to murder, kidnapping, sexual contact with a minor." He stopped reading. "Do you really want me to go on?"

"Lies. They're all lies. How can you possibly believe such things after all I've done for the people of this city?" The two officers flanked him, each holding one of his arms and guiding him out from behind the desk. "It's her word against mine. You have no proof."

"On the contrary." Elaine rummaged through that hideous purse he remembered tossing into the weeds. "I tried to bargain with you. Remember?" She pulled out a small square SD card.

"What's that?"

"It's a memory card. Roy had one just like it where he kept all the evidence he collected over the years regarding the disappearance of Jenny Ortiz, including what he uncovered to solve the mystery. The police have it now. This is just a new one, but that valuable little piece of technology was hidden in this purse, the one you tossed away because you were in a hurry."

Ted could almost feel the blood drain from his face. If what she said were true, they had enough to send him to prison for the rest of his life. He'd be ruined. His reputation, his influence, the lifestyle he enjoyed would all come down like that imploding building. He'd be everything his brothers said he was—incompetent, a failure, an embarrassment.

No, he'd not give them the satisfaction if he could get to the gun he kept hidden. He inclined his head toward the door to his right. "May I ask one favor? I'll cooperate and come peacefully if I may use the restroom first. I don't guess there'll be much time in the next hour to relieve myself."

The Superintendent shook his head. "Sorry, Your Honor. Not until we get to the station." He gave a signal, and the officers prompted Ted toward the door. Elaine backed out of their way. He stared straight ahead, but felt her gaze as they passed through the door into Patrice's office and continued into the hall.

News spread quickly. Though normally quiet and deserted, the hallway took on the semblance of a parade route with staffers lined up on both sides to view the coming attraction. Heads poked out from offices, and gasps and whispers reached Ted's ears as he was escorted to the elevator. He bowed his head to avoid the curious stares, fixing his gaze on the carpeted floor. In the past, he'd always considered such a posture indicative of guilt and defeat. Not this time. Not defeat. Not if he could help it.

Silence rode the elevator with him all the way down to the lobby. The doors opened to a sprinkling of family members of those on trial, lawyers, and staff anxious to get home and start the weekend. Another elevator opened, and a news team exited, reporters here to gather news on pending court cases.

"Hey, isn't that Judge Owens?"

They swarmed around him like hungry mosquitoes at the scent of fresh blood, shouting questions, snapping pictures. The Superintendent moved out ahead to clear the way, and the officers at his side closed in, their free arms holding back the onlookers.

Outside the building, several squad cars waited at the curb. More officers worked to hold back the growing press of reporters and curious passersby. The drumming in Ted's ears rose to a crescendo until it nearly drowned out the voices swirling around him. His temples throbbed, and sweat drenched his Armani shirt as the officers escorted him to a patrol car. The back door stood open. If he gave in and sat on that hard plastic seat, his future was sealed. He'd spend the next twenty to thirty years in an austere, solitary prison cell, his every movement watched. He knew what happened to people like him in prison.

The officers angled him sideways toward the back seat. One released his arm while the other guided him into the car. Ted hesitated until the former officer backed away. Then, bending over as if to sit, he positioned his foot against the doorframe and propelled himself into the belly of the officer still holding him. Twisting, he wrenched his arm away and kicked one foot out, connecting with the knee of the first officer. With his wrists cuffed behind his back, he lost his balance and fell against the squad car. Half rolling, half walking, he stumbled around the rear end and lurched into the street.

"Stop him! Catch him before he—"

The shouted orders were lost in the screams and pandemonium. Ted darted among the traffic, ducking behind cars and trucks, moving along beside them. He envisioned the officers drawing their pistols, assuming the shooting stance. Brakes squealed and tires screeched against the pavement as he dodged this way and that, weaving his way through traffic, waiting for just the right moment. The fog was his friend.

"Don't shoot! Hold your fire."

They wouldn't dare shoot into traffic. The resulting injuries and possible deaths of innocent citizens would be the Superintendent's nightmare. But he wasn't interested in death by cop. Still jittering his way through traffic, he heard the sound he was waiting for—a car's powerful engine accelerating, coming closer, faster and faster. He caught a glimpse of the red sports car—a moment before he stepped in front of it.

CHAPTER 29

I dropped the last impatiens plant into the spot Amanda had prepared for it, and packed the dirt around it. The entrance to Anthony's house looked infinitely more inviting with the addition of several flats of these colorful flowers. I still tired easily, a lingering effect of the hypothermia, and with my ankle still sore, I relied on Amanda to do most of the digging and soil preparation. We both stood back to admire the view.

"That looks so pretty, Mrs. Sutterfeld. I just know Mom would be so happy to see this." Amanda brushed dirt from her hands, scraping some from under her neatly trimmed fingernails.

"Thank you, dear." I picked a wilted leaf from one of the plants. This was the least I could do after Anthony graciously offered to let me stay with him and Amanda until I could find a place to live. First, I'd need to decide whether to stay or go back to Texas. Amanda sat on the front step, took a drink from her water bottle, and replaced the cap.

"Is it hard to stay here, having to look at what's left of your house every time you come outside?" She patted the spot next to her, and I accepted the invitation.

"Yes, and no. It hurts to see the charred timbers and everything in ruins. But it's still the place I lived with Roy for thirty-five years. In a way, I think maybe seeing it helps me grieve his death as well the loss of the house. It forces me to realize I have nowhere to go but forward." I studied the burned-out shell of my former home, trying to accept and absorb the ache rather than deny it.

"Do you think you'll rebuild?"

"No." I sighed. "I don't have the patience to deal with all that would entail. And without Roy, I don't know that I'd be able to keep up with all the maintenance a house requires anyway. If I stay in Chicago, I'll look for an apartment or townhouse where someone else takes care of all that." I looked at her. "I hope I haven't caused too much upset staying here with you and your dad."

Amanda paused before taking another sip of water, cocked her head at me, and leaned backward. "Are you serious? I love having another female around the house. I mean, Dad's great and all, but he's such a guy, y'know?"

I laughed and hugged her shoulders while she drained the last drops from her bottle. Anthony's arrival stirred our laughter. He emerged from the car in his blue uniform, a quizzical look on his face as Amanda and I sat there giggling.

"What's so funny?" He reached in to retrieve his backpack.

"Nothing." Amanda shrugged her shoulders and lapsed into more snickering.

"If I didn't know better, I'd think you ladies were laughing at me." He rested the backpack on the trunk, then leaned against the car and waited for us to finish the joke. His expression sobered, and our laughter faded. I didn't wait for him to explain.

"Is it done?"

He nodded and scuffed the sole of his spit-shined shoe against the pavement. "The DNA matched. She was right where he told you, buried under a beautifully landscaped flowerbed in his backyard. Her parents have been informed. They're planning a memorial service and a proper burial. They asked me to convey an invitation to the service so they can thank you in person."

"That's not necessary, but I'd be honored to attend."

Birdsongs, a squirrel's chatter, and the sound of city traffic filled the silence for several moments. Elbows on her knees, Amanda stretched her arms out in front of her, wrists crossed and fingers intertwined. "So what's next?"

Her question made my breath stick in my throat. I knew this day would come, but I hadn't the motivation, the heart to prepare for it. I took a deep breath. "I guess that means I need to decide if I'm going to stay here or go back to Waco."

"You'd consider going back?" Anthony looked at me, his eyebrows raised.

"I've thought about it. Such a short time there, but I grew very fond of Ruby, Kim, and Jean. Even Maxine. I could help Kim manage the home, maybe provide a little extra supervision for Jean to stall her need for a memory care facility." I picked up a stray twig and poked it into the dirt beside the step.

"Would it bother you to leave Roy, I mean, his grave up here?"

I nodded. "Yes, it would. And I'd miss you two."

Amanda leaned into me. "At least we'd be able to see you whenever we visit Grandma."

"I'd like that very much." I patted her hand then turned to Anthony again. "I never realized how small my world had become. My one concern was Roy. Without him, I don't know what to do with myself. I might be able to substitute teach, but no one's going to hire me full-time when I'm almost at retirement age and haven't been in a classroom for the last twelve years."

Anthony reached into his uniform shirt pocket and pulled out a slip of paper. "I have something that might interest you."

I took the paper from him. It held only a name and a phone number. "What's this?"

"Someone who wants to talk to you."

"About what?"

"A job."

"What kind?"

Anthony shouldered his backpack and stepped around me to the door. "She runs a private home here in Chicago for girls who've been rescued from sex trafficking, somewhat like Jenny. The girls are too traumatized to go to either public or private school, so they're taught there at the home. This woman needs an experienced teacher."

I twisted to face him. "But I haven't taught in over a decade. I'd need to go back to school, update my skills. I—"

"She's expecting your call." Anthony opened the door and disappeared inside the house.

"But I—"

Amanda clapped her hands on her knees and pushed to her feet. "Makes sense to me, Mrs. S." She, too, slipped into the house, leaving me with the torn piece of white paper. And a glimmer of hope.

In the reception area outside the small chapel where the memorial service took place, pictures of Jenny crowded a table. At one end, a computer played a loop of home videos from when she was an infant, a child, and all the way up until her thirteenth year. The end of the loop showed her school picture taken a few months before she disappeared. She wore the pendant carved by her dad and presented on her birthday. That picture was the way I'd always remember her.

"I repaired the pendant," Mr. Ortiz explained, "before we

buried it with her remains. It was hers to begin with, and now it will remain hers. No one will ever again misuse it in such an evil way."

Jenny's mother dabbed her eyes. "We can never thank you enough. All those years, it seemed everyone else had forgotten our Jenny. But you remembered, you and your husband."

I hugged her. "She's been on my mind every single day of every year since she disappeared. Like you, I couldn't find any peace until I knew what happened to her."

Mr. Ortiz withdrew a gift box from his pocket and placed it in my hands. "For you." I objected, but he insisted. "It is with gratitude from Jenny's mother and me. Open it, please."

I untied the red ribbon around the box and lifted the cover. Inside, a carved wooden heart, similar to Jenny's, lay on a bed of soft, white cotton. The asymmetrical teardrop shape was the same, but instead of inlaid initials, an intricate carved outline of a young girl's head adorned the center of the heart. The image grew blurry as tears filled my eyes.

"May I?" Mr. Ortiz took the pendant from the box and slid his fingers along the chain until they reached the clasp. He moved behind me and draped the chain around my neck. Standing back to view his work, he swiped a finger under his eye. Jenny's mother murmured her approval.

I pulled the pendant away from my chest to admire the design. How appropriate. Not only a lasting reminder of Jenny, but a symbol of the future. I couldn't wait to meet the precious girls I'd be teaching at the rescue home, and this pendant, with Jenny's memory, would always hang close to my heart.

I'm honored that you chose to read this book. If you enjoyed it, would you consider leaving an honest review on the website where you purchased it? Just a sentence or two about what you liked (or didn't) would mean a great deal. Reviews are gold to an author.

Thanks again!

ALSO BY M L HAMILTON

Middle Grade and YA

by

Mary L (M L) Hamilton

The Rustic Knoll Bible Camp series

Hear No Evil, Book 1

Speak No Evil, Book 2

See No Evil, Book 3

The Rustic Knoll Bible Camp Collection (all 3 e-books in one)

ACKNOWLEDGMENTS

A Note of Thanks...

To all the people who helped me write this book.

Wayne, Daniel and Lanae, Beki and Tim, and Matt: Your encouragement means the world to me. I'm so thankful for your support and enthusiasm. Love you all!

My extended family and friends: Your interest in my writing and your encouragement keeps me going through the dry seasons. Thank you.

Scooter Radcliffe: Your fingerprints are hidden in this book. Your help in answering my questions about police procedures and offering great suggestions was invaluable. Thanks so much!

Ronda W: The medical knowledge you offered came not only through education but also through personal loss. Thank you for being willing to share a few details with me.

Tim Allen: If I ever get trapped in an abandoned well, I'm counting on you to get me out! Thank you for your insight and know-how.

Kelli Hughett and Beki Allen: You waded through a mostly unedited draft and pointed out trouble spots. I am most grateful!

Peggy Wirgau and Deb Garland: What would I do without your tireless critiquing and searching for typos and other errors. I can't thank you enough!

Kathrese McKee: Thanks for an awesome editing job!

Amanda L. Mathews: You are one talented cover designer. So glad I found you!

Any errors in this book are mine. Anything praiseworthy, I give the credit to my Lord, Jesus Christ, who, through the process of writing this book, taught me much—not the least of which is patience to wait and listen.

ABOUT THE AUTHOR

Monsters under the bed never bothered M L Hamilton. What kept her awake was the man hiding in her closet, waiting for her to go to sleep so he could jump out and stab her. She never did figure out who he was, how he managed to hide in her messy closet, or why he wanted to harm her. But since then, she has imagined all sorts of other scary situations, which she hopes will provide the basis for more mystery suspense stories.

When not writing, she enjoys non-scary things like time with her family, reading, knitting and amateur photography. You can see some of her photos on Instagram (mlhamiltonauthor) and Pinterest (mhamiltonbooks).

She and her husband live in Texas.

You can find M L Hamilton in these places:

www.maryhamiltonbooks.com
mary@maryhamiltonbooks.com

Made in the USA
Columbia, SC
09 November 2020